IN *Pursuit*
OF AN
Emerald

JACQUELINE
FREEMAN WHEELOCK

Scrivenings
PRESS
Quench your thirst for story.

Published by Scrivenings Press LLC
15 Lucky Lane
Morrilton, Arkansas 72110
https://ScriveningsPress.com

Printed in the United States of America

Second Edition
Paperback ISBN 978-1-64917-129-0
eBook ISBN 978-1-64917-130-6

Cover by Diane Turpin, www.dianeturpindesigns.com

(Note: This book was previously published in 2017 by Mantle Rock Publishing LLC and was re-published when Scrivenings Press acquired the publishing rights in 2021.)

All scriptures are taken from the KING JAMES VERSION (KJV): KING JAMES VERSION, public domain.

Published in association with Joyce Hart of Hartline Literary Agency, Pittsburgh, Penn.

ACKNOWLEDGMENTS

I must thank God for allowing me another opportunity to write in His name. Further, I should thank my husband, my children and their spouses (Thank you, Demond, for twice lending me your name), and my entire extended family for their consistent encouragement throughout all the years I have chased this dream. Finally to the Cretsingers of Mantle Rock Publishing and to Joyce Hart of Hartline Literary Agency, all of whom have been exceptionally supportive, I thank you.

CHAPTER 1

Monday night, November first, 1869
Riverwood Plantation
Natchez, Mississippi

iolette McMillan pressed her back into the wall space just above the floor, the familiar pain twisting up her spine like a hostile whirlwind. There had never been so much as a bench to sit on in this cold, small space. Neither had there been a man to share it with if that coveted resting place had ever existed. She hunched forward. Rubbed the sides of her arms to fight the chill. Eyed the span of the tumbledown room.

What I wouldn't give for just one padded chair.

But as for that species called men, she planned never to entangle herself with them again.

Seated on the splintery planks, Violette resumed her evening ritual of reading—tonight racing against time to finish the last few pages of a chapter of *Uncle Tom's Cabin* before the wick of the lamp licked up the last bit of oil. Her lips moved in step with Augustine St. Clare's monologue as she nodded to the brutal truth of the character's words . . .

"If I was to say anything on this slavery matter, I would say out, fair and square, 'we've got 'em, and mean to keep 'em,—it's for our convenience and our interest—'"

Oh, no. Not the lamplight.

Violette pushed her face closer to the page. Squinted as she watched St. Clare's words become one with the blackness. She grasped the lamp's tiny metal knob. Advanced the wick.

Too late. The sooty fire of the coal oil lamp was expired, Violette's attempts to keep St. Clare's words alive through her own hot whispers of resentment falling dead right along with the flame. She knew she would be fired if Susan McMillan ever found out she had been taking more than her allotment of fuel. But Violette had been left no choice. Winter had brought on early darkness that now came long before her daily washerwoman duties were over. And if she couldn't read a few pages each night before sleep, she would simply dry out like the many yards of soggy clothes she intermittently hung on clotheslines for twelve long hours every day.

Grieving the sudden loss of the character's words, she arched her aching back. Slid her thumb along the sturdy rib that held the book together and shouted to the collection of pages as though it were a live thing.

"Why is it your spine gets to stay so straight when my back has ever been curved under the weight of slavery?"

The rage in her voice shocked the small room. Mercy. She gasped at the broken silence she had just created. Holding her breath against the possibility of awakening Emerald, she pushed the book to her chest. Monitored the sound of the girl's even breathing. Exhaled a slow breath and tried to walk back her crazy musings. Slavery is over, Violette. Do you hear? It's been over for four years now.

Thankful that she had not disturbed Emerald, she allowed her fingers to further explore the surface of the book as she pondered the words of its famous author, Harriet Beecher Stowe. Had "another and better day" truly dawned for black people, the way Stowe promised between these covers? If so, then why did Violette feel such a smothering loss tonight? And why after four years did she not have a penny to her name?

Crack! What in the . . .?

She held the book a bit firmer. Told herself the noise must have come from one of the limbs constantly falling onto the near-ruins of the former plantation called Riverwood. The place Violette had been forced to call home for nine years.

Something of the bereft passed over her, leaving her spirit restless, her body colder than the November night that seeped into the room. Again, she forced her back into the chill of the old brick dependency. Stretched her legs along the bleached planks and tried to force a yawn. The death of the reading flame meant there was nothing left except sleep.

But Violette could not sleep. Did not want to sleep. Not yet.

Eyes adjusting to the night that had invaded her space, she sighted the outline of the narrow floor mattress she shared with her daughter. Soiled. Scratchy. Curdled. Jammed against the opposite wall, it held Violette's most precious possession, thirteen-year-old Emerald. Not a bit the kind of bed Violette had hoped for her child —danced and clapped her hands for that spring night four years ago when she had reckoned herself a free woman. Then swiftly and utterly went out and destroyed hers and Emerald's future.

She shifted her hips along the scratchy floor and settled *Uncle Tom* onto her lap. Watching the lamp put forth a little cloud in the darkened space, she tried to pray but was overcome by a silent, bitter lament wrapped in the lingo of the slave she had once been.

Ha' mercy, Father. After nine long years, Emerald and me, we still stuck upstairs in this here room in back of Riverwood. Still stuck like common slaves.

Another loud, unbidden protest forced it way past her lips.

"Well, what's it going to be, Lord? Is it like Miss Stowe

3

predicted? Are we free, I and Emerald, or was the whole thing just a ruse? I want to know. I have to know—"

"Oh, good gracious, Vi'lette! Can't a person ever get a little sleep 'round here without putting up with you talking to yourself all the time? You making me crazy. You and them books. Both of y'all makes me plumb sick."

Scalp tingling, Violette listened as Emerald turned onto her side to face her. "Did you hear me, Vi'lette?"

Vi'lette. The hacking-off of her name each time Emerald called it mirrored the cuts to Violette's insides. Would the day ever dawn when her daughter would call her what she was? What she slaved to be every day of her life?

I. Am. Your. Mother.

The mother Emerald still believed to be her sister after all these years.

The girl's familiar scowl, though hardly discernible in the pitch of the room, was palpable. An icy rebuke. A precursor to the sharper one sure to come.

"You done gone to sounding like some of them whining white women you always reading about. All the time using words like 'ruse.' What that mean anyhow? As for me, I'm glad it's over."

"Glad what's over?"

"Glad the coal oil you stole along with that book is finally used up. Now maybe somebody can get some rest 'round here without that mumbling and play acting you do all the time while you reading." Emerald pitched her voice higher. "If you go'n read every blooming night, can't you just read to yourself?"

Violette's anger flared like the head on a matchstick, reminding her of her former self. Blooming? Why was the girl drawn to such language? And why did Violette put up with these remarks from her own child? A child born when Violette was no more than a child herself. She flexed her fingers—still intertwined—wrinkled, weather-worn digits of the lonely, unpaid washerwoman she had become.

4

Why don't you just tell her to shut up?

Give her a good whipping. Shout at her the way some of the slave mothers used to do back on the plantation before Riverwood, until Emerald understood that reading aloud at night, after bending her back and plunging her hands into other people's sweat all day, was the only way Violette kept her sanity. Help me, Jesus. The only way she was able to provide food and shelter for Emerald.

But she could neither do nor say any of these things. Didn't have the right. She placed the book against the wall. Knelt at the mattress's edge. Inhaled long and deliberately.

"Begging your pardon, honey, but I'm not stealing these books—"

"Stop calling me honey! Like I'm your little girl or something. If you want to say something sweet, then answer that letter from Aunt Dinah and Uncle Jonathan. Tell them we be glad to come to New Orleans and move in with them." Emerald gave Violette her back. Punched the lumpy mattress and started to cry.

"I j-just don't understand you, Vi'lette. Don't n-nothing h-happy ever happen out here at Riverwood. Ain't nobody even passing by on that road out there no more."

"Somebody must be passing for you to keep picking up words like 'blooming.'"

Emerald ignored her—as Violette knew she would—opting to avoid discussing how she had taken to hanging around the road lately, flirting with anything in britches.

"How c-come everybody be free to go wherever they please except us, Vi'lette? How come we ain't moved to town or some-where like the rest of the slaves what used to stay out here?"

Violette's stomach churned, the truth pushing against her breast like greens gone sour. How to explain to this child-woman that it was a simple matter of God's vengeance? Unpardonable sins in Violette's past that haunted her every waking hour. Most recently that night four years ago, when in one reckless hour of freedom under the hill, Violette had given up the privilege of

5

guiding her child. The child she never should have conceived in the first place.

No. No! She shook her head in the dark. Would not add that haunting beast to tonight's burgeoning list of hellhounds.

She leaned in close. Smoothed Emerald's thick, wiry hair. The only drop of pride Violette had left was this pitiful hermitage she had established for herself and her daughter on this relic of a plantation. A place where neither of the three men who had used her could touch her and her child. Since the war's end, she had been taking in wash loads every day including Sundays in exchange for room and board from her former owners, the McMillans, who still lived here. Money never crossed Violette's palm. No. Paltry though it was, this was the only protection she had to offer her child. This would have to do.

I won't go begging to Dinah and Jonathan even for you, Emerald.

"I told you, hon . . . Emerald. We won't go down there to New Orleans until we are able to pay our own way. Go on back to sleep, now."

Violette hushed. Waited. Prayed she had stemmed Emerald's latest tirade. She settled back onto her haunches and listened as Emerald's crying gave over to soft even snores. She stood. Stared at her child who was no longer a child. Body contours that Violette's mind steadfastly resisted had sprung up overnight, causing her to wonder how long the two of them would be able to share that narrow mattress. Violette had cried last week at the onset of her baby's menses. No question now but that Emerald was touching womanhood.

And she is touching beautiful.

Even the mistress of Riverwood had commented. "Quite alluring," she'd said, stopping short of the word beautiful.

Alluring. A potent, frightening word for a disgruntled yet budding young girl with no way of taking care of herself. No way of understanding the constant lecherous motives instilled into men. All men.

Yawning in earnest, Violette grasped the tail of a shift Dinah had made for her years ago. Maybe she could finally sleep. She pulled the shift over her head and—

Ummph!

She halted the shift in midair. Another noise? Not the split of a limb this time. More like a hissing, grunting scuffle in the narrow stairwell leading to her room. She tugged the shift back in place. Tried to think of the last time she'd heard anything of that sort at Riverwood.

Suddenly, the scent of two of the men from her past, Jethro McMillan and Eli Duggan, filled the space—the natural darkness that had claimed the room moments ago now a brooding presence around Emerald. No longer the absence of light, but a harmful, hovering thing shouting obscenities to Violette about the future of her child . . .

Soon she will be just like you. Only worse.

Calm yourself, Violette. You're imagining this. Eli is dead for sure. And you've not heard from Jethro in years.

She tiptoed backwards toward the wall and slid to the floor. Tried to create in her head the ending scene of the chapter she had been forced to forsake. This was just more silly imaginings. She needed to think concretely. Times like these made her wonder if Dinah's teaching her to read had been a blessing or a curse.

There it was again. The scent of imminent male aggression.

"Emerald. I have to save her. Somehow, I have to rescue her," she whispered.

Nonsense. There was nothing out there. She scrambled to her feet. Set out in a three-step pacing pattern. If only she could find a way to finish the chapter in *Uncle Tom's Cabin*, divert her thinking until sleep overtook her. Easing back to the floor, she felt along the wall until she found the box of matches she had used earlier. Matches she could ill afford to waste since there were only three

7

JACQUELINE FREEMAN WHEELOCK

left. Still, she had to have light to read, light to distract her from this craziness. Light to dispel the stench of what men—slave owners like Simon Legree in *Uncle Tom's Cabin*, slave drivers like Jethro, slaves themselves like Eli—had done to women like her and her mother. And would soon do to her child if she didn't do something.

Whoosh! She struck the match afire, looked at the thickness of the book, wondered if she was losing her mind. How long would a single match last? How many pages?

"Well, I'll just find out. First I have to find the page I last read."

But how to do that with a fast-dying match in one hand and a book in the other? She knew better than to crease a page in a book borrowed from the McMillan library. She would never have risked her reading privileges in such a manner. She grabbed the volume by its cover and shook it open hoping somehow to land where she'd left off.

Silly thang. How you expect to find a page like that? A thin bit of torn paper slipped from the back of the book. *Dearest Sarah Susan,*

A letter to Mistress McMillan? "Ain't got no business trying to read this."

The heat of the matchhead now unbearably close to her finger, she blew it out. Breathed heavily. Tossed around the idea of why an ex-plantation owner's wife would bother to read a book like *Uncle Tom's Cabin* in the first place. But truth told, Sarah Susan McMillan, strict though she was, had always had a little of the compassion of *Uncle Tom's* leading lady, Emily Shelby, in her. Violette struck her second match.

I thought you might want to know that a most troubling group calling itself the American Missionary Association of New York has purchased the bulk of our dear friend's, Mr. John Boddie's, former home in Madison County to start a school for the freed

Negroes. Though the property, I understand, was no longer in the name of Boddie when purchased, I'm certain your heart will be pained as is mine to learn of the fate of a place where such a good man set his hopes. I am told that they have already begun mutilating the mansion in preparation for the accommodation of the so-called students whose intellects will likely force them to take years to conquer a basic reader.

Liar. Violette had learned how to read in a matter of weeks. She hesitated then struck her last match.

Can you imagine, dear sister, the place of a man, almost sacred to us, now used to educate the uneducable? I know you don't quite agree with my assessment of the capabilities of Negroes, but bear with me in my candidness. Whether the portion of my information about the mansion is true I do not know. I can only rehearse what my husband has told me.

I hear the missionaries are quite avid and purposed, practically offering to give away their services to the Negroes. My heart bleeds for yet another fine Mississippi citizen whose heritage has been swallowed up by the leavings of the war.

Once again Violette pressed her back against the wall, the ragged edge of the truncated letter loosely held between her fingers, the lingering smells of smoke and male encroachment keeping her mind aflame. Jackson might as well be China for all the resources she had to access it. Yet for the first time, she saw a path, dimly lit but a way nonetheless to put miles of earth between Emerald and men like Eli and Jethro.

And Chester Singer. The last man with which she had passed that senseless hour on her one night of freedom.

Ideas tumbled over themselves like the waves of a spring flooding. If she could just earn enough money to get her to Jackson. If she could just find a way to make real money rather than trade her services to the McMillans.

If I could just. . . . Suddenly she had to find a way to feel coins in her hands. Any way. Except the one way that had gotten her into this fix in the first place.

Men.

CHAPTER 2

Tuesday, November second
Nine o'clock in the morning

"*N*ow you listen to me, boy. The only way to be a man in this world is by the strength of your own mind, the trigger of your own weapon, and the power of your own two fists."

Pieces of his dead father's philosophy floated in upon Benjamin Catlett's thoughts as he crossed the once familiar expanse of Riverwood Plantation. He pushed away the words as the useless flotsam he knew them to be. He didn't believe Rogers Catlett's arrogant, ungodly riffraff about the requirements of manhood. Nor the necessity of owning slaves.

Never had. Never would.

Steadying the toe of his polished boot on the edge of a magnolia stump hidden from view, he stood on the front acres of the plantation. Stared at the near side of one of its old servant dependencies. Caught himself talking out loud.

"Why in the name of all that's noble am I thinking of my father today?"

Why, indeed. Benjamin hated everything Rogers Catlett stood

for. Had left the state of Virginia meaning to never lay eyes on him again. He tapped his toe. Chafed at the way the day was going so far.

"And how did I manage to allow myself to be talked into visiting a woman who once tried to ruin the best friends I've ever had?"

Bent on clearing his head of these disparate thoughts, he set his mind to measuring the once exquisite Riverwood with a stick that no longer existed. Under different circumstances, a man might be a little saddened by the ruins. Gone were the magnificent landscapes, the unbroken whiteness of the skyward columns, the untainted red bricks that Benjamin had last seen years ago before Appomattox. Instead the land beneath his feet was hay. The trees and shrub an unkempt beard to the aging face of a mansion gone awry.

Curving a finger over his mustache, he rested his chin on his thumb. The aftermath of war had plainly left its mark on what had once been one of Natchez's finest dwellings. And truth be told, Benjamin Catlett really didn't care. The disturbing thoughts he held for the hundreds of people once enslaved by the owner of Riverwood were as palpable today as they were a decade ago. Though he would never admit it to the scores of white customers whose furniture he had crafted over the years, he hated Riverwood Plantation and all its ilk, strewn from Maryland to Texas. To his father's plantation in Virginia.

He smoothed the underside of his well-shaven chin. Only to please his best friend Jonathan Mayfield would he have traveled the mile or so out here to this deserted place. Only to satisfy Jonathan's wife Dinah, who urged Benjamin to test her best friend's arithmetic skills, would he speak to a woman as vicious as Violette McMillan. Any woman, for that matter, about the job of bookkeeping.

Well, not quite true. He wasn't solely out here to do the Mayfields a favor. As much as he hated to admit it, the cabinet-making business he managed, the very enterprise Jonathan had worked so hard to establish, was slipping into a mathematical morass, and Benjamin needed help. Though traffic was still fairly good, the bookkeeping was not. And if he didn't do something soon, the very business Jonathan had entrusted to Benjamin was going to be in peril. Jonathan's words from yesterday's letter had seemed timed for the moment.

"Despite what you believe, Benjamin, deep down Violette is a good person, and she and her little sister are in dire need. She could take care of the books if you are of a mind to allow it. All she needs is a week's worth of refreshing of her training, shall we say? And according to Dinah, perhaps a sizable dose of convincing that your offer isn't one of pity."

Refreshing? What did that mean? Benjamin looked up at the November sky. Filled his lungs with the crisp air and released it slowly. What would an uneducated, conniving ex-slave, and a female at that, already know about keeping books?

Jonathan's odd terminology aside, rumor had it that Violette McMillan had become an eccentric, reclusive washerwoman, causing Benjamin, who had thought of her often since the war's end, to keep his distance for years. Though his last memory of her was pleasant, his dominant recollection was filled with her malicious ways. He would always remember how she had exposed Jonathan, revealing that his manumission papers were burned and placing his hard-won livelihood as a free man of color in danger. Benjamin still didn't understand how Jonathan could forget.

An unexpected smile bloomed. Jonathan had mentioned Violette's little sister. The one good thing Benjamin's mind could hold on to about Violette McMillan was that darling of a baby sister she took care of.

"Emerald, was it? Wonder what's become of her?"

Removing his foot from the stump, he straightened his pant leg thinking, if Dinah says it's worthwhile talking to Violette, well . . . then . . . it must be true.

What did he have to lose? At the least, the part about the bookkeeping skills merited a try. He'd just have to be careful not to stumble upon that fierce pride the Mayfields had mentioned Violette possessing.

Somewhat heartened, he straightened his cravat, dusted his dustless hat, and rounded the corner that placed him at the edge of a small square between two dependencies. And nearly gasped like a woman.

"Great day in the morning!"

This part of the once immaculate estate was more derelict than any plantation he had seen since the war. Deader, more run down than he could have imagined from the front. Could this be where poor little Emerald was being reared?

The half-naked Virginia slave children he had been brought up around stepped in to replace Emerald in his thoughts. He had not been allowed to play with them. But he had watched them, their bare bottoms sliding down the hill behind the house. He had watched them perhaps too often. Especially a girl named Lucie. The girl he had wanted to marry. Lucy. Different spelling, but wasn't that the name of Emerald's rag doll? A question Benjamin had avoided for years pushed to the surface. And what is the reason you've deserted little Emerald all this time, my man?

Feeling far more uneasy about Emerald than he'd counted on, he turned to face the first building. Let's just get this over with. He placed his hand on the shaky knob. Took stock of the familiar door.

"No, no. This is where the kitchen used to be."

He turned back toward the small quad between the two dependencies. Footsteps from the stairwell to the right of the kitchen grabbed his attention.

"Help you?"

A young girl in a stunning woman's body placed her hand on one of her hips, leaned the other into the stairwell wall, and greeted him with sad, sultry eyes. He smothered a grin. Unpolished flirtation if he'd ever seen it. Yet something about the antic reminded him of Violette all those years ago. He would guffaw at the attempt if the scene wasn't so pitiful. But the girl, seemingly unaware, advanced her questioning toward what she obviously hoped would be her benefit.

"And who might you be looking for, suh?"

The urge to laugh persisted. Benjamin continued to stifle it.

"Well, I might be looking for anyone—the seven dwarfs, St. Nicholas, Simon Legree—anyone, but specifically I'm looking for a woman named Violette McMillan."

"Oh. Her."

Benjamin lifted his brow. "Do you know her? Is she here?"

The young girl brightened. "Wait! I know Simon Legree."

"Pity. Don't we all in some form or other. But it's Violette McMillan I'm looking for right now."

The girl frowned. Then, offering her best effort at advertising her developed curves, slowly made for the matching dependency on the other side of the mangy square. A hostile, demanding tinge colored her call as she neared the building.

"Vi'lette! Vi'lette, I know you hear me, girl."

Benjamin followed the girl to the leftmost door of the facing dependency and into the hot, sudsy smell of a laundry room. Bundles of what must be unwashed clothes in drawstring bags lined one wall, while large tubs of water and a hot stove obviously used to heat it held up the other. A petite woman leaned deeply over one of the tubs along the row, her sleeves rolled to the curves of her upper arms, her plaits unbound. She never looked up.

"What is it now, Emerald?"

Emerald? Benjamin halted his stride. Turned to reexamine the brash youngster who had slacked her pace. It cannot be. His little Emerald? Last he'd seen of her, she was still clinging to that ragdoll named Lucy and the miniature "big house" Jonathan had made for her. The girl standing in front of him was beautiful, looking anything but Violette's sister, choosing nothing of Violette's golden color and oval face. Instead, this new Emerald could much more easily belong to Dinah Devereaux Mayfield.

Tall, elegant, striking, Emerald and Dinah were of a piece. In a world where the very color of black seemed always used to paint the ugliness of life—black heart, black soul, black sheep—those two were born with velvety skin and dark, lengthy limbs that dared anyone to refute the God-crafted beauty of blackness. The smaller woman with the soft voice—wonder who she was?—continued without lifting her head.

"Whatever it is, honey, you don't have to scream my name. I think I'll still recognize it in a milder tone."

Wait. Benjamin took a quick survey. Debated if it was possible to overlook someone in such a close space. Where is . . . Was this soft-spoken woman supposed to be Violette?

She was half Violette's size. Her words sounded nothing like the Violette of old. Shot through with traces of defeat, the utterances were soothing, throaty—as though her very vocal apparatus had been refined by a merging of pain and beauty. And love.

But the poundage? What happened to the . . .? Poundage, smoundage. Away with the woodworking talk, Benjamin! What had happened to the plain old fat?

Benjamin repented. Redoubled his effort to be sober. Of a certainty, Violette had begun to slim down last time he saw her in that kitchen across the way. But this—this was beyond any change he could have conjured up. Violette was as beautiful as her little sister, only in way that spoke an ocean width of difference.

"You got company, Violette."

He could but gaze as, hands fixed on the washboard, the woman turned her eyes toward where he stood. Her expression revealed instant recognition, for she, too, Benjamin guessed, must be remembering the passionate sparks that flew between them the last time they met just yards from this room. Still, despite her beauty and the passable work clothes she wore, her eyes bespoke the need Jonathan wrote about.

"Mr. Catlett. Mr. Benjamin Catlett. Why, I haven't seen you in the longest time." Her speech was fluid. Studied. Remarkable for a slave. "I thought you had moved on. What on earth are you doing way out here at Riverwood?"

His mind pitched like a ship in a storm. What *was* he doing out here? Images of his Lucie—the myriad kinks of her hair pressed flat to her head, her full-figured body confined behind a set of Benjamin's mother's stays—assailed him. Violette looked nothing like Lucie. Yet the familiar pull on him to make things right for her, to perhaps fix things for this woman just as he had wanted to do for Lucie all those years ago. . . He fought for some semblance of comportment.

"Well, the fact is I came to see if I might add myself to your docket of laundry customers."

Great thunder, man!

As if this poor girl would know the meaning of the word "docket." An inanity if he had ever heard one. Inwardly, Benjamin groaned. What Violette needed right now was not a lesson in vocabulary. What she needed was help. His help, the same way he had helped talk sense into Jonathan's head when he was about to lose Dinah. The way he had helped his new northern white friend Paul Boatwright understand southern culture. The way he had tried to help Lucie. If only. . . He steered his mind away from Lucie.

Yes. It was clear that what Violette McMillan needed was guidance. Benjamin's guidance. And he would remedy that need. Now.

"Violette? Would you be able to wash for me?"

CHAPTER 3

*V*iolette lifted her hands from the slick, brownish-gray water and stared at a part of her past. Uninvited, the memories came rushing back. The way she had treated Dinah Devereaux when first Violette had met her—meanness fueled by the sheer force of Dinah's elegance and the fear that she would steal Violette's newfound job in Riverwood's kitchen.

And steal Eli Duggan. A man Violette wouldn't accept now if he were offered to her on a golden platter.

Then there was Violette's loud deliberate exposure of Jonathan Mayfield's lost freedom papers in front of dozens of other slaves, knowing the revelation could mean the end of the business he had worked so hard to establish.

Finally, there was the poignant memory of Dinah's soft heart when she found out Emerald was not Violette's sister but her bastard child by Eli Duggan. Dinah had to have figured out that, if discovered, both Violette and her child could be returned to the fate of another lust-driven slave named Jethro who also happened to be a slave driver. Yet she exacted no vengeance.

Still, something was wrong with the reason Benjamin had just given for being out here. Too many struggling washerwomen in town for Mr. Benjamin Catlett, who to Violette's knowledge hadn't bothered to set foot on Riverwood since '61, to show up of a Tuesday morning eight years later looking for someone to launder his clothes.

And speaking of clothes, the man was even more handsome than she had remembered in those errant dreams she was forced to tolerate every now and again. While Jonathan Mayfield was exceedingly tall, Benjamin probably shied away from six feet by an inch or so. Just right for Violette's height. He wore tan pants and a black coat, set off by a cherry-red vest and a white cravat. He stood with one knee slightly relaxed. One of his shoulders listed toward the ground, giving him an undeniable look of dapperness that flew in the face of that image of a common laborer he once projected. He had always worn his clothes easily as though they were tailored, not just for the svelte body he was in, but for the essence of the man. For the first time, Violette was prompted to probe the reasons why. Why had he always owned an air of superiority? Who was Benjamin Catlett really? Nobody she could remember had ever seemed to know. Not even Jonathan Mayfield, the man whose business Benjamin now ran.

She corralled her thoughts. Glanced down at her dripping, soapy hands. Suddenly aware of the crisscrossed lines that were her skin, she plunged them wet into her apron pocket and straightened to face him. Curiosity too far gone to resist, she decided to go along with his request for a laundress.

"I'm afraid you would have to see Mistress Sarah Susan about that. I'm not in business for myself. I wash for the McMillans."

"Oh?"

She knew she had thrown him. Definitely had his interest. For the fun of it, she would see how long she could keep it. Though the workloads seemed to become fewer by the day, still this was her only means of feeding herself and Emerald. She really didn't have time for these games. But she would make time, just this once.

"Yes. Haven't you heard? I'm afraid my ex-master has come

19

upon hard times since the war. Something about throwing all his good gold after bad Confederate banknotes. And now he and Mistress McMillan are left with only their house and Emerald and me. We have an arrangement. The mistress decides for whom I wash. I do the washing for room and board." He seemed genuinely surprised.

"I—well—I did notice the condition of the grounds. No one else on the place except the four of you?"

"A handful of hired ex-slaves are in and out, but I and my sister are the only permanent ones left on the premises."

Violette felt the coming interruption, saw Emerald batting her eyelids with the rapidity of a hummingbird's wings.

"And I'm bound to change that 'cause I'm leaving Violette right here in this lonely place, soon's somebody ask me to go with him."

Violette's stomach lurched, Emerald's suggestiveness tilting the game in Benjamin's favor. Blessedly, he ignored her.

"But how is it that you do not take in your own work? It seems simple enough. You do the laundry. You earn your wages. You pay your rent, buy your food."

Violette cocked her head to the side. Shot him a calculated frown. He might look good, but the arrogance, plainly leading him by the nose, grated her. He reminded her of Augustine St. Clare in *Uncle Tom's Cabin*, a concoction of innocence and haughty confusion, somewhere between compassion and nauseating condescension. If she wasn't looking at his color, she could almost believe he, like the character St. Clare, owned slaves and was just about to make excuses for it.

"Spoken like a free man who never really understood the mind of the slaveholder, Mr. Catlett. You don't quite grasp it, do you? In the McMillan's minds, I still belong to them, especially Mr. McMillan who, though perhaps a good man in the paternalistic sense, has always and will continue to put his, his children's, and Miss Sarah Susan's welfare first. It's as simple as that. So I wash and they keep the money, offering me only room and board for myself and my dau . . . sister."

Oh, lord. Had she just almost stumbled into the word, daughter? Rarely talking to anyone at length anymore, she had nearly forgotten how to discipline her thoughts before releasing them. She had become more vulnerable, especially with the habit of reading aloud, to thoughts slipping into sound. Oh, Lord.

"I should say right now that even if the McMillans did allow me to wash for colored people, you would have to bring your things out here. I have neither the means nor the desire to wash in town."

He stared right through that blatant lie about her desire. She stared right back, damp hands firmly in her pockets. Until he shot forth a question as far-fetched from the present conversation as was the idea of landing on the moon.

"Are you any good at tallying numbers?"

Violette averted her glare. Allowed her mind to calculate. Men! This irrelevant question smacked of Jonathan Mayfield. Had his well-meaning, male-dominating signature written all over it.

"And may I ask why you are asking?"

BENJAMIN WAS STEAMING. How dare she insult and then question him. He? Not "understanding the mind of a slaveholder like McMillan?" Oh, yes, he did. If this woman only knew. Paternalistic? Indeed! Who did she think she was? And from whence comes a word out of an ex-slave's mouth—well, maybe Jonathan's and Dinah's, but they were the exceptions—like "paternalistic?"

"Don't pay her no mind. She can do whatever you ask. She got the brain for it."

Emerald. Again. She seemed to be immensely enjoying the insults flying between Benjamin and her sister. And oddly, where

Violette spoke with studied polish, the younger sibling seemed to wear her broken speech like a defiant badge.

"She read all the time. Just ask her what she reading now. A body can't hardly get no sleep at night for her whispering, most times loud, always using up what li'l lamplight we might need later on."

"Emerald, that's enough. My reading habits are no concern to an important man like Mr. Catlett, nor would he be interested in what I read, I'm sure."

And what was Benjamin supposed to do with that leading statement? Perhaps say "Au contraire! I'm dying to know how you have managed such a cultural change out here on this deserted estate. And furthermore, how did you turn into such a beauty in the meantime?"

Oh, but she was manipulative. Beneath that veneer of self-refinement was the same old cunning yet volatile Violette, making him the enemy here, and he wouldn't stand for it. Either she wanted a job or she didn't. He would get it out of her right now, and whether it was an up or down answer, he would leave this heaven-forsaken place immediately.

"You've not answered my question. Are you good with numbers?"

"Dinah says I am."

Her eyelids lowered. In hope possibly? Benjamin would never understand women if he lived to be a hundred and ninety-six.

"She says I have a natural ability with figures, though my preferences are history and literature."

"And how would Dinah know?"

She glared at him with a half-smile. "As if you don't already know, it's because I kept the books for Jonathan a while, before the war was over."

"And, Mr. Catlett, I bet you don't know that shortly after the war was over, she and that old man went down—"

"Emerald! Do. Not."

Violette flushed like a white girl, fear glistening in her eyes. But Benjamin was too shocked by what he'd just heard about her bookkeeping experience to pay attention to Emerald. So that was what Jonathan meant by refreshing her training.

"You did what? B-but how could you have worked for Jonathan and I know nothing about it? I'm always there, have been since the late fifties."

Violette quickly reset.

"That I don't know. You would have to ask him. He is still the owner, isn't he? And you two are still friends, I suppose? Otherwise, you wouldn't be here. I know Jonathan and Dinah put you up to offering me a job, but I don't take charity even from my friends' friend."

"And you were paid—for keeping the books?"

"Do I look like I've been paid anytime during the last decade?"

"As a matter of fact, you do."

He paused. Wondered about the sudden flare of her nostrils. Studied her and Emerald a bit longer, relieved to find something to hang a plausible argument upon.

"Those clothes you're wearing aren't exactly the kind of plantation issue many ex-slaves are still wearing."

That familiar gathering of fine wrinkles between Violette's brows was instant. Benjamin knew he had somehow pushed her back a little. Good. He was tired of being against the wall in this interchange. Tired of being outmatched by this little washerwoman. After all, wasn't he the one who had come offering compassion and good will?

"Again, not your concern. Sir."

Sir? She was toying with him again. Memory crept beneath Benjamin's red vest and up past his immaculate cravat. Coldstopped him. He had needled Jonathan with that term countless times in the past, and somehow Violette knew it. Thinking back on it, why had he done that? Was it because somewhere deep down he was ridiculing his friend? Felt a little superior to "ex-slave" Jonathan? To Violette right now?

Ludicrous.

"Mr. Catlett?"

"Huh? I mean, I beg your pardon, Violette. What did you ask?"

"I didn't ask anything of you, not yet. Rather you asked something of me. And I've already answered. Yes. I do know numbers. It just sort of comes naturally to me. And now I have a question: since you've come looking for a laundress, what business is it of yours whether I know numbers or not?"

VIOLETTE'S HEARTBEAT ticked upwards at an alarming pace. How dare he? Of course, she had been paid for her services during the time she had worked for Jonathan and Dinah. But it wasn't anyone's business, especially not Benjamin Catlett's, that she had not a dime of it left. Had squandered it on something so utterly irresponsible, with someone so utterly reprehensible, that only a snatch of its memory sent her into a panic.

If he only knew how careless she could be with money. How careless she had been that night with Chester Singer. She resented the fact that in Jonathan's attempt to sell her as a laundry woman, he might have tried to enhance the recommendation by mentioning her skill with numbers.

Hoping her shaking hands had dried out enough, she lifted them from the apron pockets trimmed with Dinah's lace. She righted herself. Crossed her arms and waited for this insufferable, self-absorbed fellow to answer.

"I—uh—that is . . . a job at the Mayfield property awaits you, if you're interested."

Back to the washerwoman job offer, then. In hard statement form, he had just reiterated his offer about a laundress. Completely ignoring her question about his strange interest in her numbers

24

ability, almost as a master would. Stripping his words of the polite humility that Violette had somehow hoped might be embedded in a simple request.

Would you perhaps be interested, Miss McMillan? Have you considered how nice it might be to view the river each day?

Too many English novels.

She felt the involuntary stretching of her eyes, but she didn't answer. Instead, she continued to stare. Too long. Benjamin turned on his heels and headed for the door, speaking over his shoulder.

"I suppose I have my answer."

"No, wait!" Violette's insides contracted as Emerald jumped from the top of an overturned tub, abandoning the evocative perch that frightened and sickened her mother.

"Violette, is you done lost your mind?"

"No, Emerald, I have not lost my mind."

Violette looked toward the tense shoulders shadowing the door. How desperately she needed this work, especially now that the very smell of Eli and Jethro had assaulted her and she was intent on taking Emerald to Jackson. But not from Benjamin Catlett.

"Just stay out of this. I have not lost my mind. And my mind, such as it is, says no."

CHAPTER 4

Wednesday, November third
Eight o'clock in the morning

$\mathcal{V}$iolette took one last look at the door to the room where Emerald still lay sleeping. Descended the stairs. Looked up at the dark, glowering heavens. Jumped at the growling thunder. She chuckled.

"At least my Creator is still talking to me this morning because Emerald certainly is not."

The child had not spoken a word to Violette since Benjamin left yesterday in a huff. Neither had sleep touched Violette's eyelids last night, its usual heavy-handedness after a long day of washing overwhelmed by a night of relentless and petty self-recrimination.

Why had she been so prideful?

"Yes, I'd like very much to hear more about the offer." That was all she had needed to say. Why hadn't she just said those few words? Would it have cost her so much?

And now this.

She splashed through the sudden downpour and crossed the

rear verandah into the servant's hall, wondering why Sarah Susan McMillan had summoned her to appear at eight o'clock on a Wednesday morning when the bulk of the week's laundry was at its peak. It had been months since she had gone into the house, one of the sporadic hires usually coming to the dependency to negotiate the laundry intake and bring her the food allotment. The disarray of the once-immaculate mansion nearly leveled her. The halls were stacked with boxes, spider webs fairly dripping from the lofty moldings. Old food smells were rampant from kitchen neglect as musty carpet, faded drapery, and chair stains dotted the interior landscape of Riverwood.

Dinah, you would be appalled.

She crossed the wide hall. Glanced at the chipped ionic columns she once so admired and tapped lightly on the pocket door to the drawing room.

"Yes, who is it?"

The voice was gurgled, near incomprehensible. "Mrs. McMillan? It's me, Violette. Is it all right to come in?"

No answer. Except the sound of a cough so violent, so lung-shattering as to cause Violette to press her fingertips to her own chest. Gingerly she pushed open the door, years of ingrained slave behavior causing her to wonder if she was doing the right thing. Or would she be scolded for breach of protocol?

Even though the woman sounded as though her next step would usher her through the gates of hell, old fear caused Violette to stop just past the threshold.

"A glass of water, ma'am?"

Sarah Susan McMillan answered with a dismissive wave, then beckoned Violette inside. Not knowing what else to do, Violette drew close to the desk where the mistress of Riverwood was seated and waited for the woman's coughing fit to subside.

"You may sit if you like."

"No, ma'am, I thank you. The wash is waiting, and I'm afraid I find myself a little behind today."

"Oh? Why is that?"

Heavens. Why had she admitted that? "Emerald and I were a bit under the weather yesterday, s-so I wasn't quite as caught up as I wanted to be when the darkness fell."

"Still you might have used your kerosene lamp. Mightn't you?"

Scattered prickles of fear lit up Violette's skin. She would not —could not afford to—tell this woman about her misuse of her coal oil allotment. Nor of Benjamin's offer. It might be considered effrontery even by a white woman as lenient as the mistress of Riverwood. Unless . . .

Does she already know about the offer? The needles of fear redoubled. Is that what this is all about?

"I'm curious, always have been. Why is your sister called Emerald?"

Violette froze just as a peal of thunder shook the panes. Thank the Lord. She had been given a few seconds to think. But when her mouth opened, nothing came. How could she explain the impression the fake green jewel she had once seen around the neck of the plantation overseer's wife had had on her? "It's s'posed to be an emerald," she had said, "a precious gem. It ain't real though."

But it was real to a twelve-year-old slave named Violette. The prettiest thing she had ever seen. Two years later, she named her baby Precious Emerald McMillan. But not until she met Dinah did she find out what a real gem Emerald was.

"No matter."

Sarah Susan's voice was raspy, her naturally diminutive frame seeming to withdraw into nothingness by the minute. She hacked again, this time a nervous empty scratching.

"Violette, I want you to hear me well. I take no pleasure in what I'm about to say, but say it I must."

A spasm of real coughing left an incalculable time gap. Violette knew she should be more concerned about the woman's health than anything else, but her nerves had so intently grabbed onto the foreboding of the little Mistress McMillan had already said until

Violette could only think of what was to come next. People who owned people, like Augustine St. Clare in the book she so desperately wanted to finish and Sarah Susan McMillan, were incapable of understanding the power of words upon a slave.

"I have a lung disease. We have sold Riverwood. We will be out by week's end."

Violette must have been staring in a brazen way because Sarah Susan looked surprised. Affronted. "Violette? Did you not understand me?"

"Yes, ma'am. Am I . . . I mean . . . are Emerald and I to come too?"

She saw the "no" in the woman's eyes before she said it. Felt it in the tremor of her own person. She had to do something. Owed it to Emerald to find a way. She reached for humility she really didn't have. Found it in a Savior she had neglected and didn't deserve.

"Please?"

Silence. As Violette's ex-mistress's peaked eyes shone with tears. "I never thought to say this in my lifetime, but we cannot afford you anymore. We can hardly afford our own groceries. Where we're going—which is to live with my sister, by the way— the laundry arrangement we have with you would simply be out of the question. I am sorry."

Violette recalled the sister's letter about the mansion near Jackson that was about to be turned into a school. Recalled the mention of Sarah Susan's sympathy toward blacks. Knew her present words to be heartfelt.

"And Violette, you may keep the book you are reading, as well as whatever else you might like from the library."

"Thank you. I believe I will. Emerald and I will be out by morning."

"Oh, no. That won't be necessary. Although we are selling the furniture and only taking our clothing, we won't be leaving before next week."

Violette backed away from the desk, a couple of times glancing up at the towering ceiling to keep from screaming. "Again, I thank you, ma'am, but we should be going on into Natchez to see what we might be able to find."

Her head held high, she turned and worked her way back across the cluttered hall into the soggy air. She managed to make it to the back of the dependency where she vomited and cried as she had not done since she was fourteen and newly aware of being pregnant by a man who once called her a pig. Unable to tell where the rain ended and the tears began, she lifted her face to the sky.

"Lord, Your word says pride goes before destruction and a haughty spirit before a fall." Talk about a haughty spirit. Was there ever a man more full of himself than Benjamin Catlett? "I go to Benjamin Catlett with nothing. Not a penny in my pocket. Not an inch of pride left in my soul. Please make him say yes."

For Emerald's sake, she would do it. Knowing Benjamin never thought her smart enough in the first place, she wouldn't ask for the bookkeeping job she'd once had. She would simply ask his help to start a washing business so that she could get her child to Jackson and into that school. And if she had to, she would beg. Beg? She had sworn she was done with that on the night she dragged herself up from Natchez Under-the-Hill, and here she was about to descend back into that slime pit for the second time in a twenty-four-hour period. Though she'd said not more than seconds ago that all her pride was gone, when she thought of facing that uppity, mysterious lady killer named Benjamin Catlett, it took her to the brink of more than she could bear.

One thing for sure, more humility than she had ever dug up for Sarah Susan McMillan was going to be needed. And soon.

CHAPTER 5

Thursday, November fourth
Mayfield Cabinetry

"*M*r. Catlett, you kinda early today, ain't you?"

Benjamin listened to the squish-squish of waterlogged shoes, as Henry, the young man who had finished one of the finest apprenticeships he had ever known, advanced across the wet threshold and into the back portion of the shop, leaving the question hanging. The rain had not stopped since yesterday morning. Instead, it had continued in a soft, straight-down direction that made Benjamin want to quit the shop. Go to Jonathan's house next door that Benjamin had occupied for years and disappear beneath one of Dinah's exquisite counterpanes.

The ex-apprentice halted. Looked rather taken aback, then pivoted around toward the wall clock next to the door.

"Is something wrong, Mr. Catlett? Did I do something wrong? Am I late?"

"No." In the years since Jonathan left, the budding artisan had never been late. Not once.

"No? Then how come you already in your apron with sawdust

riding your eyebrows? Ever since your trip out to Riverwood the other day, you've seemed a little put out. Everything turn out all right out there?"

"I'm fine, Henry. I think I just said that, didn't I?"

"Uh, no, suh, you didn't. All you said so far this morning was 'no.'"

All right, so maybe he had just thought he said it. Hoped the preemptive lie he had practiced in his head for Henry would keep him from having to discuss the last couple of nights at all with their total absence of sleep and constant wonderings about Riverwood's resident washerwoman. Why had she been so adamant? Benjamin had expected resistance, but not like that, not a bloodless "no." As clean cut as a sawn piece of fine oak. For the first time in nearly forty-eight hours, Benjamin chuckled. Determined little thing, wasn't she?

A trace of irritation shadowed Henry's face. "Did I say something that made you laugh, Mr. Catlett?"

Benjamin schooled himself. Tried to suppress this new heart disturbance that surfaced when he thought of Violette. Violette. A yellow-colored girl with a purple name. He paused. Had Henry just raised his voice?

An image of Benjamin's father, whip partly wrapped around his knuckles, assailed him. Rogers Catlett would never allow a raised voice from someone who took orders from him . . .

"You're too soft, son. You'll never make a leader. You have to show them or they'll show you."

The memory shocked Benjamin. He stiffened, so much so that, for a second, he wondered if he would ever be able to propel his body forward again. He tried to concentrate on the sound of the rain. Useless. He was not a slave owner. Had left that life behind—spent over a decade in the Deep South trying to make up for being born into slaveholding. He gave himself a mental shaking. What was happening to him that would make him even think of his father's disciplinary methods? Raised voice notwithstanding, Henry was owed an explanation.

"No. Nothing funny coming from you. Just a minor distraction in my head is all."

"Yes, suh. I be about my work then."

Henry slid a ridiculous-looking homemade mask onto his face as he settled behind the work table. Benjamin tried to smile. The boy had come a long ways—no longer a budding artisan, really. Once a naïve and gangly slave apprentice to Jonathan Mayfield, Henry Livingston had grown into a smart and robust man quite capable of starting his own business. Henry had turned out pretty well under his tutelage, Benjamin mused, even if Benjamin had to say it himself.

Granting himself that pat on the back, Benjamin inched further, recalling how much sweat he alone had put into the boy's future as a free man. Of course, Jonathan had helped. But it was Benjamin who in the last two years had taught the boy the finer points of cabinetmaking. Benjamin who had begun to polish the edges of an ex-field slave hired out as a potential furniture maker before the war. For weeks, he had been waiting for just the right time to reward him. Why not now? Not only would it bless Benjamin's protégé, it would stem the questions about his failed venture the other day to help an ex-slave. He pointed toward a bench.

"Sit down, my friend."

"Have I done something?"

Palm raised, Benjamin stayed the muffled interruption from behind the mask. His heart rate surged again causing him a moment of dismay. Why was he so excitable lately? Something about this—the power to shape lives—split the difference between comfort and dis-ease. Just happy for the young brother, that's all.

"Have a seat." The boy pushed the mask to his forehead while Benjamin paced—strutted?—rather like an overinflated rooster. "For some time now, I've been thinking of going back to Virginia where I was born." He paused for the boy's reaction. Received none. "So. Since the war is over and my mother is still there, I was thinking of talking with Jonathan about what to do with the business should I decide to make my departure from Natchez and return to my native—"

Henry pulled down his mask. His eyes shifted between the side door to the shop and Benjamin. "Uh, Mr. Catlett."

Blast! As it stood already, Benjamin wasn't the best at this speechifying thing the way his father had been. Could Henry not wait until he was done?

"What is it, Henry?" Benjamin's voice took on an edge that surprised even him. "And please take off than mask."

"Yes, suh. But uh, ruh, I believe you have company."

HEAD TILTED BACK to the point of neck strain, Violette stood in the relentless rain and stared at the two-story home before her, then jumped at another raucous sound coming from the Mississippi River.

"Goodness gracious, them whistles is loud." Emerald stuck her fingers in her ears and giggled. "Where they coming from?"

"Boats, I guess."

She would never get used to this incessant racket. All of it—the muddy streets, the animal sounds, the closely-spaced houses, even the occasional laughter—sounded to her like one big murky threat, surrounding, oppressing, and entering her soul at once. Would Jackson be like this? And the men. How was she going to navigate being around a bunch of men?

Emerald's voice cut into her apprehension. "Ain't it all just so grand, Violette? I can't wait to meet some of the town folks."

Recalling that she'd only been in the town of Natchez twice while her daughter, for all intent, had never really even seen the place, Violette chuckled.

"I guess you could call some of it grand, the homes and the

riverboats if nothing else, though some of the cities I've read about —New Orleans among them—would likely put Natchez's grandeur to shame."

Emerald spread her arms to the dripping sky. "Uh-umm. Can't nothing be grander than this here." As though their thoughts were synchronized, they both resumed their stares at Jonathan Mayfield's home, now turned Benjamin Catlett's.

"Violette? You sure this where Mr. Benjamin live? Goodness, what I wouldn't give to live here."

"I'm not sure. Just going by what I was told by one of the workers out at Riverwood. He said it was next door to a Mr. William Johnson's house, a colored barber who once did real well for himself."

"What do you mean by 'did well for himself?'"

"He was a barber and he owned—"

Violette caught herself. No. No-no. Though she admired much of what she had heard about the Barber of Natchez, she would not poison her child with the knowledge that this black man had once purchased some of his own people. She herself had never known a black slave owner, and she didn't want to. Ever.

"Vi'lette?" A shot of curiosity, something other than romance, seemed to claim Emerald. "Well, what did he own? I hate it when you stop your talking right in the middle like that. I ain't no child no more, you know. How did he build his house? Is any other black people living in houses like these two?"

"One question at a time, honey." Emerald cast her a daggered look. "All right, I take back the 'honey.' He, that is, Mr. Johnson, owned a lot of—uh—property. Anyway, it doesn't really matter now. He's been dead nearly twenty years." Violette cleared her throat. Changed the subject. "It's time for us to talk to Mr. Catlett, see if I can build a washing business with his help. I believe the shop is behind the house here."

Violette turned into the narrow lane running parallel to the house. She directed Emerald to place the small bag of belongings next to the outer wall underneath the eaves and searched out the entrance to the famous cabinetmaking shop she had heard so much about. In truth, there were two side doors, the first one seemingly leading to the customer's side of the shop while the other must have gone directly to the workshop itself. Fear rushed her along seemingly with the same wind that slanted the rain. She tried to put her arms around Emerald, for her own comfort as well as her daughter's. Emerald would have none of it.

"Stop that! What if someone sees us all hugged up like I'm a baby. I'm near 'bout a woman, Vi'lette. When you go'n understand that?"

She would never understand that. "Sorry. I'm just a little nervous."

Squaring her shoulders, Violette grasped the doorknob. Entered the smell of moist sawdust and looked into the shocked eyes of Benjamin Catlett. Barely saw the man who, wearing some kind of mask, had turned his back and gone into a corner to work, she guessed. She walked up to the long table of tools and machinery where Benjamin stood.

"I came for the job . . . that is, if you still want . . . I mean to say . . . need me."

WANT. Need. Words with which Benjamin had cut off familiarity. Ever since the tragedy with Lucie, he had guided his life by what he deemed others might want or need. He was a fixer. Wants and needs had no place in him. He was a builder not just of tester beds and wardrobes but of lives.

Except for Lucie's.

Quick. He had to be quick about it. He snatched the rag from his pocket. Was the moisture in his eyes coming from inside? No. Of course not. It was the air around him. It's humid in here. Yes. Humidity along with the ever-present sawdust fumes.

"I do still want, I mean, need you." He conjured up a laugh. "All you have to do is look around at that desk, and you'll see the need." A puzzled look covering her face, Violette leaned in to do just that.

"Are you saying I'll be working out here someplace or would you prefer I do my job in your house? That is your house now, out front there?"

"Yes. No. The house still belongs to Jonathan, but we have an arrangement."

"Oh." Her eyes brightened. "And the profits? Is the business still making money as it was with Jonathan and Dinah?" She pressed her fingertips against her lips. "I'm sorry. I shouldn't have asked that. It's no concern of mine."

Lucie would have asked an unladylike question such as that, that is, before Benjamin and his mother would have rushed to correct her. Still, it was a worthy question. Benjamin knew his friends depended on the Natchez shop in case something went wrong in the fledgling New Orleans business. They had hinted of rumors of white backlash. White business owners were becoming increasingly hostile toward men like Jonathan and Benjamin, spurred on by secret ex-Confederate soldiers and ex-planters whose hate for ex-slaves and the Federal Government was boiling to overflow. The result was the flaying of backs as badly if not worse than slavery time. The crushing of spirits that had just emerged from the wombs of rebirth.

"The profits are fine at the moment, though more and more disgruntled southerners seem to be involving themselves in secret revolts against black business and politics, due to what they see as unfair government regulations."

Silence.

"Uh, Mr. Catlett where will Emerald and I be staying?"

~

VIOLETTE WAITED. And waited. Hours—days, perhaps?—passed before he answered her. Finally, he turned back toward her. "It's simple really. Our books are in something of a . . . ahem! . . . tangle."

The rain had picked up. She stared at him. Strained to hear him. She'd asked him about a place to stay. He had answered something about books. Was the man not understanding her? Did he need a—what was it Sarah Susan McMillan called it—a librarian? Why, as much as she loved books, she could never do that. Didn't know how. She'd come to wash his clothes!

"I didn't come to dust off books." She thought better of it. "But, of course, I will if that's what you want."

"You misunderstand me. I'm not looking for a housekeeper."

"I don't . . . then why are you needing me?"

"Well, I'm sure, if you're as good as Jonathan says you are, you know that any business needs to monitor its earnings and expenditures at all times."

Not really. Violette had only done what Jonathan had directed her for the relatively short time she had worked for him.

"Good books, bookkeeping, if you will, mirror progress or the lack thereof. Violette? Are you comprehending what I say?" That old air of slave master condescension dug into Violette's nerves. She wanted to bolt. Looked at Emerald. Couldn't.

"Violette? Shall I continue?"

"Continue."

"While business still runs briskly, Henry and I are too busy to—"

"Are you good with numbers?" That's what he had asked her two days gone. It couldn't be that . . . could it be that he truly wanted her to keep books?

"—monitor our profits tightly enough."

"Oh yes. Yes, of course."

Benjamin smiled, all traces of a slave master gone. "Then you will do it?"

"I will."

"There's only one thing, then, two really. I would need you to start right away." He halted. Did Violette detect a bit of nervousness?

"And, uh, I suppose you would have to move onto the Mayfield properties until we could find other arrangements."

A sharp sound split the air as Emerald clapped her hands and danced around the sawdust-matted floor, skidding to a stop in front of Benjamin.

"Well, cursed be Canaan! If that ain't the best news I heard in a month of Sundays."

Cursed be Canaan? If there had been hesitation about the offer —second thoughts about moving her child into Natchez and ultimately to Jackson—they fled at the utterance of only three words. So, it was true. Emerald had been listening to her nightly readings, "Cursed be Canaan," an exact rendering from *Uncle Tom's Cabin*. Trouble was, poor little Emerald had no idea what it meant, neither its origin nor the twisted way it had been used to justify African enslavement. More than ever the moment was weighted with the need to save Emerald. Violette thought she just might scream. Instead, she reached inside for the vision of a lady that Dinah Devereaux Mayfield's very bearing had unwittingly etched onto her faculties.

"If it is to your liking, sir, my sister Emerald and I are ready to move in today. Will we be upstairs or down?"

CHAPTER 6

ove in? What had he just promised? Benjamin hadn't given the slightest consideration to the fact that Violette and her sister might think he meant the main house. He was speaking of placing a couple of cots here in the shop until they could find a boarding house or something. He had simply assumed, as with any hire, she would at least aid in looking to her own housing.

She's a slave, man. Slaves know nothing of how to do these things.

He chanced a look at the two of them standing there like the bookends of beauty. One thing for certain, he was going to have to reverse this. They could not stay with him in the big house. Benjamin was too used to his own space. The only-child in him— the slaveholder's son in him?—demanded his privacy.

Banish the thought. Hadn't he worked alongside slaves and ex-slaves like a common laborer for over ten years, proven himself as black as the next man?

He reined in the creeping disturbance. He had to work this out. Perhaps Henry. Yes, Henry.

"Henry!"

"Yes, suh."

Benjamin noticed that Henry had not said a word in the last half hour. Sat as frozen as a Canadian river. "You're mighty quiet over there.

"Sorry, suh."

"Henry, we're going to need your help here, but—uh—first I should introduce you, shouldn't I. And please remove that mask." Benjamin hooked his fingers into the sides of his apron bib. "Henry Livingston, Violette McMillan and her sister Emerald. Violette and Emerald, my very capable assistant, Henry Livingston."

Henry grinned. Grinned like Benjamin had never seen him grin before. "Vi'lette. Girl. I ain't seen you in I don't know the day. Just waiting for a chance to say howdy. Almost didn't recognize you 'cept for that cute li'l frown you always had between your brows."

Violette's smile fairly dried up the rain clouds.

"Henry? Is that you?" She covered the room in a quick, graceful sweep. Benjamin's assistant receiving a hug in a way Benjamin himself might only dream of.

"You two know each other?"

Violette smiled even brighter, her whole distracting body exuding a comfort he had never seen in her before.

"For certain, sir. We've known each other since—"

"Since we was both just tall enough to—"

"Shake hands with Master McMillan's puppies," they both said in unison.

Bursting into a bevy of chortles and giggles, they shared some kind of history that set Benjamin's ears to pinging.

"And what about me?" Emerald swayed her lithe body over toward Henry. Her hands behind her back, her bosom thrust forward. "Don't I get to be better introduced by my sister?"

An awkward moment passed between Violette and Henry, leaving Violette with a quiver in her voice. "Oh, of course. I'm sorry, honey."

Emerald employed the rapid-fire eye-batting again. But this time Benjamin was not at all amused. "Now, don't chu be honeying me, Violette."

"Oh. Forgive me."

Violette clutched the sides of her wet shift. The same one she had worn when he last saw her. So unnerved he'd not really thought of it, it occurred to Benjamin that she and Emerald must have walked here in the rain.

Moved by a sudden urge to protect them, Benjamin wanted to run. Instead he willed himself to listen as Violette looked on her sister with a love so strong it nearly flattened Benjamin.

"Henry, this is my younger sister, Emerald. Where I go, she goes and vice versa. Emerald, this is my childhood playmate, Mr. Henry Livingston, from a neighboring plantation next to Mr. McMillan's country plantation where I was brought up."

"You and your sister 'bout the prettiest things to grace this place since Miss Dinah. Ain't that right, Mr. Catlett?" Henry smiled at Benjamin. Beamed at the girl. Turned to Violette. "Vi'lette, you was always squishy cute, but you've turned into a really pretty woman."

"Aw, Henry."

Was that a blush? Violette had the misfortune in that moment of being light-skinned enough not to be able to hide it. Benjamin stepped forward.

"Well, I'm happy to be privy to this little reunion, but I'm afraid there's been a slight misunderstanding about the housing. The problem still remains." Immediate regret cut through. Benjamin saw the change in Violette as she jerked back into her seriousness.

"No need to worry about us, Mr. Catlett. Emerald and I will find a place to stay."

Henry laughed out loud, as though the whole discussion were ludicrous. "They sho will. They go'n stay with me."

VIOLETTE WHIRLED TO FACE HENRY. All lookers-on, including Violette herself, reacted at once.

"Suh?-Huh-What?"

"That's mighty kind of you, Henry," said Violette, "but I'm afraid that won't do. And you know it. I believe I can—"

Benjamin jumped in before she could finish. "She's right, Henry, the first reason being the size of your place. You barely have room enough to move around in there yourself, though we both know you don't have to live quite that cramped."

Henry looked embarrassed. "Trying to save a little money is all."

Men again. Always stepping in to fix what's not yet broken or change what's already satisfying in order to satisfy themselves. Eli, Jethro, the McMillan plantation overseer . . . always looking to use and then toss away what they had no right to in the first place. Now Benjamin Catlett and Henry Livingston would arrange things for her just to assuage their own male missteps and misgivings.

"Gentlemen. As I was saying, I believe I can find my own housing." Though she had no inkling how or where, except for Natchez Under-the-Hill, and she would never set foot there again. "Anyhow, it's unseemly for an unmarried woman and a single man to share the same roof."

"Oh, close your mouth, Violette. You been reading too many of them old-timey books 'bout white folks in England and New England, whatever that difference s'pose to mean. I been hearing you every night for years, and you done forgot that we just ex-slaves. All that proper stuff don't matter to womens like us."

Violette stared at her daughter. The gem and the bane of her existence. Images of war flared, a war so fresh that Union soldiers were still about. A war whose relics, Confederate and Union, of one-armed and crazed men, endless death and destruction, which Jonathan Mayfield glimpsed during his brief stint with Tecumseh

Sherman near Vicksburg, still so overwhelmed him that he sometimes screamed in his sleep—according to Dinah's letters—never realizing his perpetual restlessness had been interrupted. Without notice, the beastly urge to slap her daughter reared on its hind legs. She sputtered and spat like a wild woman.

"We . . . we are n-not just ex-slaves, Precious Emerald. We. Are. People. And d-don't you ever forget it!"

"Don't chu be telling me what—"

Too much for Violette to swallow. She swung her arm back. Brought the flat of her hand forward with force she did not know she owned, only to find her wrist halted in midair by a strong steady grasp.

"Violette. Don't."

The touch of his hand quieted her. Shamed her. Reminded her of her old self, the one she thought she had shed. And, conversely, that old once-upon-a-time sweet Benjamin she had chanced to encounter all those years ago in Mama Tavie's kitchen at Riverwood.

"I'm sorry, Mr. Catlett."

And she was. Except that the trials of Uncle Tom, enigma that he was, were too much in her head to allow her daughter to declare that common decency, dignity, did not matter to the stolen African, slave or free. She pulled her hand from Benjamin's grip.

"I am sorry I nearly slapped my sister. I am not sorry about what the slap intended to say." She looked at her daughter. "I will use my mouth to say what I can say much better than with my hand. The dignity of all humankind matters, and that includes every black man, woman, and child on this earth."

Uneasy quietness ruled the room. Henry harrumphed. "Uh, we still ain't solved the problem 'bout where y'all go'n stay."

Emerald lifted a tentative questioning hand, causing Violette to suspect her of attempting to trade sullenness for cunning.

"I got an idea. Since Mr. Livingston's house is too little and unseemly, why come we can't stay with you, Mr. Catlett? All we need is one room and something to eat now and then. We used to that. And we would stay on a different floor, so that would make it seemly, wouldn't it?"

Violette sensed the bridled laughs. She herself almost chuckled at the absurdity. Until Emerald leveled the eye-batting thing again. Violette looked closer at the fresh lovely eyes. Were there tears this time?

~

BENJAMIN WINCED. Scratched his head. Would have laughed himself ill if he wasn't so furious. Playing games in the dark, he had stumbled into a trap of his careful construction. And now a girl nearly half his age had released the spring.

But he couldn't do it. What would his father have said about keeping them in the house with him?

"I apologize, but I . . ."

"Oh, it is fine."

Violette grabbed Emerald's wrist. She had started dragging her toward the door when her sister, a half head taller, wrenched herself loose.

"This is rude, Violette, just when Mr. Catlett was about to apologize. Don't look at me like that. You the one always saying something was go'n have to be done 'bout my manners if I ever got a chance to need some."

Ah, but she was a wily one, that Emerald. Benjamin gazed at her. Remembered her sitting on his knee, Lucy held by a foot, squealing and squirming admiringly at the scaled-down replica of Riverwood Jonathan had so painstakingly made for her as Benjamin peeled away the last of its wrapping. Clearly this grownup child was in a fight for her soul. He had always had a soft spot in his heart for her. And not only her but all children of his race born into slavery. He was bested. He had to fix this.

"Why, thank you Emerald. I was about to say I apologize for

not thinking of the invitation earlier. I'd be really pleased to have you two stay with me. My housekeeper has left Natchez," he lied. "Perhaps between the three of us we could restore the livability the place exuded when Dinah left it. The wages I paid the house-keeper, I'll pay the two of you."

VIOLETTE, too, had been bested, the offer of extra pay too much aligned with what her prayers had been for Emerald. Still, she protested like a headless chicken.

"I don't know. This is still highly irregular."

"Please, Violette? We would be working there not living there."

Genuine. For some reason, this was important to Emerald. Violette may have made a mess of her child's manners and sensi-bilities, but she knew when the layers of meanness were stripped away. Still stunned that she had almost slapped her dearest trea-sure, she felt herself relent. She startled at Benjamin's voice.

"Matter of fact, there is an 'apartment' of sorts downstairs, if calling it that would make you feel better. A guest room and a smaller adjoining room Jonathan designed for guests with chil-dren." Fear and excitement mixed themselves into a strange new hope.

"Would, would I . . . that is . . . am I to prepare meals?"

A strange question, she knew. But the fact was Violette was an even worse cook than Dinah had been, and if this was a part of the deal . . .

A sharp rap on what must be the counter out front refocused Violette's attention along with everyone else's.

"Anybody working around here today?"

CHAPTER 7

*V*iolette sighed her frustration as Benjamin's face lit up with a smile. Would they ever get this living arrangement settled?

"Coming right out," said Benjamin. He untied his apron. Slid it from his waist and disappeared through an inner doorway.

"Paul Boatwright! Good morning, my friend. It's been a while since I've seen you."

Despite the fresh onslaught of rain, Violette could distinctly hear the good-natured backslapping. A man with a touch of laughter in his clipped, hurried way of speaking responded quickly.

"A wet one, eh?"

"That it is, my friend. That it is. What brings you into town on a morning like this? What can I do to help?"

Violette looked around at Henry. She felt sticky with sweat. Her breaths were coming short. Quick puffs like those of the iron horses she'd read about. Too many men in here. She retreated toward the work bench. Wondering how she would ever survive in an environment like this, completely dominated by men and from the sound of things occasional white men at that. The man Benjamin called Paul loosed a hearty laugh.

"I could certainly use more friends like you, Benjamin. But before I answer that, meet a new friend of mine, a recently-established banker here in town and a unionist during the war. Benjamin Catlett, this is—"

A new round of thunder rattled the windows, causing Violette to miss the banker's name.

"Nii-ice to meet-cha. Y'all got yourselves a ree-yal nii-ice place here. A man oughta be able to get some fine office chairs made here."

The banker's accent was as familiar to Violette as the rain outside, now coming down in restless sheets. The voice quality was so languorous, so generally southern-white, that it stunned her. Made her wonder if somehow she . . . knew this man? No. Having only heard the educated speech of Sarah Susan for so long, she had put aside other voices necessary to forget. Voices like that of overseers and drivers. Oddly, she was catapulted back toward the ever-present fear of enslavement and what men like *Uncle Tom's* Simon Legree could do to a black woman. Lord. Would she have to deal with this many white men on the job she had just accepted? All the time?

Calm down. You'll have nothing to do with the front of the business.

She turned toward the small littered desk in the corner upon which Emerald had seated herself.

That will be your place.

A place where she hoped she would be invisible.

"Violette?"

Benjamin. Calling her. For what? Fear marched double time up her spine.

"Could you step in here for a minute, please?"

Absolutely not.

She flexed and fisted her fingers. In and out. In and . . . In truth, what else could she do? She now worked for him. He was her new master. *Boss, Violette. Benjamin is your boss.* Inexplicably, her thoughts jumped to Chester Singer. Jethro's boss. Known to most people outside the McMillan plantation as Chet Mack, Mack being a short reference to the fact that though Singer was white, the McMillans had practically owned him too. Jethro's boss. The plantation overseer of her childhood who laughed with Jethro as he struck Violette's already-addlepated, pregnant mama to see if he "could get her brain working well enough again to pick that usual three-hundred pounds."

Addlepated because, except for Violette, every child her mother had borne had been recently sold.

Why did my mama have to take that?

A kinship to the complex character of Uncle Tom in the book she was still trying to finish made Violette clasp her hands to her midsection. Push in on whatever was trying to expel itself. She hardly noticed Emerald slide from the edge of the desk where she had remained swinging her legs ever since she had gotten her wish to move in with Benjamin.

"I'm coming too."

"No, ma'am." Violette marveled at the decisive growl coming from her own throat. "You. Will. Not."

Her daughter, eyes bulged with disbelief, stood down. Slowly worked her too-full hips back onto the desk's edge.

"You done took a mean turn lately, Violette."

Violette wouldn't answer that. She crossed the middle threshold. Trembling, she stepped into the room of men. Outraged at having to do so many things in the last two days that she detested.

"Yes, sir."

"Gentlemen, I'd like you to meet my new worker, Violette McMillan. She'll be taking care of the settlements from now on. Violette, this is my good friend, Paul Boatwright and his banker friend, Mr.—"

The banker stepped forward before Benjamin could finish. Tapped the triangulated scar that covered the right side of his forehead. Examined Violette with eyes so hotly probing she could

49

wonder if it were they, rather than the rainy weather, that were producing the room's steam. Eyes that made her want to gather up her child and run. A cold thrill beset her. She didn't know this well-dressed, clean-shaven older man, did she?

But I do know him. I know his eyes. His filthy desires.

"A female bookkeeper? How ver' unique. Any connection to the slaves of the Riverwood Plantation the McMillans used to own outside of town?"

"No." Benjamin edged closer. Placed a steady hand at her elbow. "At least not anymore."

"Oh, goodness. Now, I hope I didn't offend. I cert'nly know the war is over. 'Course you know, bein' a unionist throughout the war, I'm on your side. Never could see tearing up the country like that. It's just that, coming from Tennessee and all, I'm still getting my bearings as to who's who around here, and I heard just today at the bank that the McMillans have lost their home." He looked at Benjamin. "A real shame, dontcha think?"

"Indeed," was all Benjamin allowed, though Violette noticed a new, disturbing set to his shoulders. Another customer who had quietly entered, a scraggly blond haired youth whose body build struck Violette as an elongated broom handle in denim, perked up.

"Tennessee, huh?" The young man glanced at the banker. "That's a right far ways from Natchez, but I understand things are beginning to cook in our favor up there."

Paul Boatwright turned to the stranger. "What do you mean by that?"

"Not a whole lot, I reckon. Just heard there are some war veterans who've formed a group up there that, for poor strapped loyal Confederates like the McMillans who gave every dime they had to the Cause, might be worth looking into."

"Oh? And what might they do for the McMillans?"

A low harsh chuckle escaped from the young man. Benjamin left Violette's side. Stepped closer and offered a tight, no-nonsense smile. "I'm Benjamin Catlett. Something I can do for you?" The youth looked from Paul to Benjamin then back to the banker.

"Uh, the weather's picked up. I'm thinking I'd best come back some other time."

Benjamin nodded. Eyes shuttered, jaw shut tight, he waited for the man to clear the room before moving back to Violette's side. Too close to her side if she had had anything to say about it. Holding the proximity to Violette, Benjamin turned back to the banker.

"Now, sir. I understand you'd like chairs for your new office. Violette, you might want to fetch pencil and paper."

"No need. Sir."

"Pardon?"

"No need." Her voice croaked. She cleared it. Spoke again.

"No need. I can figure it without pencil and paper."

Benjamin, along with the others, took a moment. Lifted his brow. Seemed to reorder his first thought.

"Very well."

He gave space for the banker's description before rattling off the specifications and the accompanying figures for each chair part. Was he trying to test her? Violette gave herself time she didn't really need as she clicked off the figures in her head.

"Other things being equal that should amount to . . . ." She stated the figures. Shrugged her shoulders.

Paul Boatwright beamed his appreciation while the banker held forth a sideways frown of shock and distaste. Benjamin squeezed her hand, threw back his head, and roared, nearly causing Violette to lose her balance to the floor had he not steadied her with a strong grip on her waist that brought unparalleled discomfort.

CHAPTER 8

*V*iolette stood in the vestibule of the former Mayfield home, her eyes testing the silken softness of a well-placed settee before greedily sweeping upwards along the carpeted stairs toward a landing and—oh, dear, what comfortable beauty must lie beyond.

So this was where her dear friend spent so many days enraptured by the love of her life. From the brass knocker on the front door to the well-lit first floor, to the lure of the second level, there was something so warm and liquid about Jonathan and Dinah's, and now Benjamin's, home. Though static, as walls and furniture appointments must necessarily be, there was an invisible flow that hinted of life and love. Sleek, understated woodwork complemented stately, eggshell ceilings, while pooled drapery and chair covers were all done in the same rose-colored silk as the room at Riverwood where Dinah and Jonathan first worked and played together. Violette smiled.

Fought and fell in love together.

Though nowhere near its size, this home drew Violette in in a fashion that Riverwood had never been able to do. She felt lightened at the fact that it had been built by a black man. For a black man. And in it, the touch of his elegant wife Dinah was everywhere.

"Violette, there go you some books to read."

Violette pivoted at the flicker of kindness in her daughter's voice. There indeed, covering the walls that embraced the staircase, stood shelves and shelves of books her eyes had somehow missed. Benjamin smiled at Emerald, then Violette.

"Only the tip of the iceberg, young lady. There's a full library forged by Dinah just off to the left, and there are shelves of books in every room. Lately, I'm afraid I don't take advantage of them nearly as much as I would like to, but I want you two to feel free to read any and all of them. Meanwhile, I'm thinking I need to show you your living quarters." Benjamin bowed. Swept his arm toward the stairs. "Ladies, after you."

What? "B-but you said Emerald and I would be downstairs."

"I've changed my mind."

There it was, that bossiness again. But what could she do? He was the boss, and he was a man. A combination that spelled ownership.

"It's occurs to me that my milling around downstairs all times of the night might prove distracting, and as I thought on it, there's room enough for the two of you to have fully equipped rooms at the far end of an adjacent wing. That way, Emerald won't be cramped. You might not be aware, but the Mayfields have anticipated a family for quite some time. It was with that hope that the rooms were added right after the war. Trust me, when you discover my sleeping habits, you'll be glad of the choice. It will be almost as though we have separate flats."

Emerald's onset of hiccups startled everyone, including herself.

"Flats!—*hiccup*—like having my own room and bed?—*hiccup*. That sounds like something big city people in the town of England might have."

Mercy. That child had been listening to everything Violette had

53

read. Though she'd obviously missed a few important geographical details.

"England is not a town. It's a country. And what would you know about big city life anyway, Emerald?"

"I know—*hiccup*—what I heard you read. People in cities don't always have houses or even whole floors to themselves, and ain't nothing improper about it."

"This is different. It might even hurt the cabinetmaking business—"

Emerald hiccupped her way around Violette. "Stay down here if you want to. I'm going to see my new upstairs flat."

Hands pressed to her waistline, awareness of the man behind her much too keen, Violette took a step or two, noting the muted homey creak of the third step as she made her slow ascent. Seeing Emerald round the landing, she called out.

"Well, miss, don't get too used to it! We'll be finding our own place just as soon as the rain stops and I get my bearings on this job."

THE GROWING HICCUPS, that's what Mama Tavie, the cook at River-wood who had mothered Violette and Dinah, used to call them. Maybe Emerald wasn't quite an adult yet after all. Violette could hope anyway.

She smiled, trailed her fingers along the bookshelf. Swung around the bedpost. Looked at herself in the mirror, a full-length mirror that showed every unraveling of Dinah's perfectly worked dress. She smoothed her wrinkled hands along the armoire with Jonathan's inimitable stamp on it. Walked to the window and looked out at the night skies.

Never had she seen anything so utterly breathtaking. The river and the fog had become one, indiscriminate lights from boats blinking like nearby suspended multicolored stars that she could almost reach out and touch. She heard the creaking stair, knew it must be her new master.

Why, oh why, couldn't she shake that feeling that Benjamin was just that, a master? She shuddered, pulled the draperies. Looked at the bed Dinah had fitted out for a queen.

But Violette was not a queen. Born a slave, she had always been subject to the Simon Legrees of this country. And war or no war, there were still some of them out there. To them, she was a slave. Always had been. Always would be.

She pulled the deteriorating dress over her head. Looked longingly at Dinah's bedcovers. Not only was the impropriety of being on the same floor as Benjamin's bedchamber niggling at her. It was the other feelings he stirred in her simply by the brush of an elbow.

A new kind of enslavement that gave her pause.

No question that somewhere in his past Benjamin Catlett had witnessed privilege. It oozed from his pores. But after all these years, Violette still could not cook any better than Dinah could on that day back in '60 when she sent her future husband's freedom papers flying into the fire. What if Benjamin expected a cook in the bargain?

She laughed at the worries. Unplaited and plaited her hair. Scolded herself with the reminder that Benjamin made chairs for a living. But no matter the parsing, she could not shake the notion that Benjamin Catlett was above her station in life—in speech, in carriage, in each and every way. And no matter the lingering attraction, he was her master. She would treat him as such until she could find a way out of Natchez and on to Jackson. She pulled *Uncle Tom's Cabin* from her sack. Stifled a yawn. Crawled into the stately bed.

"And I will get through this episode of Simon Legree's cruelty tonight. If it's the last thing I do."

∾

Friday, November fifth

VIOLETTE GRIPPED the candlestick with wet, soap-slimed fingers, the stench of human odor seeping from the pores of her hands, the dying flame's dance against the walls becoming weaker and weaker. What had possessed her to wander the halls this way? This late at night?

A meanness equal to Simon Legree's drove her forward. Pushed her through the dark corridor with the force of a cyclone. Fear she had once held for her master had turned inward, metamorphosing into a clawing, demanding thing. Causing her to forfeit sleep in search of what the new, unfamiliar surroundings would yield and match them fear for fear.

The candle flickered. Died. She stepped into one of countless rundown rooms where Dinah's rose pink had recolored itself into blood red, and the hem of Dinah's well-made work dress Violette wore snagged a floor, cold and splintered. Clinging to the candlestick with its smoking nub, she glided toward a slit of a window and looked out. Through the darkness, she spotted hundreds of slaves all dressed in white. One-eyed, one-eared, one-armed. Running. Screaming.

"There a haint in there! We seen her! Done come for our souls! Tell Massa Legree!"

Plop!

"Oh, have mercy." Violette gasped. Struggled to figure out her surroundings. Indeed, she had not finished reading Legree's meanness. Had imbibed just enough of his crazed mulatto concubine's revenge to nearly send Violette off her own rocker. She gripped the soft sheet now damp with perspiration. Spotted the book that had fallen to the floor. Sucked in her breath. Recognized the best-smelling food since Mama Tavie's.

"Who's cooking like that? What time is it?" The rain was over, sun was up. "And where's Emerald?"

With speed she had not used since she was a girl playing with

56

Henry Livingston—who truly had turned into a good looking boy —she flung water at her body and jumped back into Dinah's dress.

"Lord, don't let me lose my chance before I even start. Don't let me end up down there back under the hill."

She flew to Emerald's room. Knocked on the door. Heard giggling below.

"Emerald?"

Slowing her steps to accommodate the unfamiliar carpeted stairs, Violette followed the sound of her daughter's laughter mixed with the tantalizing smells of fried pork and biscuits. She inhaled deeper. Grits with butter? Eggs? She stopped at the threshold of the first kitchen she had ever seen integrated into the main floor of a house—so like Jonathan—and listened.

"Mr. Catlett, you must be funning me. You ain't never seen no singing haints practicing on their harmonicas at the graveyard for the next service."

Emerald leaned into the table where she mutilated a potato with a paring knife—just like Dinah had before Mama Tavie taught her to cook—a scattering of quasi-shredded peelings marring the beauty of the wood, her recent seductive behavior plainly vanquished for the moment.

"Really? Is you funning me, Benjamin?"

Violette cringed at the use of his Christian name. Benjamin chortled. "I swear I fun not." His back was to the door as he lifted sizzling pieces of ham onto a platter. "Except I should probably admit 'h'aint' been no real ghosts I know of making music save the ones in my childhood nightmares in Virginia eons ago."

"Benjamin!"

He laughed. Ducked. As though he expected Emerald to throw a potato. Violette had thought him appealing the other day in Riverwood's wash house, but standing there in his shirt sleeves more at ease than she had ever seen a man in a kitchen in her life, she thought him simply wondrous. A mixture of manliness and sensibility to tuck away for eternity.

"Potatoes ready to fry yet? These ham drippings are sure ready for them."

Benjamin tested a slice of the thick ham. Wiped his hands on his apron. Realigned his seasonings. While Violette, her heart doing funny little things that made her want to cry, stepped into the conversation.

"Good morning. What's all this talk about haints?"

Heart dancing around in her chest, Violette's eyelids lowered of their own volition, the same as they would have done for any master.

"Am I . . . am I late for work?"

CHAPTER 9

*S*he looked nervous. Tired. He had been glad to see her sleep late. Glad to have a chance to unearth a bit of the charming child he had once known in Emerald. Glad not to have to face Violette yet and confront his fascination with her.

Tired and beautiful. Eyes puffy, unbound hair disheveled. Beautiful. Benjamin dropped the meat turner. Emerald scrambled to pick it up.

"It's perfectly fine. Henry knows how to carry on. And, yes, your sister and I have had a ghost of a discussion. We're about to have breakfast. Join us?"

"I . . . well, yes. I believe I will. Not over much, though."

She was putting up a strong front, but Benjamin could tell that, like her sister, she had not had so much as simple fare like this in Lord knows when. He would fix that. And soon.

THE SUN WAS OUT, and things were popping. The scratching sounds of a saw and several men's aggressive laughs greeted Violette's ears as she entered the shop through the rearmost door along the side of the building, Emerald at her heels. Dust from the saws and other sources ruled the air, witnessing that the whole place was groaning for a good cleaning, but it was the noise that grated her. She stopped. Took a step backwards. Slammed into her daughter.

"Oww!" Violette turned to see Emerald cupping her mouth and nose. "What chu doing, Violette? You done near 'bout broke my nose." As usual, her daughter exaggerated, and Violette accommodated her.

"Sorry . . . achoo!"

Violette's sneeze went unnoticed, Henry never even looking up. Her mind, soul, and body continued to recoil from the sounds. For years, her washer's world had been quiet, gradually refitting her to the isolated environs of wind sounds. Birds. Squirrels. What had she been thinking?

This is a world of men. I can't do this. I cannot again submit my will to whatever they demand of me.

Benjamin looked over his shoulder toward her. Pointed to the empty space where the desk had been.

"Removed to the customer's side," he shouted.

"But I thought—"

"It will be fine."

He whisked her through the connecting door. And into the face of the banker from yesterday. If she had thought her gut had curdled from the noise in the back room, this man ratcheted her fear to a new level. Panic and resentment pummeled her from both sides. Why did he rattle her so? Why did Benjamin move her without asking?

Because he's your master, that's why. Despite the war, nothing had changed. Nothing at all.

"Morning. Ma'am."

Forced. Something no southern white man would say, war or not. The banker had choked out the "ma'am" like rotten meat. Benjamin's friend, Paul Boatwright, smiled. Tendered a soft bow.

"I was impressed with your gift of calculating yesterday."

It occurred to her that, once home, Benjamin had not said a word about that. "Thank you, sir."

"There now, sit down," said Benjamin, who pointed her to a chair behind the relocated desk and brought around two more chairs to the front of it. "We'll get the furniture rearranged directly. Now Violette, the banker here has decided on a new desk in addition to the two chairs he mentioned. He thought it best he look at some more wood samples this morning and have you calculate the new costs."

"Certainly, sir." Violette had never seen wood samples in her life. Wasn't sure she even understood what Benjamin was talking about. "Mr. Catlett? If I could speak to you for just a—"

"Mornin', Mr. Benjamin."

"Hey, again, Mr. Benjamin."

Dual greetings beset Violette's ears from either side of the room. A lanky, serious yet pleasant-faced youth entered the shop through the front door as Emerald's voice simultaneously sliced through Violette's attempt to corral her new job. Emerald stopped. Slacked her jaw. Seemed to realize she had neither time nor the surplus wit to put on her female wiles. Lit up like a bevy of fireflies and wrapped a separate greeting around the young boy who was so plainly on the cusp of manhood.

"H-hey . . . everybody."

Boatwright offered an indulgent grin toward Emerald. The banker colored with consternation, as Benjamin obviously scrambled to bring protocol to the black and white world that was Natchez, Mississippi.

"Davey. What can I do for you this morning?"

"You sent for me, suh."

"Oh, that's right, that's right. I did. I'm afraid it'll have to wait until tomorrow though."

Violette tautened as Benjamin seemed to take note of the two youths who gawked at each other.

"Meantime, meet Emerald. Emerald, this is Davey. Davey, Emerald."

Emerald fairly skipped toward Davey as Violette moved to cut her off. "Pardon me, but I think Emerald had best go back to the house and work on her letters. Emerald—"

"Or," said Benjamin, his eyes apologizing to Davey and maybe even a little to Violette herself, "you can hang around until I'm finished here. But wait in the workshop. I don't want you on the streets. I hear Jethro's somewhere close to town."

"Jethro?" Violette flinched at the shout of her own voice. Heard it tremble. Could not stop it. "Did you say . . . Jethro? Jethro who?"

"Jethro McMillan."

Benjamin dipped his head. Jerked it back upright, delayed recall etched across his brow.

"Jethro McMillan."

Likely he didn't know what Jethro had done to her. But of a certainty,

Benjamin knew what he had tried to do to Dinah. And he knew that she knew.

"Davey is his son."

Mr. Boatwright appeared utterly confused while the banker who had yet to reveal his name to Violette wrinkled his nose as though he had found himself stranded in a locked outhouse.

Jethro. Satan's very spawn, who all those years ago had said she didn't have sense enough to take care of Emerald, so she would have to leave her out at the country plantation while Violette was sent to Riverwood. She glanced at her daughter glowing with some kind of worrisome anticipation. Had he been right after all?

Jethro. The slave driver to whom she had consented to give her all so that he'd agree to let her bring Emerald with her to River-wood, but only until she was fattened up enough for him to take to market.

Jethro. The traitor who had tried to have Jonathan sold based

62

on information Violette herself had supplied about Jonathan's missing freedom papers.

Jethro. The rapist who had come within an inch of stealing from Dinah what Violette had unwillingly sacrificed for a few years with her daughter.

She had thought—prayed—that he, like Eli, was dead. But no. Here he was in the flesh. At least, flesh of his flesh. The boy moved as if he would draw near to her daughter. Somewhere in a muted part of Violette's brain she sensed he wanted to offer some kind of explanation. Some kind of unwarranted apology. But she couldn't access it. Couldn't separate the boy from his father. She felt her language reverting to the Violette of old as it often did when she was upset.

"Don't. Chu. Touch her. Don't chu ever touch her or I will kill you. I swear it."

"You will kill no one." Benjamin spoke through clenched teeth as Violette looked around at the utterly dismayed faces. The banker left abruptly while Mr. Boatwright took a seat and lowered his head to his hands.

Oh, Lord. What had she just done? She had not meant to embarrass Benjamin like that.

"You're fired."

"What?"

"Have you become such a scholar that you no longer understand plain-spokenness? I said, you're fired."

CHAPTER 10

*P*ausing under the night sky to examine the bare branches of a sweet gum tree, Benjamin wondered how the day had ended up like this. He had reasoned. Apologized. Pleaded. Reasoned again. Done everything except dropped to his knees. But pacing the vestibule this afternoon, she had vowed she and Emerald would be leaving in the morning. She showed no signs of anger toward him. If anything, it was more embarrassment. Resignation. Just needed to figure a few things out, she said. Then she would finish up her one workday in the shop. Would Benjamin be kind enough to let her stay the night here at the house?

He snapped a twig. Kind enough? After the way he had treated her? Lord. Talk about Simon Legree! The look on her face when she asked him to stay the night was his undoing. Hadn't Jonathan and Dinah warned him of her pride? Why had he behaved in such a manner earlier back there in the shop? Firing her as though she were a found-out harlot?

The scene back at the house following the firing assumed a cruel relentless loop in Benjamin's head.

"I didn't mean it, Violette. Can't you see I didn't mean it? It was just that . . . the poor boy . . . I've become fond of him, and you were about to jump him as though he were a common criminal."

"That's not it, Benjamin, and you know it." Her voice was so very subdued. Benjamin pleaded within himself.

Please be angry with me. Please.

"Well then what is it? You do need the job, don't you?"

"I do need the job. But I made you ashamed of me, and that's something I won't do again."

How had it gone from the warmth of female company in Dinah's kitchen this morning to the biting chill he had left behind in that vestibule? All in one day. And why had Violette seemed so disappointed in him as though he had planned for Davey, who was really nothing like Jethro, to choose that moment to appear? Hadn't Benjamin sent for the boy simply to try to help him? Fix his life by maybe offering him an apprenticeship? More to the point, hadn't he simply been trying to do for Violette what most men would never do? Placing her out front like any other male employee? Her words had cut to the marrow.

"I made you ashamed of me."

Benjamin cringed. Tried to escape the taunting refrain. Slammed into another senseless phrase. "Any other male employee?" Crazy talk. If it was anything Violette McMillan was not, it was a male. In fact, each moment he spent with her was so painfully tantalizing that—

"I won't think about it. I will not. I came down here to clear my head. See what else I might do to persuade her. And that's what I'm going to do."

He resumed his climb away from Natchez Under-the-hill. The sun had long since slipped behind the banks of the Vidalia, Louisiana side of the river as he made his way up and back to the house that had over the years become home. Why had he behaved in such a manner earlier back there in the shop? Firing her as though she were a found-out harlot?

Except for the time he had fixed supper, he had been gone all afternoon into the night. Walking. Sorting. Remembering Lucie . . .

She sat with her wrists overlapping, fingers splayed across her lap. At sixteen, she still hadn't much lap, thighs so thin until Benjamin wondered if her skirts were filled with air. Skinny as a sapling and nearly as bendable. And though she had known only the fields all her life, she had the frailest hands he had ever seen. He smiled at her.

"Lucie, darling. Loosen up. This is the wonderful gala we've been waiting for."

"Don't call me darling. It don't fit, Benny. I'd rather words like sugar or pumpkin. They don't sound quite so sophisticated."

Indeed, the words sounded country. He knew they did. But Lucie was smart. She was charming. She was what he wanted, no matter how much Rogers Catlett was bound to rail against it. All she needed was help from Mother, and Mother was doing all she could. After all, Anna Benjamin Catlett was a remarkable woman —nothing like Father—one Benjamin was honored to pattern his future wife by. The soft whimpering sounds Lucie was making— made only when she was upset or hurting—pulled him from his thoughts.

"You're doing it again, darling."

Benjamin hated peppering her with the darlings when she had asked him not to. But it was Mother's orders. "A few more of the proper epithets here and there, and she will forget her aversion to our ways of endearment." Mother would be a worthy ally against Father after tonight when Benjamin posed the big question. But even Mother had her lines that must not be violated. And "pumpkin" would cross the line. What his Lucie was getting in the trade, when Benjamin made her his bride, would far outweigh the loss of a few cultural nicknames.

"Doin' what, Benny? What am I doin'?" She looked so troubled sitting in the Catlett drawing room, almost as though she were in pain. Could she be—in pain, that is?

"Moaning, darling. You're doing that low moaning again. . . ."

Benjamin kicked the edge of the fence. Opened the gate to the yard. Arrogant pig-headed lout. That's what he had been. What he was beginning to look like again.

Still, all his questions had not been answered. Why did he yet want to punch somebody?

"You know why. Stop walking and kicking things and admit it. You care about her. You've admired her ever since you saw her interact with a younger sister with so much care all those years ago."

Benjamin exhaled a decade of suppression. Yes. He admitted it. He was attracted to her, but he could never be with a woman of Violette's temperament. And practical thinker that he had always been, he knew what he had to do about it. Theirs could never be more than a workplace proximity.

"But from the looks of things, hers and Henry's certainly could be."

That's it. The best way to rid himself of the lingering attraction was not to fight the solution but to embrace it. If he could just convince her to stay, he would pair her with Henry. And if it was one thing Benjamin knew about himself, it was that once Henry and Violette discovered their interest in each other, he would never set to naught a healthy budding romance. Never stand in their way.

It was what he had to do. The lingering question was, did he really know why he was doing it?

PEAR PRESERVES, bread, cheese, ham left over from breakfast. All laid out for supper when Violette walked from the shop back into the kitchen, complete with checkered napkins that she didn't know what to do with. How had he learned his way around the kitchen like this? At times, Benjamin seemed to know everything. Think of everything. Other times, nothing. It didn't matter. She knew he

67

would probably fire her again as soon as he returned from wherever he had gone after their talk. And she deserved it. Yet she wasn't quite sorry for keeping Emerald away from Jethro's son, and she would make the best of the time she had left in this comfortable home.

She ate. Looked in on Emerald who lay sulking over Violette's treatment of Jethro's son and the resultant firing. Best not to broach it this evening. Violette was too tired anyway. She grabbed her copy of *Uncle Tom* which she just couldn't seem to ever finish. Sank down in the lovely ladder-back rocker in her room. She opened the book to Legree's increasing fear of his slave mistress, Cassy. Closed it.

"My soul is so restless."

A little mind-numbing exploring was what she needed. She only wanted to see the house, not soil it. Had wanted to as much as Emerald ever since yesterday. She wouldn't touch a thing. Would not lay her wrinkled, water-damaged hands on a single thing except the stair rail. She would simply record it all with her eyes so that on cold, lonely nights when she had long since moved from here, she could pull it out from that little drawer in her memory and know that she and Emerald had spent two nights here.

Book in hand, she climbed the forbidding steps to the attic at the end of the main upstairs hall. She'd had to light a lamp, so dark it had become, and now she had found a window seat, higher, of course, than the one in her room. An even better view of the river. Hopefully she would see or hear Benjamin when he came home and beat him back to the second floor.

"Oh!"

There he stood, dimly lit. Completely owning the role of the master he was. Sullen yet in complete control. Her head swam. Her senses fled, but she clung to the book.

Reading. The master has caught me reading.

Her head swam. She would be whipped for this.

Massa won't do it. Too much of a gentleman. But Chester

Singer, Massa's overseer, he will. The one what sold all Mama's children except me, he will . . .

What? Confusion had set in. Violette's head felt twice its size. Her senses fled, but she clung to the book.

"I won't give it up. Mistress McMillan, she give it to me. You can ask her, suh. She said I could have it. Forever."

HE HAD MEANT SIMPLY to retrieve Lucie's harmonica from the window seat in the attic. Turn it over in his hand and heart. Repent once more for the tragedy he had heaped upon her.

Now he had run squarely upon Violette. Nearly run into her. He stepped back from the seat, struck by the way she had looked seconds ago before she had known he was there. Knees drawn to the book's cover. Skirts securely tucked. Braid grazing the globe of the oil lamp. She was a vision. Seemed almost dozing, her lips moving as though she read aloud in a dream. Yet her face had remained close to the book as though too much space between them would have caused pain.

Eyes flooded with fear and defiance, she now crouched into the window seat as frozen as the petrified forest he had heard about further north in Mississippi, her lamp handle held high for the best light.

"I won't give it up, suh. Will not."

"Give up what, Violette? It's late. What are you doing up here?" He placed his candle holder on a nearby stand. "Here, let me have the lamp." He removed the wire handle from her clutches. She blinked. Stared. Glared and spoke half-sense.

"It's . . . it's the river. I can see it better up here. I won't come again, but I won't give up the book."

Why was she talking about the book? Was she still asleep? He felt some kind of compulsion to scold her. When all he really wanted to do was join her on that window seat. Beg her once more not to leave. Find out what she was reading, what had her so utterly absorbed that a man could have kidnapped her. Fled to the West Indies with her. Heaven's sake! He, too, was running off the rails here.

"It is a better view, I suppose. I don't get up here much."

"I will leave now, s-sir." Her studied speech had returned. "Let you do whatever it is you've come to do." She scrambled from the padded seat. Nearly knocked the lamp from his hold. "I need to check on Emerald."

"No. Wait."

"No?"

"Yes. I mean, Emerald's fine. I just passed her room on my way up. All was quiet."

"Was Lucy with her? She gets scared sometimes without Lucy."

No longer a question in his mind. Violette was beyond petrified. She was terrified to the point of temporary regression.

"Is there anything I can get you, Massa?"

Massa. Benjamin stared at her. His heart spinning like a lathe. Massa. She didn't yet realize she had called him Massa.

His eyes fell on the book she held to her chest. *Uncle Tom's Cabin.* Ah, so that was it. She was so deeply submerged beneath the cruelty of Simon Legree that she had probably lost her way in some kind of a dream state. Forgotten that the war was over and there were no more masters. He pointed toward the window seat she had just vacated.

"Sit."

Benjamin winced. Was that an order he had just leveled? Certainly sounded so. "You just called me Massa, Violette."

Her nostrils flared. "No, sir. I did not."

"Yes. I'm afraid you did."

"So I did, then. Massa, boss. What's the difference?"

Stricken by the implication of what had just come from her

lips, he thought of what she had said to Emerald a little more than a day ago right down there in the shop.

"Well. It doesn't seem quite fair that Emerald would be nearly slapped because of her loosely constructed account of what slavery meant to its victims. Yet you, a survivor of a way of life probably accountable as the worse blight on this country, haven't learned the difference between working for someone and slaving for him."

Tears pooled at the bases of her eyes. Benjamin marveled that she was somehow actually able to command they drip no further. Emotions he had thought exorcised years ago gripped him. He wanted to cry with her. Hold her. Instead he stood there, knowing that if he moved to her, he might lay claim to things for which God's law said he had no right. Which was exactly what his slave-owning father had probably done the better part of Benjamin's life. He dared not move as Violette reclaimed the window seat. She seemed to as Violette sat down. wade through the thick silence before finally speaking.

"I've never lived without a master. I-I don't know how to own myself."

"Violette. I don't want to be your master. I . . . if the desire to be a slaveholder ever once crossed my mind, you would never see me again. I would never contaminate a smart, beautiful, precious woman like you with my presence again."

Their eyes locked. Questioned each other as to what to do with the returning gap of silence. "What are you reading?" As if he didn't know.

Her visage darkened. Then just as quickly brightened with excitement. "*Uncle Tom's Cabin.* I intend to read it again, next time to study it. Have you ever read it?"

"I have. In fact, some feel it was instrumental in starting the war."

"Oh?" she laughed sheepishly. "I do realize I'm reading it a bit late."

"Never too late to read a good book."

"I admit I have become like a wadi. Each time I lay aside a completed book, I dry up inside until I can enter the pages of another. Do you know how many countries I've traveled to in the past decade? Twenty-seven!" She turned her face up to Benjamin, opening passage into a smile from which he never wanted to return. "Much more than that, if you allow England to be counted more than once."

A scowl erased what must have been enthralling journeys abroad. She rubbed the spine of the book in her possession. "I confess I hate Legree with a pure hate, but Augustine St. Clare, whom some might call a good guy at heart, frustrates me. At times disgusts me. Oh, listen to the way I go on."

"Quite all right. I assure you." He felt he could listen all night without saying another word.

"It's just that my curiosity consumes me. I have yet to under-stand how a country—the symbol of freedom—how a race of people could have become slaves in a country like America in the first place."

Benjamin shifted. Set his weight upon one leg. Then another, thinking, you should ask Rogers Catlett, one of northern Virginia's foremost slave owners . . .

"The only way to get somewhere in this world is by the strength of your own mind, the trigger of your own weapon, and the power of your own fist."

"I find I want to help. Like an ant, I want to push my small crumb forward through Emerald. So that we can do our parts to restore the independence our people once knew."

She struggled to hold on to the tears. Gave up and gave them a vicious swipe. He eased down beside her. Delightful, dangerous territory. Placed his hand atop hers which still clung to Harriet Beecher Stowe.

"You're quite the spokesperson." Quite the woman. The temptress. "You know that?"

She held his gaze, as though willing him to say what he would not, forcing his attention toward something else, anything else. The matching window seat he had nearly forgotten did the trick. A small box he had left there years ago still sitting upon it.

Lucie's harmonica. The reason he had come up here in the first place.

He hadn't realized their fingers, his and Violette's, had become intertwined. He unfurled them one by one.

"I really must be leaving. Stay and read as long as you like."

She looked crushed. Frightened. As though he were the master, lording it over her again. Why did he feel she was right?

"But Violette, please don't leave in the morning. I need you."

CHAPTER 11

Monday, November eighth

$\mathcal{I}$ need you.

The magic words that had made her relent. Gingerly, Violette sat down to her desk as though she expected to encounter hidden tacks. She still had her job. Her only chance, she had decided, to get Emerald to that safe place in Jackson, away from the pernicious influence of men like she was sure Jethro's son would turn out to be. Yet this morning, in an atmosphere so quiet one could hear the sawdust hit the floor, she felt more put out to pasture than if she had been fired all over again.

Despite the other night, Benjamin's invisible line of authority was back in place. All weekend he had been surly and short-tempered. All business. Like a master might be with one of his slave lovers the day after a night of sin.

She thought of the window seat. Felt ashamed. Once more used, like with Jethro on the plantation grounds and the overseer on the night of freedom. All these years, since Chester Singer took her to that room under the hill, she had always dripped cold sweat if she so much as got within a three-foot radius of a man alone. She had been sure, when the day came, she would be thoroughly repulsed if she found herself in such an attic room with any male. But she had been drawn to Benjamin's strength. Wanted him to sit with her. Wanted his maleness to cover her.

What was happening to the fear and hatred of men she had coddled so?

And after experiencing all that, all Benjamin had said when he left the shop a while ago was, "If there's anything I can make clear in those ledgers . . ." She had shaken her head, no.

"Morning, Vi'lette."

She startled at Henry's voice. Turned to find his work mask lowered beneath his chin, one muscled arm leaned into the door-facing between the two rooms.

"Good morning, Henry. I didn't know you were here. Something I can do to help?"

"No, no. Just got caught up in a little too much mind searching. Thought I'd come in to say howdy, business being slow like it is. We didn't get much chance last week."

Violette, not knowing how to begin explaining her behavior last Friday, balled a piece of paper. Tucked her chin.

"Aw, now. C'mon, now, Vi'lette. This is Henry." He took her hand and tugged her to the crate in the workshop. "You ought to know I ain't looking for no reasons why. I know Jethro as well as you do. Every black person in Adams County know him, 'cept maybe Benjamin—not that he don't know what he tried to do to Miss Dinah, his own best friend's wife, and Lord knows how many other people. He just can't feel it like another slave. It makes him mad, but it don't make him mad *and* scared *and* crazy. Reckon 'cause he wasn't brought up like us."

For the first time since she had set foot in Natchez a few days ago, Violette felt herself able to relax without a book in her hand. Something about Henry's speech said he understood how displaced she felt. How lonely. Yet it was Benjamin's approval she wanted.

"Thank you for that, Henry. Will you tell me about your life all these years? When did you get to be such a talented, important fellow?" He studied his boots. She had unintentionally embarrassed him. Sweet.

"'Fraid that credit goes to Mr. Jonathan Mayfield. Best cabinet-maker this side of the Miss'sippi." He chuckled. "As I think on it, I reckon I don't know anything about the other side of the river. Never even been to the town of Vidalia. Seen it a thousand times across the river, but I ain't never set foot in it."

Violette laughed out loud. "You always did have a way with phrases. 'Member that time you blamed me for catching a cold? Told your mama I had put my snotty nose right up against you like a tick on a dog. Mama and your mama laughed 'til they cried."

Violette and Henry did much the same. Only when their laughing tears stopped, they remembered their deceased mamas and cried for real. Henry swatted away the renegade drops.

"Must've got that sawdust in my eyes again." He fumbled with his mask. Pushed it to his forehead. Scowled. "What happened, Vi'lette, that made my mama sit and cry 'bout her friend from time to time 'til she died? I mean. I ain't never really understood."

"No. You wouldn't. I'm older than you."

"And not nearly as pretty."

"Oh, stop it, boy." Violette flung the piece of balled-up paper at him. Found herself having fun. "Seriously, did you ever know our mothers were cabin mates once?"

"For true?"

"On the McMillan plantation. Before your mama got married, she often shared a cabin with Mama while my father was rented out. Helped with the children. That way, they both saved on the little fuel they had. One day, so abruptly it was almost like an eye blink, Mama said, your mama was sold to the neighboring plantation where she met your father, but it was still a year or two before you came along."

"Ah, so that's how come she was always wanting to visit your mama, sometimes getting real low when she couldn't."

"Um-hmm. She had come to love Mama's children way before I was born, not knowing that all of them except me would eventually be sold by that devil of an overseer. By the time of the selling, I'd got to be a big girl, and I reckon you were apprenticed or something 'cause we wasn't seeing each other anymore. Seemed like you just fell off the side of the world, but Mama, because of the sell-off, had gotten too mixed up in her head to explain your whereabouts to me even if she knew."

"Near 'bout did, fall off the world, that is. Like your papa, I was rented out when I was young so I couldn't visit you all no more. Mama took that pretty hard, but she perked up a lot when I got the chance to learn a trade under Mr. Mayfield."

An awkwardness ensued as Henry returned to the work table, fumbled around, Violette waiting for more of his words like an enrapt child.

"Hard to get them slavery memories out of you, ain't it?"

"Right at impossible, Henry. I imagine it will take centuries, if ever, to get that slavery hurt out of us. But we will be found trying, don't you think?"

"Yes, indeed. We go'n be found trying."

Violette batted her eyelids. Pulled back the fresh tears. Wrapped Henry in her arms. Looked up into the angry enticing eyes of Benjamin Catlett.

Wonder what he heard?

She stared down her boss. "That's right. We go'n be always trying."

IT WAS PROVING to be one of the longest mornings he had ever spent.

Benjamin walked through the back door to the shop as though he had not been listening to the close camaraderie going on between two people he truly cared about before walking in on the embrace. Crazy unwarranted jealousy coursed through him like a swollen river. They seemed so right together, reminding him of his childhood isolation when he was the master's heir prohibited from the slave children's playground group. He took a moment. Remembered the pain of exclusion that Jonathan once mentioned. Thought to himself.

Is this the left-out feeling Jonathan tried to tell me about when he found himself in the company of black brothers and sisters who were yet slaves?

Of course. The pain of exclusion. That's all Benjamin was feeling. Nothing more. Time to execute his plan. Stepping into the shop, he meant to be casual with his employees. Instead a snarl issued forth.

"Don't you two have anything better to do?"

"Morning, Mr. Catlett. Uh-ruh, could I talk to you for a minute?"

"Yes, Henry, what is it?" Henry looked confused by the clipped tone Benjamin was powerless to drop. He glanced over at Violette. Pressed on.

"Uh, about that talk we had the other day."

"What talk?"

Violette rose from the crate she had claimed. "Perhaps I should step back into the office."

"No, no. You two seemed quite cozy when I came in. No need to break that up. What talk, Henry?"

"Well, matter of fact, we didn't really have a talk. You did most of the talking, suh."

Benjamin felt a knee quiver. That talk. Eons ago. Before the breakfast with Violette and Emerald. Before the window seat visit.

Before Benjamin realized how perfect Henry and Violette were for each other.

"If I'm remembering right, you said maybe you might be thinking about . . . I mean it sounded like you might want to go back to Virginia and would maybe be looking for someone to take over the business."

"Ohhh, that talk. I'm thinking I might have overstepped, Henry. I can do nothing here at Mayfield Cabinetry without first talking to Mr. Mayfield." Benjamin scolded himself. Why was he referring to Jonathan as Mr. Mayfield as though Henry was being trained for an English social season?

Henry looked as mortified as Benjamin felt. He inhaled. Stuttered. "B-but I th-thought I remembered . . ."

Assuming an innocent impatient stare, Benjamin dug into Henry's confidence. Lord, what was happening to him?

The knives Violette threw with her eyes, based on the way her childhood beau was being treated, caused Benjamin's knees to want to give to the floor in apology and prayer. Instead of reneging on his offer, why wasn't he moving forward to get the romance going?

A knock sounded from the front.

Benjamin struggled to turn his attention to the customer, then stepped through the middle doorway.

The banker? Again?

"What can we do for you today, sir?"

"Well, truth is I wanted to talk to Vi-i-lette in private for a few minutes. I promise not to keep her long."

Benjamin felt his hackles rise. He didn't know why yet. He just knew he didn't like this man. He felt a lift to his brow, a fierce sense of alarm replacing the jealousy he had felt a minute ago. He reached for every ounce of authority Rogers Catlett had taught him as a youth in Virginia. Found it still there.

"You will pardon my rudeness, Mr. Singer, but what private business would you have with Miss McMillan?"

Violette rushed into the room, alarm stretching her eyes. "Singer." She gasped the name nearly imperceptibly. But Benjamin heard it. Wondered if this was the first time she had heard the banker's name.

"Miss McMillan just entered my employ a few days past, and I hardly think she would have anything to speak to you about that would not first need to be spoken to me."

The man looked explosive, as though Benjamin had spat in his face. Benjamin sensed Henry's awareness. Saw him move to the pistol drawer. They had been fortunate these several post-war years to have had only minor incidents. A few eggs splattered against windows, a need to wash away words from the fence every now and then, a miniature, black effigy next to a dead black cat. But they both knew the lingering hatred—blame, really—anchored in the devastation of the South went much deeper. Was as real and palpable as a pit of snakes.

And what Benjamin had heard Henry say about him just minutes ago had been dead wrong. Benjamin was scared. But he wouldn't show it. Not now. Not ever.

Singer glanced past Benjamin at Violette. Schooled his features and tugged his vest over his ample paunch. "Kindly accept my pardon, sir. I thought to steal this arithmetic wonder out from under your nose, but I see my chances of hiring her are slim to none." He tipped his hat. Shot another look at Violette.

"Good day to y'all. I'll be awaitin' the furniture. Fine work I know it'll be."

Benjamin nodded. Flexed his fingers.

"And a good day to you. Sir."

VIOLETTE CLUTCHED THE COUNTER. Stared past the determined set of Benjamin's shoulders. Waited for him to round on her. Her heart beat out of rhythm, her hands as wet as they had been each day all day in Riverwood's laundry room. If only she had listened to her heart, gathered up Emerald and their small belongings, and fled Natchez when first she spotted those eyes. How could she have not recognized the man?

What are Precious Emerald and I going to do now?

Chester Singer had changed. Put on weight, shaved his beard and lost his hair. From the looks of things, started wearing expensive-looking suits. How had he fooled everybody in Natchez? For one thing, he had acquired that triangular scar. For another, who expected a mean, low-talking plantation overseer, always hidden beneath a brimmed hat, to reappear as a banker after seven years and the ending of the war?

Still those icy gray eyes, had she only allowed them to, could have propelled her to flight. They alone marked him for the soulless man he was. Jethro's trainer, her mother's murderer.

The man I followed under the hill.

But it was all empty thinking now. If she tried to leave, Benjamin and Henry, especially Henry, would worry that something terrible had happened and likely follow her. That would not be fair to them. Either she stayed a while longer or at the least told the two men who were concerned for her welfare why she was leaving.

Her heartbeat now pounding in her ears, she continued to wait for Benjamin to ask the question, most likely demand the answer, given he was most assuredly acting the part of a master today.

"How do you know that man?" he would ask. She would either have to lie or tell the truth. There would be no room for middle ground.

"Well," said Benjamin, finally turning to face her, "that went swimmingly. Somehow I think that's the last we will see of that customer." He rested his fists low on his hips. Smiled at her. Genuinely smiled. Chucked her chin, then leveled her with the most beautiful eyes she had ever seen.

"Let me know if he or anyone else is ever unkind to you again." Violette closed her eyes, her hands volunteering for a position of prayer.

Lord, Jesus. Does that include him?

"Violette?" She opened her eyes. Benjamin smiled again. "And that includes me."

Violette smiled back at him. Knew there was no further use for denial. For all his arrogant inconsistencies, the man had a heart. And he was making short work of picking up the pieces of hers—which he had unwittingly shattered nearly ten years ago—and placing them squarely into his pocket.

She felt like giggling. Skipping as she did on the night of freedom. As she had not done since. Something truly delicious occurred to her: a recipe in one of Dinah's cookbooks with all the ingredients listed in Dinah's hand and attached to the ensuing instructions in *Miss Leslie's Directions for Cookery.* For certain, Violette was not a cook. But who needed further guidance for soup when the ingredients were right there before you? Any dunce knew that all you had to do was boil it all together. So why not prepare supper? For Benjamin, tonight.

Why not indeed.

CHAPTER 12

*V*iolette lifted Dinah's ingredients list from atop the first page of the recipe and scanned the initial line of print: BEGIN THIS SOUP THE DAY BEFORE IT IS WANTED. She would simply ignore that wisdom nugget. After all, how much time could it possibly take to cook soup?

Ah! Fine beef soup. Just the thing to counter the November air that had turned quite crisp the night before. The ingredients, or at least most of them, were readily available. And the main one, beef, she had purchased with the money Benjamin had advanced her. Or at least she hoped it was beef she'd bought. Her mind stepped back out onto the busy street a half hour or so ago. Her eyes recalled the window sign.

SPECIAL CUTS! CHEAPEST PRICES YOU'LL FIND ANYWHERE IN MISSISSIPPI!

She had overheard the meat vendor, a smirk on his face, whisper to his helper that, in a pinch, there was nothing like a good deer to make a better cow. And now that she thought on it, why had the beef been so cheap?

Truth was, except for the few times she had stolen a plug or two from Mama Tavie's kitchen for herself and Emerald all those years ago, Violette had no experience with beef. But right now, that did not signify. She didn't have time to think about anything except that Benjamin and Henry would be here by nightfall, and she wanted with all her heart to please them.

She washed the meat and the vegetables. Checked the fire. Rewashed the pot. Glanced back at the recipe. Noted again the first-line instructions from the cookbook saying the soup should have been started the day before.

"That must be some kind of friendly precaution for the extremely slow and fastidious cook." Which Violette was not, not yet anyway.

Scary joy flooded her. She wanted to whistle a jaunty tune like a man. Tonight was her chance to show Benjamin she was a changed woman, more than a sullied human adding machine—that in spite of it all, she was like her friend Dinah in this one point, capable of showing warmth and appreciation where it was warranted and even where it was not. Wasn't that what the Lord wanted from her? From us all? She settled for humming. Set a cool smoothing iron on the edge of a page of *Miss Leslie's Directions for Cookery* to keep the pages in place.

Cookery. What a strange word.

Foolery. That's what this idea was.

Terror flirted with her. What had come over her anyway? Had she been out of her mind to volunteer for tonight's supper? She had touted it as "A light supper," trying to sound Natchezian. And what would she, a newly minted ex-slave, be knowing about what rich folks ate in the town of Natchez?

"Father. Give me strength. I think I might have run out ahead of you."

You can do this, you can do this.

"I can do this," she mumbled aloud. "If Benjamin did it, and he looks no more like a cook than—" Footsteps bounded down the stairs. Emerald stopped and glared.

"What chu think you doing, Vi'lette? You know you can't

cook. Wasn't for the cooks what came and went out at Riverwood all the time, we would've been starved to death long time ago."

Violette groaned her displeasure at how much her daughter sounded like the Violette of old. How she had hoped Emerald would turn out differently. A fresh coat of perspiration crept across her forehead, dampened her upper lip.

"Evening to you, too, Emerald. Now, honey, I want you to listen to me. You're going to have to either sit there quietly or leave the kitchen. Or show me you can help. I can't be bombarded with questions right now. Start by looking for soup bowls in that cabinet right there." She pointed toward one of the exquisitely carved china cabinets that again spoke of Jonathan Mayfield.

Where were the pot lids like Mama Tavie kept? Would she even need one? She would have thought Dinah kept them in a more obvious place. She allowed her eyes to race down Miss Leslie's directions, something, she argued with herself, she didn't have time to do.

"Allow eight or nine hours."

Eight or ni . . .! "Well, my apologies, Miss Leslie." She did not have eight or nine hours. The vestibule clock chose to sound the quarter. Mercy. She did not even have two.

Placing the pot next to the ingredients, she began examining the vegetables.

"I suppose these tops need to be removed from the carrots." And the turnips—should she use the tops, bottoms or both? She knew enough about turnips to know Mama Tavie had cooked both ends, but whether to use them both in the soup . . .

"Mercy." She glanced up at Emerald, hoping to find a bit of encouragement.

"Don't be looking at me. You told me to hush. I hushed."

Fine. She would just dump it all in. Big chunks of meat. Vegetables like carrots, turnips, onions, celery. She covered it with water. Added a dash of salt. And a more than generous amount of pepper. If all else sank into flatness, pepper would save the day.

Wouldn't it? Though she really had not . . . well, not thoroughly . . . read what the cookbook lady said about it.

She hoisted the pot onto the trammel. Watched until it started to simmer. Adding a pint or two more of water, she settled the lid. At least it smelled good. She sat down to catch her breath. Perhaps she would read the instructions a bit while she rested. Change what might need changing.

"BREAK UP THE BONES." The bones? Violette hadn't done that. Couldn't change it. Didn't know how.

"PROPORTION THE WATER TO THE QUANTITY OF MEAT . . . CAREFULLY SKIMMING OFF ALL THE FAT THAT RISES TO THE TOP."

Mercy.

DO NOT, ON ANY ACCOUNT, PUT IN ADDITIONAL WATER TO THE SOUP WHILE IT IS BOILING. Violette glanced at the pint jar she had used to add water at will.

Double mercy.

AFTER THE MEAT IS REDUCED TO RAGS . . . Rags? Did that mean the meat should be falling off the bone? Or should it simply be stringy? Or . . . Her meat pieces looked like tree stumps. Stew. That was it. This was going to be stew she was cooking. Like Mama Tavie's. Wasn't it? How she wished at this moment that little lady and her husband James had not moved to Jackson.

STRAIN IT INTO A LARGE EARTHEN PAN. No time. She had no time a'tall for straining. Maybe everything, vegetables and all, would just blend together the way Violette envisioned.

ON THE FOLLOWING MORNING—the following morning! —BOIL SEPARATELY, CARROTS, TURNIPS, ONIONS, CELERY, AND WHATEVER OTHER VEGETABLES.

"Alas!" Violette borrowed drama from the dozens of novels she had read. "I am ruined . . . I am ruined!" And Benjamin would be here any minute.

"Told ja. You just ain't cut out to be no cook," said Emerald.

"Ummm. Something sure smells inviting."

Reeking of sawdust, Benjamin and Henry materialized out of nowhere. Benjamin strode across the floor and peered into the pot. Henry nodded his assent.

"It do, don't it. I'm way-yonder hungry too."

"We'll just wash up over there at the sink, Violette, if you don't mind." Benjamin set about to help. "How about we all eat right here in the kitchen. I know we're a little early, but I can't wait."

The stack of bowls clinked loudly as Violette moved them from the work table where Emerald had left them and tried to arrange them in some semblance of wishful anticipation for the partakers. The group, even Emerald, fairly ran to the table as Violette brought over the bread and lemonade left over from yesterday. And finally the soup that Violette had been too discombobulated to taste. Benjamin asked grace. Rolled up his sleeve and passed around the large wooden bowl of steaming liquid.

It started with Henry, who choked a bit, then teared up, then chewed and chewed. And chewed. Benjamin, his first spoonful suspended in midair, took notice.

"Henry? You all right?" Henry shook his head. Up and down. Side to side. Kept chewing. Crying.

Then Benjamin. At first he tried to suppress the cough. But his eyes teared up to the point where the water was ready to roll into the soup. Like Henry, he commenced to chewing the tree stumps amidst the crying.

But it was Emerald who squealed foul after the first bite. Gagged and left the table for the back door. Ran back and slammed her hands on the table.

"I told her she couldn't cook! What you want to go and try it for, Vi'lette? Now we all go'n die. Right here in this big old pretty house they go'n find us with our toes pointing to the roof. Just like Ananias and Sapphira in that Bible story you like to read sometime."

Without a word, Violette dipped into the soup. Boiled leather. That's what she had called Dinah's early attempt at preparing collard greens shortly after they had met. But those greens didn't hold a light to this meat. This was true boiled leather. And not only was the meat tough enough to walk alone, the soup was pepper hot!

Violette swallowed the meat then started to cry. All her attempts at dignity and domesticity shouting back at her from the soup bowl before her.

"A-and t-to think how I tr-treated poor Dinah w-who probably had m-more cooking in her little finger th-than I'll ever have."

Emerald looked stricken. "I know it's go'n be the road for us this time."

Without another word, Emerald turned out of the kitchen. Henry, his awkward attempts at cough suppression hanging amongst the pungent smells, followed suit looking over his shoulder.

"It'll be all right, Li'l Vi'lette. It ain't all your fault. It's just meat. And deer meat at that."

∽

LEFT ALONE at the table with Violette next to him, Benjamin wished she would scream, but all she did was tuck in further to his chest and softly sob as Henry made that unwitting yet stinging remark and left through the back door.

It really shouldn't be that difficult. Violette was quite fixable. With a little recall of Mother's advice on how to become a lady, Benjamin could repair much of the damage slavery had done to her in a matter of weeks.

"We can still make something of the dish. A few more hours of simmering. A little water here to, um, soften the meat. A couple of Irish potatoes there to absorb some of the pepper."

She looked up at him. So much like the Emerald he once knew that he almost wanted to take her to his lap.

"But Miss Leslie said to strain the meat first, then add the vegetables the next day. It's too late now. We will have to throw it out."

"Now you tell me." He grinned. "Just teasing, just teasing. I don't care what the cookbook writer says, we can fix this." She stood from the table. Wrapped herself in her arms.

"Don't tease, Benjamin. You don't know what it feels like to fail at everything you do." Inadvertently, his shoulder glanced hers as he started to clear the tables. She was as stiff as an oak plank while he felt as malleable as teacake dough. He placed the bowls back on the table.

"Oh, is that what you think?" Gently, he tugged her by the hand. Edged her into the vestibule and onto the settee. Placing her on his lap was out of the question. So he gathered her again to his chest.

"I am so very, very sorry for what I said to you Friday. I don't think I can ever forgive myself—"

"Benjamin, what's happening to me?"

"No one, not even Mama, has ever held me like this." Shaking all the way down to her soles, she seemed not to hear him, not to speak directly to him but to the world.

"N-no one, n-not even Mama, has ever held me like this." Against his better judgement, he continued to hold her, a bit closer. She inhaled way too loudly. Forgot to breathe.

"Breathe, Violette."

"Yes, sir."

"And get rid of the 'sir,' will you? "

He lost track of time. Something the Catlett heir would never do. The house was quiet as he lifted a sleeping Violette, arms clasped about his neck, around the creak of the third stair and on to her room. A tear touched her hair.

Truth told, not once—not even in the case of *his* mother—had anyone ever held Benjamin this way either.

CHAPTER 13

Tuesday, November ninth

"Seem like we right back where we started from."

Henry's face was swollen. Not from a punch or a kick—or even from a vicious bite—but seemingly from some kind of mind poisoning that chilled Violette's soul. Taking measured steps toward the work bench where he stood, she stopped short of the defeat emanating from him.

"What is it, Henry? What's wrong?"

"It's Davey. They done hung one of his brothers. Strung him up like a hog at killin' time." Henry yanked off his mask. Slumped to the table. "Davey found him back of that stream behind the McMillan plantation 'bout two hours ago. Somebody had drawed a picture of a Union soldier and put it in his hand."

Fear she had not felt since the day her brothers and sisters were goaded into an auction-bound wagon sloshed around in Violette's belly. She had never seen a hanging before, but she knew of them. Everybody black knew of them, had images of hot, swollen bodies swinging from southern oaks somewhere in their minds. And Henry's words, confirming for her that Harriet Beecher Stowe was most likely wrong about it all being over, sent spots across her vision. Sweat gathered in secret places it ought not. She wondered if incontinence would betray her right then and there. She should hug Henry, shouldn't she? Do something. But all left to her was to stare through the spots and stammer out the obvious.

"Why? What did he do?"

Henry dragged a hand down his puffy face. She thought she saw a tear.

"Dunno, but I can imagine. He always got a lot to say, that one. Ain't never been quiet like Davey. Got a mouth like his pa but spewing better stuff. And the war ending like it did ain't helped him none. Been telling everybody that would listen that he was free and meant to talk about it whensonever he pleased." A sigh like Violette had never heard from Henry broke from his chest, part tremulous, part proud.

"No, sir. Wasn't nobody go'n tell that boy what to do. They tell me he fought like a wild boar with the Yankees at Milliken's Bend. Still just a boy. But no other soldier, black or white, topped him."

Violette looked up. Found him looking at her, eyes near begging her to wake him up from the nightmare he had entered. But for Violette, the spots of her own eyes had increased. Was she dying? Were they both dying of despair? Or was it simply that her system had taken such a jarring until her very eyes didn't care to look even upon a friend?

Lord, this poor, dead soldier boy Henry describing sound so much like Emerald.

"Me and Benjamin. We had wanted to fight so bad. We even set out one time in early '63 in the dead of night to catch up with Grant's army up near Vicksburg, but a couple of old slave patrollers, who forgot they didn't have much of a job no more, chased us back into town before we was two miles out. Benjamin got knocked about something bad at first. But then he give 'em back pretty much the same fight he got. By the time I turned back round to help, they'd slunk back into the woods. Dinah had to take care of Benjamin for weeks before he could come back to the shop. Blessing the town's folks didn't ever find out what we was about, or the business would've gone down further than it did."

Violette focused. Remembered, even through the spots that now seemed to want to claim her brain, what Jonathan Mayfield had said once when he had ridden out to Riverwood in the wee hours in early '63 and knocked on her dependency door.

"I need you to look at these books, but remember to always keep them hidden. We've had a little trouble with Benjamin. I wouldn't want anything to happen to you too. No matter how benevolent"—Violette had blinked at the unfamiliar word—"you think the McMillans, they are still slave owners, and they are convinced they know what's best for you. You must not let them know your gift of numbers."

So that's why Benjamin never knew about Violette's book-keeping work. He'd been laid up from a beating, and Jonathan had chosen not to tell him the risk of what he and Violette were doing behind the McMillans' backs. Violette inched closer. Finally found her voice.

"Now, Henry, you just listen." Not fully aware, she completely reverted to her first language. "We strong people, Henry, if God ever made any strong folks, we it. Who else could put up with what we have all these hundreds of years, except maybe the Hebrews, and still be going on? We made it through the war and we go'n make it through this. It's go'n blow over."

"Naw. Naw. Not true." He shook his head, sending sawdust flying into the spots still lingering in her eyes. "Whites just biding their time 'til they can completely get rid of the blue army men. Still madder than a cold setting hen. I overheard one say the other day that white men can't afford to continue supporting coloreds like Benjamin when there's so many of their own race who don't have food on their tables because of that useless war. They coming for us, Violette. Believe me when I say it." He reached for his mask. "I can't talk about this no more right now."

Violette turned toward her desk with a thousand more questions. She wanted to go back inside the house. Check on her little girl. Hold her so tight until they were one again the way they were when she carried her. That way, she had known. Could always be sure her baby was safe. She jumped at the sound of Benjamin's voice.

"Morning, Henry."

"Morning, suh."

She waited. Was Henry not going to tell Benjamin what happened? Well, if he didn't, she would.

"Been meaning to ask you about those orders collecting over there in the overflow."

"Yes, suh?"

"That armoire and matching daybed have been finished for some time, and what about the walnut rocker? Wasn't it ordered around Easter? And the cribs for those redheaded twins?"

The quiet was thick with uncertainty and confusion. "Henry?"

"They done hung him."

"What? Hung who? The twins' father?"

"Davey brother. They strung him up."

Violette bit the inside of her jaw as Benjamin swore. Bellowed like an enraged bull. Swore some more. "Why?"

"I can't be telling the story no more today. Ask Violette. She tell you what I said."

Dread sheathed the fear that had already gripped her. She didn't want to talk about it either. But she did. Told it exactly as it had been told to her. Saw the pain in Benjamin's eyes and wanted to hold him as closely as she wanted to hold Emerald. Benjamin set a frantic, angry pace. Pulling out drawers. Straightening and re-straightening papers. He stomped to the window.

"Violette? Do you think . . . could it be that these orders are not being picked up on purpose? Has the residual hate boiled to a point where . . ." He slid his hands into his pockets. Shrugged. Reminded her of the sweetest little boy. "I wonder if it's time for me to return to Virginia."

Oh, but if he did, what would happen to her plans for Emerald? What would happen to her heart?

"Mr. Catlett, from what I've been able to see, there is a serious lack of cash coming in right now. I heard Jonathan call it a cash flow. And I think as soon as those orders are picked up—and I am sure they will be or else we sell them—all will right itself. After that, there should be no problem, sir."

She didn't believe that, and she knew he didn't either. In the land of her birth, the daily rising evil against her and everyone like her was palpable. Had been for some time. She crossed to the window. Took Benjamin's hand. Moved him to where Henry stood frozen behind his mask. With her free hand, she took Henry's. Standing between them, along with Henry, she wept for what might have been.

BENJAMIN MUST EASE his and Violette's intertwined fingers apart before her touch became his undoing and he unmanned himself and started to weep like Henry. If there was one thing Rogers Catlett despised more than a thinking slave, it was a weeping man of any color. But Benjamin didn't care about what his father would have thought, did he? He braced himself for the shudder that always came when he thought he might have imbibed even a single sip of his father's ways.

My father. My African father. My African father, the owner of African slaves.

Thank heaven Benjamin had been able to escape the plantation with none of his father's traits. It was Mother—her impeccable skills in running the house and later helping him place freed slave children—that he admired. Patterned after. He battened down his thoughts. Pulled his attention back into the space of

Henry and Violette. Violette questioned him with her eyes, then her voice.

"Are you all right?" As though not to cry suggested something was wrong.

Still holding onto Henry, she reached out to regain Benjamin's hand. Her roughened palm in his felt like nothing he had experienced among the black elite in Virginia. Not even Lucie's hand, which had had a similar field-worn surface that always made him so tenderhearted, was as rough. And he wouldn't risk that sensation again. Yet what did it matter? It was Henry's touch Violette really wanted. Benjamin refused her hand.

Time to advance the inevitable.

They were a perfect match. It was now or never. "Never" was his preference. But "now" was the only real possibility. The only thing that would have made sense to Father.

He stepped back from Henry and Violette who were now wrapped in each other's arms. Watched one of her braids spring loose from a pin Henry had obviously disturbed in the embrace.

"You two pair off nicely." They jerked apart. Slapped away tears. Looked at each other, then back at him as though he had sprouted the antlers of a ram.

"What?"

"No, really. You do. I had not noticed before." Liar. "But you make a handsome couple." He managed a wink at Henry. "What's the story with you two anyway? Past and present if you will. Neither of you has told me yet how the two of you met." They glanced at each other again, clearly discomfited. Well, too bad. It was out now. They might as well find their ease.

"Uh. Uh-ruh, I mean to say—" Try as it may, Henry's steadily-lengthening mouth failed to yield anything intelligible.

"What story, Mr. Catlett?"

So Miss Violette McMillan would be coy, would she? Why did she look so beautiful standing there? Her hair. Braids not even pinned and she hadn't even noticed.

And he didn't care. Actually liked them wild and bold. But he would not admit that to himself and anyone else. What would Mother think? Violette was the antithesis of Mother, who never stepped outside her bedchamber undone, though he had seen her with a mysterious bruise a time or two.

Blast! He didn't have time for all this ruminating, neither about Violette's coyness nor the stubborn sidestepping of his own thoughts into what it would feel like to touch that persimmon-colored skin of hers. Or did he? Perhaps he should just play along. Force her into that same kind of senselessness Henry had uttered moments ago.

"Oh, come now, Miss McMillan. Busyness is not synonymous with blindness. I do make it a point to focus on my customers, but that doesn't mean I have not seen the two of you on more than one occasion acting quite common, bursting with the need to speak to one another. And what lady would allow herself to be embraced such as I just witnessed without an understanding of some sort? Oh, and one more thing. This is not Riverwood Plantation, and you are no longer a slave. A lady never allows her hair to just go willy-nilly in a public place like this. I would have thought you alert enough to take some basic cues from Dinah."

Willy-nilly? Had he just said willy-nilly? He had lost his mind. The longer he talked, the sillier he sounded. But it was too late. He was too far in.

"One last point. In your quest to be a lady, you should try hair grease. 'Oil' sounds better, I suppose. Maybe even a hot comb. My mother was able to secure one from Europe. It wasn't easy, but I hear once you try it, it does wonders for unruly African hair."

He halted. Felt the weight of regret as he had not in a very long time, even the moment when he had fired her. Why was he saying these things? Was he still holding what she had done to the Mayfields against her when they themselves clearly had set it in the past? In truth, he actually liked unruly African hair. So why?

The answer seemed to come from his very soul. "Jealousy, my son. It is cruel as the grave."

~

"OH. EUROPE, YOU SAY?"

Violette decided to pull from the little knowledge of British English she had learned from her novel reading.

"Quite the thing, really. Why, I skip over to England all the time. As a matter of fact, Emerald and I had just returned when you found my ladylike hands submerged in a tub of tepid, filthy, wash water last week. Mr. Catlett, how did you guess? Was it the gowns I wear? Or perhaps the clink of the coins always bouncing around in my reticule."

Violette warmed to her performance which, in its anger, was really not an act at all, while Benjamin tried to find his signature smirk. Failed.

"Now, just a minute. I think you misunderstand—"

"Just the thing, you know, for entertainment on a winter morning when the chill of the Thames is still in one's bones."

"That is not how I meant it at all. I only meant to say, to help you—"

"To help? To HELP? Calling me everything short of an under-the-hill apprentice—how, pray tell, does that help? Questioning everything from my boots to my wild hair. How do you propose to help with that?

"But I . . . I . . . that is, in truth, I like your hair. I really do. I just thought—"

"Thought what? That it was jolly good for you to embrace me in an isolated vestibule but not for ex-slave Henry to do so after learning that a boy had been hanged for nothing more than un-corralled talk?"

Henry's eyes bulged. He flexed his fist. Violette checked herself and gave him a calming pat.

"It's all right, Henry. It's all right."

She stepped over to Benjamin. Looking up, she stared until she commanded his regard, then jabbed the pencil she'd grasped toward his chest.

"Now you listen to me, Mr. Benjamin Catlett—whoever you are and wherever you came from. I. Am. Not. A. Lady."

Violette's insides twisted at the sound of her bitterness and the resulting shame. She had given herself to Eli, Jethro, and finally that night under the hill she had given up her last chance to the loss of whatever she had regained in between. But this morning, sawdust reaching her ankles, she would let the hurt and disappointment gush—this once and for all—and then she would gather her child and leave.

"I may have to swallow the condescension of well-meaning people like Miss Harriet Beecher Stowe simply because the plot and the hope so engulfed me that I could not put it down. But I don't have to put up with it from you. If I am going to be talked to like a slave, then it might as well be from someone whose cruelty I don't question."

"Violette? What ch'all fussing 'bout? What's this I heard about Davey's brother?"

Emerald. Her usual, inexplicably ill-fated timing disrupting the flow. "Go back to the house, Precious Emerald, and put your things in a sack." Emerald didn't move.

Benjamin looked stricken. A bell tinkled in Violette's head. A warning that she might be stepping into a graveyard with hidden live bodies. A sense that she had struck some dissonant chord whose vibrations were irrevocable. But she was just too angry to look out even for the ones she loved.

What? I do not love Benjamin Catlett. Unlovable lout.

"Were you ever a slaveholder, Mr. Catlett?" Lies she had spread about Jonathan once wanting to own slaves tried to halt her from proceeding with this line of questioning. But she was past warning. "Or did you just aspire to be a black slave owner. Buying up the souls and bodies of your own people like the barber, Mr. Johnston, who once lived next door to this very place?"

Benjamin crossed to the other side. Sank to the chair he had placed behind her desk. She followed him.

"No. I am not a lady. What I am is a slave who as a child happened to play once in a blessed while with another slave child named Henry Livingston of a Sunday afternoon—into the twilight —while we both were shamelessly naked except for a shred of cloth hanging from our shoulders waiting to be replaced at the overseer's whim. But alas! When we thought nothing could be mean enough to separate us, Henry was farmed out while I was sent to the fields with the promise of house duty. I was the fortunate one who got to stay in familiar surroundings while the overseer sold every sibling I had along with my father, leaving my pregnant mother and me to wonder in stark grief—pain more naked and offensive than mine and Henry's children's bodies had ever been." She yanked her braid to the front of her shoulder.

"Far more offensive than my naked, ungreased hair."

She stalked toward the door. Heard the beginnings of a sob barely caught. Felt the shift of her heart. Could that have been Benjamin's cry?

Certainly not. Benjamin Catlett never cried. She continued out the door.

CHAPTER 14

Wednesday, November tenth

*P*lease, Violette.

It seemed to Violette that Benjamin's eyes had pleaded those very words when last she'd seen him, but his lips had remained silent. She tapped her fingers on the desk. Spoke her frustration into the empty space.

"Why could he not have asked? Just this once?"

But instead of asking her to stay, he had flat refused to let her go. Argued she owed him at least another week.

Said with a catch in his voice that she must never call herself a slave in his presence again.

Now, Violette found herself alone in the shop, Henry having gone to the docks to supervise an offloading of lumber, Benjamin several miles south of town trying to negotiate a rare deal to furnish a new house being built way down in Baton Rouge. Though she had been at Mayfield Cabinetry only a short while, it was plain to see the business had slumped in recent months, the books showing two times more in the purchasing column than on the profit side of the accounts.

Despite the anger still smothering her at times, she felt a bit sorry for Benjamin. A grudging smile claimed her face. He could be rather sweet when he had a mind to. Turning her chair to face the house, her smile widened, reminiscence about the night of the failed soup suffusing her with an inner glow.

He would have been well within his rights to scold her, she knew, especially given the money she had wasted, not to mention the mess and the hunger everyone was left with.

Knowing the things he still held against her, a good tongue lashing at the least would have begun evening the score for how she had driven Dinah to distraction to the point of accidentally burning Jonathan's manumission papers. Plus all the other meanness.

Instead Benjamin had held her as though she were a delicate precious stone, the younger sister he never had.

"And therein lies the problem. I don't want to be his sister. And he doesn't want me to be anything else. Wants me to be a lady, so I can marry . . . Henry?"

Heavens.

But maybe, if not a lady, she could have become, a decent enough woman. If only Jonathan had not come to Riverwood on that day of freedom with yet another ledger, smiling and whispering to Violette that she was now a free woman. If only she had not listened to Singer that night when, unbeknownst to her, Mayfield Cabinetry and much of its ilk had become mired in the mud of bitter resentment and bigotry, just as it seemed to be today. A chill passed over her. She let her eyes roam the few elegantly understated furniture pieces in the front of the shop used as advertisement.

Lord? How much longer could Jonathan's dream and the hopes of countless others like him outlast this hatred?

But that one night of freedom had been so joyous. It didn't matter, the rumor that the surrender had occurred weeks earlier at a place called Appomattox Courthouse, Virginia. Violette, yet confined to an isolated life at Riverwood, had not even known of the speculation until that morning when Jonathan showed up, more animated than she had ever seen him.

She had grabbed eight-year-old Emerald by the hand. "Please, Jonathan. Please let me go to town with you." Jonathan had been hesitant.

"I don't know that it's a good idea right now. Dinah and I are sticking close to home." He looked at the wagon bed where he had delivered a load of wood to the McMillans as an excuse to bring the ledgers back to Violette. "Much of white Mississippi is not in a good mood. And until we know for sure that the word of the war's end is true, McMillan might not take kindly to this notion."

She begged like a hungry puppy. "I and Emerald, we don't want to be by ourselves right now. It's a happy time. We can't stand to be by ourselves." Jonathan stared interminably. Nodded toward the back of the wagon. "All right, you win. Bring the ledger so you can work on it. And don't leave behind the money you've saved."

My savings. The money I set aside on the off chance I could get me and Emerald to the north where we could start all over again.

Her insides whirling, Violette's head jerked up to the sound of the opening door. A new customer?

"Good morning. What can I do for—"

Chester Singer.

"You can do a whole lot for me, bookkeeping girl. I know how you enjoy a good time. Ain't that riii-ght?"

"Mr. Catlett's not here." As soon as she said it, she knew it was a mistake. "B-but Henry, he's—"

"At the dock. No need to crank up them wiles of yours, little lady. I been watching for days. I know when them two biggity white-man pretenders is here and when they ain't. It's darkies like Benjamin and that there Henry, and now you, that's got men like me running around pretending to be what we ain't so things can get back to the way they were meant to be in the first place."

The triangle on his forehead faded white. A side of his mouth kicked up in malice, all semblance of the new banker's speech flung aside. This was the Singer Violette remembered.

"Pretty soon it ain't go'n matter no how."

Don't ask what he means. Best not to ask. "What do you want, Mr. Singer?"

Whatever it was, Violette knew it meant no good. Simon Legree might have been fictional, but his type was as true and consistent as a snake's venom. And here stood his embodiment in the person of a man whose cold-blooded strap flung warm blood against tree after tree out at the McMillan Plantation when she was a child. She had never thought about whether Master McMillan sanctioned it, her brain yet too resistant to pain to ponder it. But whether the master approved or not, it appeared he never questioned the methods as he looked the other way toward the fat accounts placed before him month after month, accounts yielding enough for him to build a town estate called Riverwood.

"Not a matter of what I want, little lady. It's what you have to do if you want to thrive in good health." Violette waited in silence. Knew he wanted her to show more fear.

"So, you won't be asking what my intentions are. That what I'm to understand?"

"I'm sure you will tell me."

He laughed. "I always knew you were a brazen stubborn thang, even when you were a little hunk of lard out on the plantation. And that evening in '65, soon as I saw you and that little sister of yours wandering around the river as though you was decent white folks, I recognized you."

Why, Savior, didn't I stay put that night like Jonathan and Dinah told me to do?

She would never allow it to escape her lips, but she knew the answer to that question. Residual resentment for a couple who had done nothing but love her almost from the beginning. That was the mean, pitiful reason she had defied their instructions. Decided to walk alone that night.

"I recollect I wasn't feeling the friendliest that night. Couldn't get my hands on Lee and the rest of them turncoats up in Richmond to try to choke some sense into them. But I was determined to show one more darkie who their god-given bosses were on this earth, and you were just the ticket. Greedy as a newborn black-haired pig. Eyes the size of a full moon at the prospect of doubling your savings near 'bout lit up the niii-ght.'"

He moved around to the back of the desk where Violette gripped the arms of the sleek padded chair undoubtedly made by Jonathan years ago. Her palms sweated profusely causing her to wonder if even the expensive lacquer Jonathan must have sacrificed for would withstand the relentless moisture.

"If you must know, little lady, I plan to be a big part of the reestablishment of the Old South. But in order to do that, I've got to remain 'incog nita' as they call it. Can't have no overgrown pickaninny like you ruining it for me and my brothers in the Cause by telling people who I really am and what my job used to be. Wouldn't want to have to trade tales with you and tell that Benjamin fellow how you acted out down under the hill that evening."

Violette stiffened. Rage flourished like a field of weeds. Miss Stowe, and Mr. Douglass and all the rest of them had been wrong. This hatred was never going to end, but she wouldn't be one to help it along by showing fear.

"Tell Benjamin whatever you like, but you'll have to beat me to it, because as soon as he gets here, I'm going to tell him myself —so that he can tell everybody else—just what a devil's spawn you really are. One who probably doesn't know the workings of a bank from a horse stall at mucking time.

"Oh, ho! Will you, now."

He placed his hands over hers. Gripped them as they gripped the chair arms. Put his eyes to her eyes, his nose to her nose.

"Now you listen to me. Don't matter, this so-called Union win. I still have my boys working for me. They still know their places and what to do 'cause I taught them real good, 'specially when it comes to roping in other loud-mouth darkie boys, like Davey's dearly departed brother, and pretty little sassy black girls who live in two-story houses. So if you don't value your life, how about li'l Precious Emerald's?"

The flow of Violette's existence stopped. Blood, heartbeat, muscle movement. Her baby. *My life, Lord. She is my life. I have nothing except my precious jewel.* Too focused on the prayer itself, she didn't hear the partial answer coming through the door. Benjamin's carpetbagger friend, Paul Boatwright.

"Chester? What on earth are you doing? Come out from behind that desk, now. It doesn't look proper. Doesn't look proper at all!"

THE DEAL TO furnish the house had fallen flat. Benjamin pressed the back of his hand to his dampened forehead, then lifted and swung another set of dressed wood planks onto the wagon, Henry at the other end of the load. Though born to privilege, if one could call it a privilege to see men who mirrored his own image under the threat of his father's whip every day, he had found there was nothing like hard, physical labor to clear the mind, soothe the soul.

"Don't imagine we be needing to make no more of these here kinds of orders for a while, Mr. Catlett, 'specially now that our one big order done flew out the window. What chu think?" Benjamin flinched at the use of his surname, noticing that since he retracted the offer to turn over the business, Henry had reverted to formality.

"So, Henry, I see it's on your mind, too, is it?"

"Yes, sir, 'tis."

"Well, I suppose it would be, given the picture Violette's been painting of the numbers and what happened today with the Baton Rouge job."

"If I may say so, sir, this picture had already started to take shape, a ways up the road before Vi'lette got here and started tinkering with them numbers."

Benjamin walked around to the other side of the wagon. Shame fixed him squarely in front of this young man whose hopes about running the business Benjamin had teased and then snuffed out. He clasped Henry's shoulder, the boy's shirt as drenched with sweat as his own.

"Henry, you are a master builder. Jonathan says one of the finest he's ever known, and I agree. Please know that my every waking moment—"well, at least the few remaining moments after those daily outrageous thoughts he'd been having about Violette "—I am trying to save Jonathan's business. Our business, mine and yours." Henry looked at the ground, his stance every bit that of the slave.

"I believe that, sir. But right now, with this part of the country turning so mean toward the freed slaves, well . . . it just don't seem possible."

Henry had an uncanny way of sizing up the heart of a matter. Benjamin felt an involuntary shiver. Turned toward the hill that led to upper Natchez where Mayfield Cabinetry had sat for a decade and a half.

"Benjamin!"

Benjamin cupped his hand over his eyes and swung back toward the docks. Who was that standing in front of Eliza's Boys' saloon, suited long arms flailing at him like thick saplings in a storm?

"Benjamin! Benjamin Catlett. I need to speak with you."

"Paul Boatwright?"

What could be urgent enough to bring him back to town this quickly and down here under the hill? True enough, he wouldn't be the first "gentleman" to be caught down here. Business wasn't as good among the brothels as it once had been, but it was by no means dead. But this time of day? Surely Paul wouldn't . . .

"At Violette's instructions, I've looked everywhere in Natchez, even—ahem!—at some places I wouldn't expect to find you."

Benjamin's insides fluttered. "Violette? Is she all right? Has something happened to her little sister?" Paul waved him off.

"Oh, they're fine, just fine. Sorry if I misled you." Benjamin said nothing. Stared and nodded Paul's continuance while his heart worked overtime to right itself into a slowed rhythm.

"No. I just felt . . ." The man looked sheepish, as though, now he was here, he wondered why. "I felt like you ought to know that, even though it has been several years since the war's end, the mood is darkening among the defeated Confederates. Rapidly. I mean really rapidly." Benjamin was about to lose patience. As sickened as everyone else about Davey's half-brother, he knew what was about to be said. Didn't want to hear it.

"Mood? Speak plainly, man."

"I overheard something today. A couple of Negroes joking about what they would love to do to you and your business. Said they were just waiting to get the word from their 'old' boss." Paul scratched his head. Made a little semicircle. "I tell you, Benjamin, it shook me. Those two weren't playing." Benjamin inhaled. Reminded himself that Paul was a trained lawyer. Suspicious of everything.

"Do you know them?"

"No. Being a northern land speculator, there are still many white faces in town I don't know, not to mention the faces of the ex-slave population that sadly move from the footpaths and still seek the ground when they pass near me."

Henry moved in closer. Tentatively raised his hand. Fought to keep his own face level with Benjamin's friend's. "Uh, Mr. Boatwright? Could you be saying what they look like, I mean them ones doing that talking about the shop?"

"No. Mostly their backs are what I saw. One was African black, the other mixed, is about all I can swear to."

Something in Benjamin recoiled. Wasn't the war over? Hadn't the thing he had moved to the South for in the first place been secured four years past? That most precious gift of freedom? Despite the horror of what happened to Davey's brother, what Paul just said could not be the future, not in a general way. It just couldn't be.

"Listen, Paul. I thank you. I do. And I know there's plenty of unrest left around here. But Jonathan and I have been working this business since before the war. We've built a clientele of some of the wealthiest people in the south, albeit many have suffered loss." He glanced at Henry. "Which is why I believe we're in an ebb tide at the moment."

"For heaven's sakes. Be reasonable, will you? That's just not the case, Benjamin. Yes, there's plenty of loss that's bound to affect your income. But you and that business of yours is not an untouchable island as far as hatred is concerned. Now, I have an offer and I want you to hear me out before you refuse. Agreed?"

Silence. Benjamin felt his jaw working out of control.

"Well?"

"All right. Agreed."

"I know you're still thinking of returning to Virginia."

Henry sucked in loudly. Benjamin ignored him.

"I think I have a solution, something that will safeguard all concerned. Truth is, I'm not making the headway I had hoped for in land acquisition, but as you know, the Lord has blessed me with enough inheritance not to be overly concerned. Why not go ahead and sell the shop to me? I'd be willing to oversee it for you, with Henry's help, of course, until some of this backlash dies down. Then if Henry can establish himself among the townspeople and you wish to return, we could talk compensation. If not, or if the whole thing turns unprofitable, I'm sure I could sell it. Write off any loss and possibly return north myself."

"Are you serious?"

Paul glared at him. He was. And so should Benjamin be.

How much plainer did it have to be before Benjamin conceded that Violette McMillan was designed for Henry, and Henry was designed for cabinetmaking?

Benjamin's time here was up. Why couldn't he just admit it?

Still, why was Paul so agitated? There was something he wasn't saying. They needed to talk further without the added pressure of Henry.

"Was that the last of the load, Henry?"

"Yes, sir."

"Then haul it on up to the shop, would you? I'll be along."

Benjamin and Paul stood like ice carvings in the latent November heat until Henry started to rattle up the hill. An old, discarded bench not far from the river's edge caught Benjamin's attention.

"Come, Paul. Let's sit down for a minute."

It was past time he told somebody why, in spite of words to the contrary, he would never set foot in his father's house again.

CHAPTER 15

hank God for Mr. Boatwright, who had looked perfectly stricken before hustling Singer out in short order, on oath begged by Violette not to tell Benjamin what little he had seen.

She trembled at what might have happened. At what had already happened between them. The look in Singer's eyes . . . Don't forsake us, Lord, me and Emerald.

She paced the tiny space around her desk like a besieged general.

How would Singer know to say the "Precious" in Precious Emerald's name? How would he know?

Mercy. How would he know?

Unless Eli told him. No one from her past knew her child's first name except Eli Duggan. She had thought it such a beautiful name. Had tried to impress him with it one of the few times she'd managed to talk to him at Riverwood. But Eli could not be the one who gave away her child's name. Eli was dead.

Wasn't he?

The shop was quiet. Other than Singer's visit, Violette had not seen a single customer since Benjamin and Henry left much earlier in the day. Words from an hour ago dropped on her like a black-smith's hammer.

"I know when them two white-man pretenders is here and when they ain't."

How? Had Chester Singer or someone he'd hired been spying them out? Waiting until no one was in the shop to do whatever awful, cowardly thing he and his "boys" were about to do? Or worse was he . . . were they . . . waiting until they were all here so that they could—

She dropped to her knees. Softly sobbed out a prayer. "Oh, Father God. I can't pretend any longer. I'm leaking hope. Fast. What am I to do?"

Face buried into the cushion of Jonathan's chair, Violette's mind calculated horrible past scenes as fast as it did numbers.

Multiple murders of McMillan slaves from the barrel of Singer's gun. Hangings near the river for all the world to see. Slavery-time beatings that would shiver Simon Legree.

Was she adding up the sum of who she was? Violette's forehead dripped with sweat. Fear binding her to a hollow frozen future like a mummy maker. Lord. *Lord. Lord. Please help me, Savior. We have no weapons. They have the power. They could kill us.*

Wait. Wait one minute. Was she still a slave so petrified with fear she could not continue the fight for what thousands had already died for, or was she a woman who had survived a dehumanizing existence and was legally and morally bound to take what was hers as a citizen of the United States of America? No. She would not retreat.

She. Was. Free.

She allowed her thoughts to travel back to when a handsome young man was all the talk of black Natchez. So proud of him they were! Despite the strands of jealousy, the black community, slave and free, looked to Jonathan Mayfield as what it might someday become. A young man who had somehow gotten himself free with

JACQUELINE FREEMAN WHEELOCK

the papers to prove it and off to North Carolina to learn the trade of furniture making. Returned to Natchez and proved himself a contender with the best the South had to offer. Not to mention marrying a slave named Dinah Devereaux who must be the prettiest woman Violette had ever seen. Not to mention hiring a suave, articulate, mysterious man named Benjamin Catlett, who had become the brother Jonathan never had.

And the love Violette never dreamed possible.

"Surely, God, you would not allow a man like Singer to destroy what these two men along with Henry have labored to build. Surely—"

Where was Emerald?

Violette shot to her feet. Poked the ledger beneath her arm and flew out the door.

∾

"Loo-see."

Sounding out the two syllables into the ears of another human being shot pain to the back of Benjamin's head.

"Lucie was her name."

In the more than a decade he had been in Natchez, he had not spoken her name to a single soul, not even Jonathan. It was too precious. Too painful. Not that he loved her like a man loves a woman. He had finally come to accept he had never loved her. He had simply used a lovely slave girl named Lucie to try to cleanse his soul. And in the bungling attempt, he had killed her.

Hands loosely clasped behind his back, Paul Boatwright had the decency to remain silent as the walk progressed up a winding hill. He looked every bit the lawyer he was. Nodding here and there while Benjamin hemmed and hawed, groping his way toward a decent beginning to a horrible story.

"I don't know if I'll ever be able set foot on Virginia soil again, slave-driven soil or free, without dying of shame and guilt. I have blood on my hands, and sometimes I think I ought to be in a jail cell somewhere.

He could almost see Paul's mind careening toward the edge, but his friend kept his peace outwardly.

"I always knew she was frail. Even before I learned my letters and she learned that she was forbidden to learn hers, even as I watched her year after year in my father's fields bending her mind and her back to the crops, I sensed her body had not the fight to survive the Catlett drivers that came and went." Paul halted. Broke his silence.

"Catlett drivers. I must ask you to explain."

Benjamin blew out a protracted breath through the o-shaped whistle his lips had formed. "My father owned slaves. Once as many as fifty. Lucie was one of them, born on the plantation."

There. He had said it. The first little piece of his scabbed-over secret seemed to fall against the packed-dirt road, making him feel a bit lighter.

"And from the first day I came into the knowledge of myself as a human being who happened to look and act just like Rogers Catlett's human property, I detested who I was. Yet all I was given, all the toys and ponies and specialty sweets, came through human enslavement. At first, I appeared to thrive on it. Ate the best foods. Wore the best clothes. Learned from the best tutors a black man could hire. At the insistence of my father, I was referred to as 'sir' by full-grown, muscled men.

"But there was no thriving in the widening gap that gradually formed between me and the slaves as I grew a little older. Just the hollow carved-out space of an only child who from a distance watched near-naked slaves who looked just like him, of an evening playing in the lengthening shadows down the hill among the cabins. A little boy who took to longingly mimicking the behavior of his father's chattel, even down to shedding his clothes within the confines of his decorated room in order to become as naked as they were, and skipping to the slave songs he tried to imitate. That ritual came to a painful and abrupt end when my father happened upon me and welted me soundly with a strap.

"Then one day a slave girl called Lucie ran. Whenever my father and his driver and patrollers met that night to discuss how best to capture her, I hid to listen without anyone's censure. I heard them say what they would do to 'break' her of what could become a lifelong habit. Unspeakable things that even now my brain registers but my mouth refuses to utter." Benjamin let his words clear the air before he continued.

"In all our heads, Paul, there are unformed ideas just waiting for the right crisis to give them full birthing. Lucie was twelve. I was thirteen. I got it into my head that somehow, if I could save her from this looming punishment, God might forgive me for the Catlett blood running in my veins. I told my father that I was in love with her and that if he would give me a chance, I—Mother and I together—would make her into a lady. He laughed. Flatly refused. I insisted, begged. He refused again. And when they found her half dead from cold, he personally whipped her until she lost consciousness. Whatever else he and the overseer did I have never known."

Benjamin heard the roughness of his own voice. Wondered if he was about to cross some kind of masculine-designated line of dignity. Decided he didn't care.

"My father had not always been that way. I would go so far as to say that he had once been loving, maybe not in an emotional way but in an agape way. He had chosen to show love, aiding others on neighboring plantations, making sure Mother kept the slaves well-fed, even though he wasn't an avid church goer. Then something changed in him. He seemed to see what power could do for any man of any color, saw that he could bark at other human beings who depended on him for life's sustenance and they obeyed like animals. The more they obeyed, the more their obedience corrupted him, elevated him in his own eyes until he started to beat his purchases for a little or nothing, all the while learning to justify it with the law and the Bible. I suspect the need for power stretched to the beating of his wife, and when that didn't satisfy, he turned to drink which eventually killed him.

"As the only son of Rogers Catlett, my guilt grew unbearable. At seventeen, I determined I would marry Lucie whatever it took. I would use her to atone for what I had been born into. Behind Father's back, I enlisted Mother's help to groom her, hoping my father would eventually come around. But Lucie, beautiful though she had become, had never recovered from the 'lesson' my father had whipped into her. Instead, she had grown more delicate over the ensuing years so that by the time I took her as a project, what she needed most were not manners and pretty clothes but bedrest.

"I remember the day as though it happened this morning. Mother had gussied and trussed Lucie in preparation for a ball among the few free and independently wealthy Negroes in Northern Virginia. I, of course, would be her escort. Lucie commenced to favoring her right side as we sat in the drawing room waiting to be fetched by a carriage driver, but I ignored her. After all, that was the night I planned to propose in front of everybody. She was only just experiencing a little discomfort for beauty's sake.

"'It's the stays,' Mother whispered as pain finally brought tears to Lucie's eyes. 'But you simply must learn to wear them if you're to be a Catlett.' All Lucie said before she sank to the floor was, 'I thought I already was a Catlett. You own me, don't you?'

"The doctor worked furiously. Said something had burst inside her, something rotten and insidious possibly poisoning her whole system. He called it an appendix. Disgusted with Mother and me, he announced that the stays Mother insisted Lucie wear could not have helped. Lucie died the following morning at seven forty-five, and for months, I hardly slept. Ate just enough to please Mother. Pondered how I might make up for Lucie's death. Mother felt it too, though not in so debilitating a way as I.

"The next year, Father drank himself to death, leaving the

wealth for me to inherit and Mother to manage until I came into my majority. I was eighteen. I wanted no part of it unless it could bring Lucie back and relieve my soul of its guilt. Father died in mid-afternoon. By eight o'clock that night, I was packed and ready to leave my Virginia upbringing and the bequest of death my father had so painstakingly put in place for me. For months, I pondered how I might make up for Lucie's death. Mother felt it too, though not in so debilitating a way as I.

"The idea struck me with the force of a rock. I would move to the Deep South. I would learn what it was like to be a slave—not to become one, but to apprentice myself to someone, working with my hands until I became proficient in something other than inheritance. Meanwhile, with Mother's help, I would rescue as many children as I could from the auction block by buying them and then smuggling them to my mother in Virginia who would, in turn, see to it they were safely placed in free states."

"Did your mother free her slaves?"

Benjamin paused to contemplate something he had thought of but only as a fleeting pest. "Oddly, no. While she treated them far better than Father in his latter days, for some reason she never let them go, and when I've tried to approach her, she has been evasive and non-committal to the point of causing herself physical pain. To this day, I don't know why she held onto them, though since the war it's all moot. Praise God."

A different kind of quietness ruled until they reached Benjamin's gate.

"I fear I have come down here for the wrong reasons." More than roughness in Paul's voice gave him away. His face, wet with tears, spoke much louder. "There's much more healing to be done in the South than money to be made."

Benjamin said nothing. Simply opened the gate and went inside, still wondering what it was Paul was not saying.

∽

SOUNDS of mewling sobs came from above stairs as waves of opposite temperatures stoked Violette's frozen body to action. She ran the stairs. Stumbled to her knees. Ran again.

Froze again.

Davey sat on the edge of Emerald's bed, Emerald's body pushed up next to his, her arm draped around his shoulder, his head resting against hers. The son of a black slave driver cozied up to her precious gem.

Jethro's son . . .

Violette had followed Jethro into the woods, her legs moving of their own volition. They were not her legs—were they?—but the legs of some other slave girl stepping in just long enough to get the job done, the same way Violette fantasized each day that it was her slave-self stepping into her body to do the killing work in the fields. A hollow-sounding chant landed among her thoughts.

"A job, a job. That's all it is. A job to get us away from here and into Riverwood." Her and sweet baby Emerald. "I do this for my Emerald. My Precious Emerald. I do this for Emerald."

"Glad you finally able to see this my way, Li'l Vi'lette. You go'n be glad, too. Help you remember old Jethro got power on this here plan'ation. Now ain't I sweet to let you have that baby sister of yours, what the law say ain't really yours, and take her to town? I say, ain't that sweet?"

"Th-that's sweet."

"That's it. Now, once we finished, you and that young'un be on your way. . . ."

Violette flew at Davey, her fingers digging into his flesh like talons. Her thoughts a tangled blur of red rage.

"Get away from her, Jethro! She's mine. Mine, do you hear me? My baby! You can't have her, too. You promised. You promised."

Crack! The sound of Emerald's palm to her jaw sounded off in Violette's head like a hunter's gunshot. Full circle. Her child had slapped her just as Violette had wanted to do to her days ago.

Clarity floated in. Blew away the rage. Who would allow their own issue to slap them? Violette had totally failed as a mother.

"Vi'lette, Vi'lette, Vi'lette. What is the matter with you? Can't you see Davey hurting?"

Oh, nooo. Noooo. In that moment of craziness, Violette had forgotten the hanging. What must this boy be feeling toward her?

"And my name is not Jethro."

"And I ain't your baby. How many times I got to remind you we sisters, not mama and child?"

The boy Davey straightened. Rose and slowly made his way to a window. He seemed to be a touch embarrassed. He was a good-looking boy, really. Tall and regal. Must have gotten it from his mother.

"I hate him."

"What did you say?"

"I hate him. Jethro. I hate him. Have hated him for as long as I can remember." He seemed to be rallying around the word hate. "I hate him and I would kill him if I knew where he was. Even if he was dead in a grave somewhere, I would exhume him and kill him again. I hate him."

Exhume. Among other things, the boy was a reader. Only reading and listening could leave a slave with a word like that. Violette took a moment. Forced herself to remember the young boy in Dinah's story, a little boy whose fear of his father seemed near hero worship. Yet in the hours Dinah had spent beneath the threat of Jethro's whip on the day he abducted her, she had seen his son's raw pain for his field-hand mother whose bruises, exposed in the sun, came not from a driver's whip but from a husband's fist the night before. Violette thought of her own mother, the ravages of too many births and only one unsold child, lying on her dying bed bereft of hope.

This poor boy.

"Don't you see, Vi'lette?"

Having momentarily forgotten Emerald was standing nearby,

Violette spun around to face her. First time she'd seen this look of pure compassion. Budding maturity.

"I had to bring him up here. Give him a hug. Don't you see? He ain't got no mama. Like me, he ain't got no mama."

Violette tested the waters. Touched her child so tentatively that an onlooker might have thought her a fine piece of porcelain. Slowly and with all the love she had stored up for her daughter from the time the midwife said, "Just pretend like the one you just had in there is your mama's baby. It'll go better for everybody that way," she coaxed Precious Emerald into her arms.

"You've got me, Emerald. You always will."

CHAPTER 16

Thursday, November eleventh
Seven fifty-nine in the morning

*V*iolette laughed out loud at Henry's makeshift mask. She didn't know why it should strike her as laughable today. Except it was kicked beyond the point of askew and he just looked cute in it, bent to his task, tongue peeping from the corner of his mouth. One end of the mask's anchoring string hanging below an earlobe while the opposite end sat atop the other ear, he looked like the picture of a little boy determined to learn how to bait a fish.

In her adult life, she had not been blessed with a brother, but if she'd had a choice of one, he would be just like Henry Livingston. During these last few harrowing days, he had been her rock. A soft-hearted weeping rock, perhaps, but a rock nonetheless. Henry returned the chuckle, obviously not knowing what he laughed about.

"Mornin' to you, too."

Violette placed her hands on her hips. Swallowed the laugh. Reverted to the language of their childhood.

"What chu laughing at? And I don't remember saying nothing to you about it being a good morning either."

"That's a belly laugh you just sucked up, girl. And most times a belly laugh means something good happening, to the mind and the soul."

That stopped her. Pulled the playful sparring right out of her. How long had it been since her mind and soul had been clear enough for a belly laugh? Since she even remembered she had a soul worth nurturing?

"I guess." She inched closer. Watched him remove the silly-looking mask he had pieced together with burlap. He smiled at her.

"What's the trouble, sis?"

Sis. Violette half-smiled back. Which one of her brothers used to call her "sis?" Junior? Jack-O? Sonny Boy?

Maybe all of them. She couldn't remember. So long ago, so far away. Yet not so distant that the sweetness didn't resonate. Like the familiar echo of the chip-fell-off-the-white-oak bird of an autumn evening back of the quarters. Bittersweet. A sharp pain moved her. A sudden need for family so vivid it fluttered inside her ears.

Violette had not forgotten what it felt like to have a mother, father, sisters and brothers, all snatched away by Chester Singer like the dead head of a useless flower. Something tore loose inside of her. Something she had forged long and hard, beating it into submission with the hot hammer of meanness and fear ever since she was fourteen. Standing there knowing Henry must be mystified, she started to cry uncontrollably.

"I'm about to lose her again."

Henry stepped from behind the work table flexing his dust-covered fingers. "Who? Lose who?"

"Emerald. I'm talking 'bout Emerald. I lost her once when I let that old lady talk me into switching her. I can't lose her again. I just can't." Strange how, after all these years, it remained a blur in Violette's mind, yet as sharp as the feel of a bucket of icy water down one's back.

It had been sticky hot in the one-room cabin. Hers and Mama's screams colliding in the night. Blood-smells bumping into each other. Violette wondering how in the world Mama had lived through this over and over and never complained . . .

Violette heard herself scream once more. She had known the moment it was over for her, the searing pain ebbing back down a watery road with the feel of a final goodbye. Then finally Mama, too, was quiet.

Too quiet.

Violette lay on her back, her body stretched in ways she had not known possible a year ago when she turned thirteen. Her newborn, Precious Emerald, was crying her lungs out, waiting to be fed, so said the midwife, while her little uncle lay silent.

"'Twas a boy." The midwife spoke. Her voice low and gurgled.

What had Mama said she would name him if he was a boy? Elijah. That's what she'd said. Elijah.

"Time to get ch'all cleaned up. I don't think I'm go'n do this here no more. My old heart can't stand it."

Violette had no desire to figure out what the old lady meant. Too tired. Too—

Why? Why was Mama and the baby brother Violette had always wanted so deathly quiet?

She turned to look at Mama. Her mouth was slightly parted, a mixture of shock and relief on her face.

"Your mama gone, honey. Her and the little one both. If I was you, I'd just act like the one you just had was your mama's. She a determined little thing. Nobody knows 'bout your mistake. Make it better on everybody. No need to get old Singer and Jethro to thinking on how they can use you before they have to . . ."

"Oh, Lord, please help me." Violette spoke aloud, barely able to recognize her surroundings. "Jethro did it. He ain't my baby's papa, but he did use me. I didn't mean to push Emerald away like that. I didn't mean to make her motherless for the rest of her life like me."

Henry closed the distance. Gently pressed her head against his chest. "Shhh. It go'n be all right. You calling on the right one now, sis. It go'n be all right. You crying out to the Savior to help you."

Violette felt herself coming around. A Savior. She actually had a Savior. All the fighting and scratching she found herself doing in her mind all the time, and all the while she had an Advocate just waiting to fight her battles. When would she ever learn?

Feeling the tension ease, she slumped against Henry. Sniffed. Opened her eyes and heard a familiar voice, though not always with this bladed edge.

"Good morning, crew. Is there something the captain needs to be alerted about?"

"FATHER WOULD HAVE BEEN HORRIFIED."

Benjamin wiped his hands on Dinah's yellow checkered dish-towel and marveled at how proficient he had become in her sunshine-colored kitchen.

"So be it. Horrible men ought to be horrified sometimes."

Thinking the house seemed unusually quiet with Violette already gone to the shop and Emerald still in her room, he took a moment to look at the beautifully appointed kitchen he enjoyed every morning. Father never visited his plantation kitchen, commanding his house slaves to deliver a simple glass of water, and forbad Benjamin to go near it. The kitchen was separate, below him. Not just physically yards away from the main house but worlds away from how Rogers Catlett saw himself. The structure called a kitchen was more or less a few steps up from a slave-quarters necessary, with far more pleasing smells.

Disgusting analogy. True nonetheless.

Benjamin jerked his thoughts back to this pocket of sunlight the Mayfields had created. Knew what had drawn Violette to attempt the impossible the other night. Allowed himself a wide, satisfied grin. Unfolded and refolded the dishcloth as he continued to speak to himself aloud.

"That soup can only be described as a classic disaster."

His grin softened, some kind of splendid sweetness tugging at everything meaningful to him. At heart, she really was a good girl. And at times so very vulnerable. Wanting so desperately to fit somewhere that it made something ache in a man. Something Benjamin would rather not confront. Violette will never become a Mama Tavie. She will never be Dinah.

"Violette McMillan was born to business."

He smiled. Saw her bent close to the desk the day before. Thought of the way she loosely held the pencil between her lips, her brow pulled into itself, a renegade braid touching the desk's edge, totally absorbed with the numbers of Mayfield Cabinetry as though she were an investor.

"She's a natural, as much as Henry is a born cabinetmaker."

An idea bloomed, blotting out all others. He put the dishcloth on the wooden peg. Grabbed his work apron and headed toward the foyer. It was time for him to leave Natchez, go to New Orleans, perhaps. Boatwright had made a generous offer yesterday, vowing he'd be a white-man cover for the business which should help restart sales. Sure, Benjamin could take the easy way out. Go home and accept the slave money his mother kept offering him. But he would never do that. Never abide himself if he spent money made from his brothers and sisters' forced labor. Besides, he might not be as good as Jonathan and Henry, but he was skilled enough to take care of himself. Leaving Natchez would not only save the business, it would save him from Violette who no matter how appealing simply was not a good match for Rogers Catlett's son.

And why was that?

He slammed the front door against that dark thought and made his way along the side of the house to the shop. What were those sounds?

Sobbing. It could only be Violette's.

Thinking her to be at her desk, he stepped through the first door. Not there. He swiftly moved to the shop area, and there she was, nestled again against Henry's chest as though she had been made for it. Strange. He would have thought this repeated scene to fit right into the plan he had formulated five minutes ago: give the business to Henry, move to New Orleans.

Forget Violette.

Instead he wanted pick a fight. With Henry. Well, that wouldn't do, but he was still the captain of this sinking ship, and he would rule it like the man he was trained to be until the waters rolled over his head.

VIOLETTE FISTED her hands against Henry's fast-beating heart and swiveled her neck back toward the front office. Despite the disgusting sarcasm dripping from Benjamin's odd captain-and-crew metaphor, she would not give in and leap from Henry's brotherly embrace like some caught-in-the-act strumpet.

"Good morning, Mr. Catlett." As though she had not eaten at his table less than an hour ago.

Henry stuttered out a greeting. "M-morning, Mr. Catlett. We was just—uh—j-just uh—"

"About to finish up our little morning devotion."

Untangling herself from Henry's petrified arms, she turned to face Benjamin. Never once blinked. Hers and Henry's *was* a devotion of sorts—they were devoted to each other. Benjamin lifted his eyebrows in shock before lowering them to that dreaded scowl of his.

"I don't think what I just saw would qualify as devotion."

"And I don't care what you think. Sir."

"I beg your pardon?"

"No need. I think your reception and interpretation of what I said are just fine, but for the record, I'll repeat it. How I spend my time in devotion and to whom I devote it is between me and the Lord."

She held her ground as Benjamin clasped his hands behind his back. Repositioned his legs apart an inch or two, as though set for some major oratory or other. "And I suppose this type of 'devotion' is a carryover from your life as a slave where you did anything doable to get your way?"

Violette felt her resolve turn to icy water. How much did he know about her past? Had Dinah said anything about Emerald? No, she knew her friend wouldn't do that.

She raised her chin to get her blood running again. "And what exactly would you be knowing about my life as a slave? Especially since your past is as mysterious as the origin of the wind."

His color changed. She had definitely hit a nerve, but she was not about to back down. She was tired of the hot and cold spewing from Benjamin Catlett's mouth. From this day forward, he would either treat her with evenhanded respect, or this was the Violette he would get. She locked in on his outraged eyes and slowly moved in his direction.

"Tell you what, sir. I'll give you a dime's worth of my dull past for a nickel's worth of yours. Who are you anyway? Were you ever a slave? Do you even know how to plant cotton? Chop it, pick it?"

She felt Henry move in close. "Now, Vi'lette, you might'a done stepped past the line. You might wanna think about what you saying."

"What did you say your mother's name is? Your father's?" Violette faked a gasp. Covered her mouth. "Oh! That's right. You've never said, have you? All these years and nobody seems to know."

Chin slightly lifted, Violette took a tiny step backwards. Her bravado was seeping as Benjamin began to close the three-foot space of sawdust separating them. He leaned into her. My, my. But he was one mad fellow at that moment! And just as handsome as he was angry, his face so close until she was forced to tilt her head up even further than she had bargained for.

"Now you listen to me. Everybody is this town knows what you did to Jonathan Mayfield, how you tried to hang his life out to dry by exposing his most damning secret of lost manumission papers. But you won't do that to me. Dig, claw, lie. Whatever you want. You'll not get a thing out of me about my background, my personal life—"

"Hey, Mr. Catlett, you thought anymore about finishing up that conversation about the business?"

What? Did Henry just bring up the idea of Benjamin's leaving the business again? Now? Violette nearly collided with Benjamin as both their bodies turned toward Henry whose mouth was set in determination.

"I'd like to know, for once and for all, if you thinking 'bout giving up this here shop like you hinted at a few days back. 'Cause if so, I want to be the first to throw in a bid. I ain't got much, but every nickel I done earned is yours and Mr. Mayfield's if y'all willing to gimme a chance."

Violette watched the fight going on in Benjamin as plainly as watching two brawlers in a street, his emotions ebbing and flowing until the one thing he didn't want to say, he said, though not eye to eye with the man whom he obviously respected deeply, perhaps even loved.

"I'll be staying on," he said. "At least for a while."

That, before he walked out the door, shoulders drooped, with Violette searching her mind for a dark hole to which she could withdraw.

CHAPTER 17

Friday, November twelfth
One o'clock in the morning

*V*iolette huddled against a wall of the attic's window seat, her lips moving in lockstep with the words of Uncle Tom's hymn that seemed to lift off the page and plant themselves into her soul. Normally she would have heard the groans of the house, the wind whistling outside the window. But tonight her world was completely Uncle Tom's. At that moment, she could not have said where she was on earth except for the plantation of Simon Legree—the subhuman archetype of Chester Singer—and his two slave-scourging black drivers, Quimbo and Sambo.

Prototypes of Jethro and Eli.

She didn't quite know yet how she felt about Tom's abject humility in *Uncle Tom's Cabin*. But she understood his fate, his plight. Knew what had happened to all slaves whose backs had become a game board for the whips of greedy, soul-less men. And it stirred her to song.

"When I can read my title clear

To mansions in the skies,
I'll bid farewell to every fear,
And wipe my weeping eyes.

"Should earth against my soul engage,
And hellish darts be hurled,
Then I can smile at Satan's rage,
And face a frowning world."

She stopped. Let herself for the first time consider those mansions in the sky which Tom sang about. Were they really there? Could the God of Heaven have somewhere out there a place of peace for her and her troubled child? Or could He still have a place of comfort for them right here on earth?

One thing certain, the recent little sand castle of Benjamin Catlett and Violette and Emerald McMillan had crumbled. They had eaten supper together in silence, sounding the final note for their cozy little arrangement. She had to find someplace to go until she could afford to take her daughter to Jackson.

Benjamin. I will certainly miss you.

Tentative footsteps jolted the small hope within her that refused to die. Benjamin?

"Vi'lette? You up there?"

Emerald.

Violette rushed from the window seat to the top of the steps. "Is anything the matter, honey?"

Her tall, graceful daughter looked so small, so frightened standing there with tears in her eyes, peering up from near the bottom of the stairs. So very open to all the Chester Singers and Simon Legrees, Quimbos and Sambos, Jethros and Elis of the world. Violette nearly swooned. Had Emerald been violated, threatened, perhaps coerced into womanhood at thirteen right under her nose?

Candlestick in one hand, nails dug into the other, Violette

forced herself to wait at the top for the bad news. Braced herself for the chastisement for the "honey" that had slipped seconds ago while. Expected her very heart to run right out onto the steps at any moment.

"No. I just . . . I can't sleep."

All she needed was Lucy the ragdoll, and Emerald would be four again. Violette wanted nothing more at that moment than to hug her, let her know they could work it out as they always had. Together. Emerald continued her trek up the steps. Worlds came and went as Violette waited.

She replaced the candle, oblivious to the hot wax that had nearly reached her fingers. She patted the window seat. "Come sit with me."

"Hey, Violette?"

"Uh huh?"

"You know what I be wishing sometimes?"

Violette paused. Reverted again to the old way. There would be no storybook language here tonight. Just the words of two ex-slaves who desperately wanted to bridge a chasm.

"No, what chu be wishing?"

"I wish we had our mama."

Silence. Before Emerald began to cry softly.

"I want to know her, Vi."

Violette's breath stopped. Emerald hadn't called her Vi since she was eight.

"I need to know something that only a mama ought to tell a girl."

"Do you think maybe I could tell you what chu want to know?"

"I ain't no little girl no more and I want to know about boys. I want to know about Davey."

Violette's supreme nightmare. Oh, Lord. Oh, Lord, help me.

"You ain't never had no boy as a friend, so you probably wouldn't know. But I want to know do they feel stuff. Do they hurt like we do sometimes?" She looked at Violette, a flicker of hope in her wet eyes. "You wouldn't know, though. Would you?"

"Well, I think the Good Lord gave them the same feelings, the same hurt we have. But I think there's just something in 'em that just makes 'em make it their business all their lives to keep from showing it."

"You think so? 'Cause since that one cry after they hung his brother, Davey ain't cried no more. It's like he's sorry he let some of that hurt out. Like he needed it inside for something. Maybe to fight with or something."

"I think you done said it right well. Don't think no woman could've said it better."

Emerald's crying subsided to an occasional jerk. She inched a bit closer. Such a beautiful girl. And wise, too.

An idea bloomed in the dark like a night flower. Violette's hands trembled like November leaves. She would try this, and if she was rebuffed, she could at least comfort herself with the memory of the trying.

"D-do you want to put your head on my shoulder? Maybe we could sit here together in the dark and sleep for a little while?" Emerald nodded and leaned into her. Violette slid her hand around her child's shoulder. Waited. Then the soft familiar snores.

She closed her eyes and exhaled. Violette didn't know where she would travel from here. Didn't know if Benjamin would keep her on until the end of the week or if she should just strike out toward Jackson at first light whose direction she couldn't describe if hers and Emerald's life depended on it. She only knew one thing. She would swim the Mississippi River to own this one moment in life, with her sleeping child nestled in her arms, one more time.

Just one more time.

~

WANDERING THE QUIET STREET, Violette half realized her mind was stuck in another world, saddened by Uncle Tom's looming fate. Propelled to the moon by having awakened earlier to her daughter's sleeping in her arms. A soft Mississippi chill had invaded the air, and she had decided to partake of the arching, blue skies and golden leaves more reminiscent of an early October morning than a November one. She had a few minutes before it was time to be at her post in the shop. Mostly she didn't want to face Benjamin yet.

She walked westward toward the river before her steps turned south. She hadn't been under the hill since that night of freedom when she had messed up her and poor little Emerald's life with Chester Singer. Wouldn't it be wonderful if she knew as little about men as her child thought she did? She knew she shouldn't head down here, but it had to happen sometime. She had to break the spell of that night if she was to ever have a chance to move ahead.

It really could be exciting down here in a chancy, daring kind of way. No matter how the nabobs felt about it, the docking under the hill was the receiving place for much of Natchez's historic opulence. She wouldn't stray far. Just stand here at the bottom of Silver Street for a minute and look at the bobbing boats. Try to rewrite images in her head. Pray for forgiveness.

Father, forgive me.

She opened her eyes. Through the gathering workers, something flashed before her. A dark-skinned man with a certain set to his body brought thoughts tumbling down upon her head like a load of bricks. There was no question. No doubt. No internal debate. It was he. It was . . .

Eli.

Her pulse arrested. Her brain did not. Instead her thoughts ran hard into each other fusing the distinguishing boundaries.

Thought he was dead. I thought Eli was dead He has to be dead He has to be . . .

But there was another man. And another and another. All huddled against a warehouse, all four backs turned, deep in conspiratorial gestures. How had she almost completely missed seeing the others? How had she missed Chester Singer and—

Jethro?

In an instant, the refreshing chill of autumn turned into sharply-pointed icicles. She took slow, backward steps up the hill, her eyes trained on the three most hateful men she'd ever known and one she didn't care to. Her own Simon Legree package prepared and wrapped especially for her by the devil himself. She continued to back up the hill despite the descending, quickening traffic of the morning.

"I can't let them see me."

She couldn't figure out quite why, but instincts said they must not see her see them together. Finally, she was able to head her body north. She took out up the hill with the force of a spooked horse, her footsteps beating out a rhythm to a single thought.

Why. Those. Three? WhyThoseThree?

Those fiendish miscreants together. Why those three? And who was the fourth one?

CHAPTER 18

Friday, November twelfth
Early evening

In the darkness, Benjamin sat on a crate in the corner, on the work side of the shop, his elbows on his knees, his stubbled jaw in the palms of his hands.

"I think I'm in love with her."

So why was he so dead set against it? And did it really matter since it couldn't be more apparent who her choice was? He had successfully avoided her for nearly thirty-six hours. Yet he knew they needed to talk. He dragged his hands the length of his face.

We sure can't go much further like this. Everybody working behind these four walls is miserable right now.

He clasped his hands behind his head. Stretched his legs to the limit and blew out a breath. They were so right for each other, Henry and Violette. Benjamin had never asked, but he estimated the two of them to be around the same age, not into their thirties as he was. This escalating resentment among whites couldn't last forever. And even if it did, there would always be some folks who wanted expertly-made furniture to the point where they would cross the color line long enough to get it. Cabinetmakers didn't get any better than his friend Henry, who was not just trained but gifted.

"They could have a good life together, he and Violette."

The words nearly made him sick. He lifted his head. Leapt to his feet as someone opened the door to his hiding place.

"Who's there?"

"It's just me, Henry, suh. I thought you might want some company."

"I don't. But thanks anyway." Benjamin resumed his seat on the crate. Waited for his assistant to leave.

Nothing.

"I beg your pardon, suh, but I'm thinking it would help you if we talked. Might straighten out your thoughts on what you saw the other day 'tween Vi'lette and me."

So. Henry was thinking he could help him forget Violette. This would be interesting if it wasn't so absurd.

"All right, Henry. Speak your piece."

Henry moved through the darkness like a cat. As though self-effacement was going to lessen the tension of whatever it was he had to say.

"I ain't in the habit of telling folks' business, but I reckon you ought to know something about Violette befo' you finish judging her once and for all."

"Make your point, Henry, or let's just take this up at another time."

"All right. That pretty little girl, Emerald, that you know as Violette's little sister is really her daughter."

The room got darker, some kind of choking cloud emerging that muffled Henry's words as Benjamin tried to keep from suffocating.

"What?"

"She couldn't have been more than fourteen or so when the baby was born. I remember 'cause I think back every now and then to how sad my mama was after Vi'lette's mama died in childbirth. They was friends, you know. Had been since before Mama was sold to the other plantation. At the time, I was just a young'un myself. Didn't really understand death pain yet. But I knew Mama had been served a hard blow.

"Not 'til the other day when you caught Vi'lette crying 'gainst my shoulder did I finally put all the pieces together. You see, I been knowing for a long time, from my mama, that Vi'lette had once been in the family way, though Mama said she never did look like it. Said even her mama didn't know."

Benjamin braced himself. Surely Henry would reveal who the father was. This time, he wouldn't push though. Just sit quietly waiting for Henry to resume. Tell him the rest of this all important revelation. Strengthen or shatter his heart.

"Thing was, Vi'lette's mama was in family way at the same time, even though her husband and all her children 'cept Vi'lette had done been sold months before. Anyways, when Mama, out of breath, came running back to our cabin on the plantation next to the McMillans' one night, hollering and screaming that her friend had died but her baby had lived, I worried what was to become of Vi'lette and her baby. That's when Mama explained to me what an awful night the midwife said they'd had and how both mama and daughter had been in hard labor together. Vi'lette's mama had died, but Vi'lette had lived. But Vi'lette's baby had died too, so said the midwife, whilst her li'l sister had held on. Vi'lette had lost both her baby and her mama and was go'n now try to raise her li'l sister. That's what the granny told my mama. And that's what I believed 'til Violette let it slip the other day that Emerald was *her* baby and that the old woman who delivered her thought it'd be best to act like the child was Vi'lette's sister to keep that old overseer and Jethro from making her a breeder right away."

Benjamin sat perfectly still. Suddenly everything was clearing up. All Violette's mean tricks of a decade ago—all the grating disrespect she suffered from Emerald now—everything was

136

becoming clear. All of it had been to somehow safeguard Emerald. Could it be that the snitching about Jonathan's manumission papers was to ingratiate herself with those goons, Jethro and Eli, for some reason related to Emerald? It was entirely possible that they had found out something about the true maternity of her baby and blackmailed Violette into becoming the surly, heartless, young woman she seemed.

Poor, poor girl.

And I have been beastly to her.

It would take a while for Benjamin to figure it all out. But when he did, he was certain he would find that . . .

The man standing in front of me is Emerald's father.

"And who is the child's father, Henry? You haven't said so yet."

"That's 'cause I don't know. She didn't say. I didn't ask."

Jonathan stood to his feet. Adjusted his pant leg. "That was indeed enlightening, Henry. Thank you. I believe I'm going to retire for the night now."

"Yes, sir. You all right, Mr. Catlett? Will I see you Sunday at the Dinner on the Ground?"

"I plan to be there, yes. Good night."

He watched his young friend leave as quietly as he had entered.

Henry Livingston might not know for certain who Emerald's father was, but Benjamin would wager that the young assistant had a solid hunch. Then again, he might be as sure of Emerald's sire as Benjamin was but simply unable to prove it. A budding revelation that would usher in a swift and certain cart-topple of the whole mess of rotten apples. Benjamin lowered himself to the crate. Clasped his hands before him and bowed his head.

"Father, God, what am I to do now?"

VIOLETTE PACED the vestibule until she dizzied herself.

"Where is Benjamin?"

As certain as she was that nighttime had overtaken Natchez, that was how sure she was that Benjamin was in danger. And she knew that the certainty had not come from her own ability. It had come from the Spirit of the Living God.

She had somehow made it through the day, though she wasn't sure how she would make it another twenty-four hours under the same roof with her employer. How angry and hurt he must be toward her and the brash words leveled against him.

"And what exactly would you be knowing about my life as a slave? Especially since your past is as mysterious as the origin of the wind?"

Whatever made her think she could say those things to him? Had she just cast into the river all the little sense she had tried to accrue in recent years? What business did she have referencing her boss's past?

And now the man's life was in danger. Chester Singer had as good as said that he was out to destroy Benjamin's business and Benjamin himself in the process. *Help me, Holy Spirit.* She had to do something. She grabbed Dinah's shawl she had found in the attic and swung open the front door. Right into the faces of—

"Mama Tavie? Mr. James?"

"How you doing, Sugar? We didn't know for sure we'd be blessed to see you here, but we were hoping."

She collapsed into the waiting arms of Riverwood's former cook and butler. No doubt the most warm and timely feeling of welcome she could have imagined. No doubt from the hand of God.

No sooner had Benjamin's knees settled into the sawdust than he thought he had received his answer. Of course. It was Henry's deep-seated slave training that caused him to keep the knowledge about who he was to Emerald to himself. The boy was afraid!

He sank to his knees again, spewing out confessions that should be to the Lord but somehow seemed tailored for his own hearing.

"I can fix this. I'll help them get together. Show them there are no hard feelings. Maybe let them use the house for a wedding. Help them find a house of their own. Emerald deserves no less"

But they don't need fixing. They are both My children, entire just as they are.

Who was that? The words weren't audible. Rather they were kind of . . . heart words? What kind of talk was that?

He rose from his knees. Ignored the jolt of that strange interlude. Covered himself with the practical mantle that suited him. That he had always worn. That he felt comfortable in.

"Yes, I'll make up for these recent missteps. Maybe even for that haunting horror with Lucie by stepping back from these errant feelings I've been having for Violette and stepping up to be the repairer God has always meant me to be."

Strange. That niggling feeling that God wasn't in this. Strange, too, that Benjamin's gut still would not allow him to consider going home to Virginia. New Orleans maybe, but not Virginia. The reason was Emerald, of course. He was sticking close by for the same reason he came to Natchez in the first place: to help the children of his race who were in peril, this time the child being Emerald. That was it, wasn't it? And he knew exactly how he would start. By inviting Violette and Emerald to the Dinner on the Ground event on Sunday. Wait a minute. Wasn't he forgetting something? Oh, yes, and for sure. Henry would be there. And that would make things just as they ought to be.

CHAPTER 19

*V*iolette would tell them everything. Almost. From Emerald's specious birth to Violette's recent observation of the triple-headed embodiment of Satan himself, Chester Singer being the main head. Everything. Except how, often in the deep of night, she still felt Singer's clammy hands along her upper arms urging her up from the felt table. The other gambler's looking away in a part-gleeful, part covetous discomfort. Little Emerald's eyes wide with terror and an innate sense of disgust.

"Get rid of the pickaninny, will you?" The gambling-room attendant sent a look toward Precious Emerald. Nodded knowingly while Singer laughed. "Don't kill her, though." He laughed louder. A scraping, brassy sound that lodged in Violette's soul. "In a few years, some lucky man might find her as useful as we're about to find her mama."

Violette pulled away from the memory. Told the part of her narrative she wanted the sweet older couple to hear. Mr. James listened patiently to the end. Cleared his throat. Bowed.

"Oh, yes, sir, Mr. James. Please pardon me." Violette smiled through her embarrassment at her lack of manners. But Mr. James was still the perfect gentleman. The consummate butler. He moved gracefully toward the kitchen while Mama Tavie, sitting next to her on the settee, looked away.

"Been knowed about Emerald for a while now. Glad to finally be able to say so."

For a fleeting moment, Octavia McMillan looked her years, the usual glow of her yellow skin waning a bit. "If you ever been a mama yourself, it ain't too hard to figure out when you looking at another one."

Through Dinah, Violette had heard that this woman had lost all her sons to yellow fever in this very county. Yet she had taken on little Jonathan Mayfield as her own when that same fever and its consequences had robbed him of his parents. Violette's heart melted. Only God could sustain a mother through that. She wanted to use some of those big words she had learned to say something about Mama Tavie's loss—at least acknowledge the residual pain —but nothing worth saying seemed to be forthcoming. She tried and choked on her new vocabulary. Used her hands instead. Pat, pat, pat.

"I love you, Mama Tavie. Other than Dinah, there is no woman I would want to see as much."

"Y'all all like children to me." Mama Tavie dabbed her eyes. "Now. Back to the subject and the verb."

Violette chuckled. "Subjects and verbs? I am impressed."

"It's James. He's been wonderful in helping me say things better. By the way, you ain't—you're not—sounding too bad your-self. Anyhow, what do you plan to do about Singer and Eli 'nem?"

"What can I do? I can't prove anything. Mine is just the word of an ex-slave against a new banker. Who's going to take my side against his certain denial of the threat to hurt my child if I don't cooperate with whatever evil he has in mind?" Mama Tavie flexed her fingers. Studied the backs of them."

"Violette, you been doing any praying about all of this?"

"No, ma'am. Not a whole lot. I've been so busy with the new job and all that I—"

"That's too busy, honey. When you get too busy to ask the Lord about it, you start spinning your wheels in life's mud, mess up everything you worked so hard to clean up with a lot of your own pitiful thinking. If you know what I mean."

"I do. It's just that I need answers. Quick answers and I know I can't rush Him."

"So you just go ahead and put things in order yourself? Is that your thinking these days? Do you usually get things lined up just right, all your little ducks paddling right behind one another when you leave God on the shelf?"

Violette lowered her head. "When you put it that way . . ."

"Let's pray, baby. Right now."

When Octavia McMillan finished talking to Jesus, Violette felt washed. Whatever the future held, it would be in the flawless timing of Christ. If only she could hold on to that. She lifted her eyes to a steaming pot of coffee. Where was her hospitality? She hadn't even invited them into Benjamin's parlor.

"Mama Tavie, what ch'all doing coming way down here to Natchez? Are y'all okay? How'd you even know I was here? Come. Let's sit in the parlor."

Mama Tavie smoothed Violette's hands. "We fine right here, honey." She accepted a cup of coffee from her husband. "Me and James, we went to the plantation and hardly nobody was there. The place looked like it had been run through by wild hogs, but one of the old servants happened to be out there doing some work for the new buyer. He told us where to find you. As for why we here?"

Mr. James brought out a chair from the kitchen. Took a seat. "Octavia's been wanting to come for some time," he said, looking as handsome and stately as ever. "We heard one of her cousins out in the country passed on some months back, so we saved up to come see his widow before it gets too cold. And, of course, I'm hoping, maybe in the spring to come back and see Dinah when she and Jonathan come up for their yearly visit."

Mr. James looked almost shy at the mention of Dinah, the

discovery some years back that she was his daughter seemingly still new and almost too exquisite to touch.

"And I couldn't resist trying to help prepare for the Dinner on the Ground celebration that some of us slaves back at the old plantation used to try to have every year on one Sunday in November," said Mama Tavie. "Only problem is I was hoping to beg use of the McMillan kitchen, and now that ain't even a part of the question."

"But this kitchen is."

All heads turned to greet Benjamin who was looking quite well. *Holy Spirit, did I miss Your guidance by that wide of a margin?* Quite excited about something, he turned to Violette and smiled.

"And what's more, I'm hoping that Violette and Emerald will come as my guests."

CHAPTER 20

Sunday, November fourteenth
A picnic area outside of town

The most beautiful of days.

That is how Benjamin would have started his poem today, had he held an ounce of the poetic within him. The river, so placid one could almost be beguiled into trying to walk upon it, reminded him of a strip of shiny, caramel-colored ribbon. The weather could only be described as balmy, as though God had drawn winter's curtains just enough to bestow that unique glow of autumn sun while permanently shutting the door against the brutal heat of a southern Mississippi summer. The boys bandied about makeshift balls′ while the girls—Emerald included—played hopscotch. Though some of the games were a little juvenile for her, Benjamin thought he had never seen Emerald this happy, either since she moved to town or before.

Wonder where is Henry?

It wasn't like him to miss something like this, a good time to further solidify his courtship of Violette.

Yet there had been a jumpiness about Violette all day—looking over her shoulder each time the whistle of a boat sounded or a distant bird cawed. He chuckled as Emerald rushed up to the quilt he sat next to, where Mama Tavie had spread out enough food to feed half of Natchez.

"Arm wrestling 'bout to begin! Girls and they papas lined up. Whosever's papa wins the most times, that girl gets to be church queen."

"What are you talking about, Emerald?" Violette seemed to appear out of nowhere. "What is all this about needing a papa?"

"Well, they say you don't have to have a real blood papa. Just somebody who'd be willing to stand in for you, kinda like the preacher said Jesus done for all of us when he became that scapegoat for all our sins.

"I need a papa, Violette, just for today. Just think. Whoever gets to be queen is go'n get a new dress made. A woman over yonder said she done wrote Miss Dinah and Miss Dinah go'n donate everything!" Emerald jumped up and down like a six-year-old. "I got to win that dress. I just got to." She laid a grip on Benjamin's arm. "Please, Mr. Benjamin. You a strong man. I watched you and Henry in the shop picking up all kinds of stuff and you both real strong. But Henry ain't here." She tugged Benjamin to his feet. "Please, sir. They 'bout to start over there."

All heads turned toward the riverbank. "Gentlemen! Five minutes before we start. Just five minutes before you make some little girl the happiest young lady in Natchez!"

Where was Henry when you needed him?

Benjamin looked at Emerald. Saw the four-year-old of nine years ago standing in front of him, reaching to be swept up into his arms so that he could show her the little "big house," a replica of Riverwood that Jonathan had made for her. And he knew he had been recaptured.

"I have an idea. Why don't we supply you with two papas?"

He grinned at Mr. James. "You up for it, Mr. James?" The old butler bowed to Emerald who giggled uncontrollably.

"Why certainly, sir. Anything to crown this young lady the queen she already is—"

"Wait . . . wait a minute."

Violette reminded Benjamin of a sputtering fire, a beautiful dancing flame.

"This ain't even fair. What are you planning to do? Serve as Emerald's double sponsor, then knock off all the opponents until you get to each other?" The two men spoke in unison.

"Exactly."

"You can do it, James! You a strong man. I know you is."

Mama Tavie looked around, obviously a bit mortified by her own enthusiasm. Violette thought the little woman more nervous than a man with six un-divorced wives on his seventh wedding day. And Violette herself was no better. She was shocked at the strength left in the older man's arm.

"How'd he learn to do that, Mama Tavie?"

"That's one of his favorite things to do, sugar. Whips everybody he runs into. Says he's been doing it since he was a boy of twelve. I didn't know it myself until after we married and moved to Jackson." This love of a woman was as flushed as a sixteen-year-old. "He some kind of man. I'm telling you now."

Suddenly Mama Tavie's hands slapped both sides of her jaw, her swaggering stance deflating more rapidly than the Sunday afternoon sun.

"Oh, nooo! James gone down."

Violette looked at the winnowed field of arm wrestlers. Struggled to keep from laughing. Judging from Mama Tavie's reaction, one could think Mr. James had just been struck down in the siege of Vicksburg. Violette looked again. Nobody was left but Benjamin and . . .

Jethro!

Her nerves rioted like jungle vines. Surely in seconds she would be the picture of a fainted pre-war plantation belle. She glanced in the direction of the two men for whom she had the strongest feelings. Undeniable affection for one, abhorrence for the other. Not even Eli Duggan, Emerald's father, measured up to the loathing she felt for Jethro McMillian. What she had done with Eli she had done willingly. But the bargain she had struck with Jethro had been murderous coercion. He had killed something in her. She had sacrificed herself for the extension of her child's freedom. But unlike the Christ, her sacrifice was blemished, so dirty and flawed that she had never been able to wash it away. Jethro winked at her —winked at her!—as he locked arms with Benjamin.

Poor Benjamin. Poor, sweet Benjamin. He didn't really know who it was he was going up against. He knew his reputation, but you had to experience Jethro to know him. Mama Tavie quailed while Mr. James seemed more ready to fight than she had imagined him capable.

Lord, please help Benjamin.

The crowd hushed. A steamboat from the north screeched a distant whistle. Emerald blew a kiss. "You can do it, Mr. Benjamin. You stronger than him."

"Better looking, too," yelled some woman Violette didn't know. The crowd guffawed. Violette froze. Was that a rush of . . . jealousy? . . . that made her want to strangle whoever it was?

Lord, please help this man I love. She didn't know why she loved him. He had fired her. Hurt her feelings. Rattled her confidence.

But Lord, please help this arrogant, wonderful, confusing, kind, handsome man that I have irrevocably fallen in love with.

The sun was about to plunge. Jethro sneered as every cord in

Benjamin's forearm expanded to meet the task. The crowd groaned as that arm sloped backwards toward his heaving chest.

Oh no, Oh no, Oh no.

"You mayst well, give it up, Mr. Big Man," said Jethro loud enough for Vicksburg to hear. "Pretty boys like you ain't made for nothing but show.

Who was he sponsoring anyway? What woman had turned crazy enough to let Jethro McMillan represent her little girl? He would demand something in return. That was for certain and for sure.

Just as the sun dipped into the territory of Vidalia, Louisiana, Violette's eyes locked with Benjamin's. Mixed their very hearts so that she knew, no matter what, the love would always be there between them. The love that in the early months of 1861 had flickered between a once-chubby slave girl and a sleek Virginia free man when Jonathan Mayfield had come to Riverwood to woo Dinah Devereaux—bringing an exquisite replica of the town mansion for Emerald—and Benjamin had straddled the chair in Mama Tavie's kitchen uttering those enchanting never-forgotten words to Violette.

"What have you done to yourself, Violette? You look different somehow. Lovelier, if I may be so bold."

No one, absolutely no one she could recall, had ever called her lovely, and she had vowed that day to remove food as her idol.

The crowd erupted. Had she mulled so deeply that she had shouted that story aloud unbeknownst to her own self? Heavens knew she read aloud all the time. No. Benjamin, her Benjamin, was standing in victory with Emerald in his arms. Benjamin had won!

She made her way through the crowd. Threaded her fingers through his.

"You were wonderful. I don't know what to say. I owe you an apology for so many reasons. In so many ways."

"I think you just read my part of the script." He tugged her and a babbling Emerald closer. "Come. Let's go home."

"Yes, let's."

It's a happy time.

Still, a painful prick kept interrupting her thoughts. Jethro had absorbed the loss with no protests. No threats. You simply did not embarrass Jethro McMillan the way Benjamin had just done and get away without—what did the novels often call it?—recrimination.

CHAPTER 21

$\mathcal{T}$here was a sliver of a moon. Soft and silvery. Not enough to give much light but enough to speak of God as the Creator, enough to silence creation in a moment of adoration.

Benjamin listened to the fading sounds of the river. Could not remember a time when he had been happier. The entire crowd heading back toward Natchez and beyond nestled in a rare moment of contentment. His joy topped itself when he felt Violette untwine their fingers and loop her arm into his. She leaned in and whispered in a serious, cottony voice.

"Mama Tavie 'nem decided to stay and help put the church back to order, and Emerald and Davey offered to assist."

He waited, nothing in the words she'd just spoken accounting for the perceived seriousness in her voice. A bevy of soft giggles escaped her, prompting a lifting of Benjamin's eyebrow.

"What amuses you? I thought perhaps something was wrong."

"Nothing's wrong. And I laugh because Mama Tavie used the rest of that chicken and cake to talk those children into helping quicker than a deer can leap a fence."

He smiled down at her. "I suspect that was by design. Mama Tavie is notorious for making matches, you know."

"What kind of matches you talking about, Benjamin? Parlor matches? Game matches?"

"Don't get cute." He elbowed her slightly. "You know the kind of match I mean." Sweet silence reigned as she leaned a little more into him.

"Benjamin, I'm a little worried about Jethro. You did know who you were wrestling against back there, didn't you?"

"Fire!"

Benjamin heard the shout from the front of the dwindling crowd that had quietly moved ahead. Saw the smoke in the distance and halted. In truth, it wasn't the smoke itself that shimmied his spine. Folks burned leaves in autumn all the time. No. it was the amount of smoke. And, more than that, it was its direction.

Oh, no. No. No, no. It's Jonathan's house.

"Jonathan's shop!"

He broke through the advancing group, neither realizing nor considering how well Violette was keeping up.

"Please, Jesus," he heard her repeat each time she garnered enough breath. "Please don't let it be."

Buoyed by what seemed a time suspension, he found himself looking at the ashes of Mayfield Cabinetry, Henry's voice cutting through the smoke.

"It's looking some better, y'all. Keep at it!"

Better? How could it be looking better when the machinery that Jonathan Mayfield had purchased with all the sweat he was capable of producing and entrusted to Benjamin to safeguard stood hot and naked, its wooden supports turned to ash while iron and metal proudly continued to take the torture of hungry flames?

"Don't stop now, ladies and gentlemen."

Benjamin had seen and heard both Henry Livingston and Paul Boatwright before they saw him, beating around the edges of a still-angry fire beginning to die down. Shouting encouragement while countless other black men and women along with a few whites dumped water, ran down the hill for more. Dumped water again. In the mix, Violette's voice managed to find him.

"Benjamin, look. Look, Benjamin. They saved the house. I don't know how they managed to do it, but the house is go'n make it." She touched his arm. He jerked away. "Benjamin? I know how bad it seems, but God's got a plan, and it is still intact—"

He rounded on her. Tore off his shirt and began to attack the dying flames. The joy associated with the twinges of pain in his forearm, left over from the arm wrestling, as illusory as the cradle of that new moon up there beginning to shroud itself with thin wispy clouds.

"Don't you dare throw religion at me right now." He beat at little fires fighting for resurgence. "Since. When. Did. You. Get. So. Holy? Huh, Violette? You of all people."

With each whack, he knew he was shattering an already-damaged soul. But he couldn't stop.

"How am I going to ever be able to tell Jonathan? Answer me that. Give me a religious platitude for that."

"I don't have one." She reached for one of the pails of water seemingly materializing out of nowhere. "All I know is the man I saw an hour ago, fighting for a little bit of happiness for my ch . . . sister—"

"Say it, Violette." He continued to beat the ground with his shirt. "Why don't you stop lying for once? Go ahead and say it? Your child. Because I already know that's who she is, and I know who the father is."

To Violette, the words rolling off his tongue must seem hotter than the fire that was just about contained. Benjamin barely recognized himself, as molten rage gushed from him. All he had sacrificed to help fight racial hate, and this was how it ended. Henry and Boatwright rushed over.

"So very sorry about the shop," said Boatwright, his words tight with emotion. His voice hoarse from smoke. His breathing labored. "But at least we were able to save the house. Had it not been for the quick thinking of Henry here."

Rogers Catlett's words waylaid Benjamin with new force.

"The only way to get somewhere in this world is by the strength of your own mind, the trigger of your own weapon, and the power of your own fist."

"I know who did this. And I intend to see him pay."

Boatwright shot him a look of concern while a small hand touched the same forearm that had been so successful a short while ago.

"Mr. Benjamin? What chu getting ready to do?"

Emerald's voice tried to cut through. Came closer than anything thus far. But Benjamin had failed again, and he had to bring about Justice. First Lucie. Now Jonathan. And yes, even Violette and Emerald. Was he not a man? As much of a man as any white man standing at the edges of this fire? As much of a man as Rogers Catlett.

More of a man than Jethro McMillan. Violette wasn't the only one who had witnessed the smirk at the end of the match, and Benjamin was set to erase it.

"I believe Jonathan's got a gun inside there, and I know how to use it. If you all will excuse me."

Henry and Boatwright stood frozen, mouths agape, while Violette followed Benjamin toward the hot smoky house. Why couldn't she just stay away from him right now?

"Benjamin, please. Please tell me what you are thinking of doing. Can't we talk about this?"

Lord help him, he wanted to slam the door in her face. But the teaching from his mother proved him enough of a gentleman, even when he craved the painful separation that awaited him from the woman he loved, to allow Violette over the threshold first then slam the door behind him. The house was so hot until Benjamin feared it, too, would catch fire any minute.

"What's there to talk about? I'm going to kill Jethro tonight.

And that banker, too, if I get the slightest hint that he had anything to do with this." He took the stairs in threes, praying she would leave and allow him to let the rage out.

"Now leave me alone. I have things to do."

∼

"He's going to do something awful, Mama Tavie."

"He ain't go'n do nothing that the Lord don't let him."

"I'm telling you he left with a gun, and he knows how to use it. I didn't even recognize that man that left here. He looked like a murderous version of Benjamin. Wearing Benjamin's clothes, copying Benjamin's stride. But a stranger nonetheless full of anger as thick as a block of hog head cheese."

"I still say we can pray our way through. We will pray our way through."

Violette looked at the little butter-colored giant sitting beside her. What would she have done without her these last few days? If she had ever wondered about God's timing here on earth, she wondered no longer. If only she could trust Him enough to risk explaining to Mama Tavie the real teeth in Chester Singer's threat. She'd been vague about why he had come in the shop that day. But she could not say it. Not if she valued her and Emerald's life.

Not if she valued the little respect Benjamin might hold for her.

More than ever, it was time to leave Natchez. Time to seek out the new school she had heard about just north of Jackson. Meanwhile she would do what she had always done, except that one time with Singer, safeguard Emerald.

Do you not think I can protect Emerald? Is she not My child first? Was she not My precious gem before you ever saw her, as I wrought her in the womb? Do you have such little regard for Me?

Oh, if she could only get rid of these drops of wisdom at times like these. "I cannot risk it. I must protect my child. She is all I have. Don't You understand?"

I subjected my Son unto Death. And I did it for you and Precious Emerald.

"Mama Tavie, what would you do if you had some information that might help lots of people avoid danger in the long run but possibly harm you and your . . . uh . . . friend in the short run?"

The question was moot. The damage had already been done to Jonathan's business, and if Singer and his "brothers" were behind it as Violette suspected, there would be many other blacks like Davey's brother who would be hurt beyond hope. But Mama Tavie didn't quite know all that. Didn't know how well Violette understood the man. Didn't suspect the loathsome secret he had concerning Violette.

Mama Tavie opened her mouth. Slammed it shut, as a hard rap on the door silenced the question. Violette stiffened. Watched with dread as Mr. James strode tall and erect to the front door as though he had been made for the job.

"I reckon I'm mighty glad to see you again, sir."

Henry.

"Henry? Come in. My, how you have matured." Mr. James led him to where Violette and Mama Tavie sat gripping each other's hand.

"Now tell us, what's the problem, young man? You look in need of a good night's rest."

"Well, uh ruh, I reckon it's Mr. Benjamin." Henry was shaken. Violette could always tell when he was rattled because he started prefacing every other point with "I reckon."

"What's wrong with Benjamin?" Violette was in her friend's face before he could defend his space. "Henry? Tell me."

"Well, I reckon—"

Violette stomped her feet. "Will you stop with the 'I reckons' and tell me where Benjamin is!"

"Oh. O' course. I reck—I mean to say . . . he in jail."

Mama Tavie gasped. Mr. James's brows shot upwards. All three spoke at once.

"For what? That cannot be. Some mistake has been made." Henry had the fortitude to hold up his hand.

"I just seen him. In jail. For murder."

Numbness started in Violette's fingers. Quickly found its way to every extremity, such that reaching for Dinah's shawl felt like trying to grasp sand. But grasp she did until she got it around her shoulders. She flew to the door, her guests on her heels. She turned to look at Henry, their terror colliding like two useless battering rams voiding each other's strength. They both had heard his declaration. Knew he had meant it. Lord, how many others had heard?

"Whose murder?"

"Chester Singer's."

As if from a distance, Violette barely felt her numb body as it sank to the floor of the foyer. Mr. James caught her. And the little delegation faded into the darkness.

CHAPTER 22

Monday, November fifteenth

Ⓘn the wee hours, Violette hurried through a dying November thunderstorm that had been unexpected like all else this day. How many more people's lives would she destroy in pursuit of Emerald's happiness? A happiness that seemed to elude her at every turn.

Again she had disregarded someone else's well-being for the sake of her child. Again someone was paying a price he didn't owe because of something she had done. Or not done. Only this time it was Benjamin. The man she loved. Charged for the murder of another man she knew, a man she'd heard state his evil intent. But not just any man. Chester Singer. An ex-slave overseer.

A dog. The one who enticed you to gamble away every dime you owned in a whore house, in front of Emerald.

Her skirt a sodden rag, she knocked on the jailhouse door. Dripped minor puddles and followed the rangy, sullen jailer into a cell that was worse than the old slave quarters out at the McMillan cotton plantation. Hadn't she seen him somewhere before? She had seen a number of new faces in recent days, so she wasn't sure. She *was* sure she'd had to bribe him with the last of her earnings, but to wait until dawn had not been a choice she could make. She owed Benjamin Catlett. She had to help him, and she had to do it now. Natchez had not had the worst of the war, but who knew whether or when a group of seething ex-soldiers and depleted planters might take the law into their own hands.

Slumped near the edge of a cot, his head hanging low, Benjamin had never looked more vulnerable. More appealing. She had loved the arm-wrestling hero of hours ago. But somehow, she loved the man sitting here even more because she knew he needed her. She pulled up a crate, nearly knocking it against his slackened knees. Walls for the clasped hands hanging between them.

"I'm here, Benjamin."

He didn't lift his head. Just spoke to the grimy floor. "I was awful to you back there at the fire."

"You had reason." She reached down. Lifted his hands into hers. Smoothed the veins that seem to stand in defiance of his defeated countenance. He allowed the gesture but would not look at her.

Lord, help me. Give me what to say to this proud man.

"Seeing the cabinet shop go down was an awful, provocative thing to see, Benjamin."

"I didn't do it. I didn't shoot him, not intentionally anyway. But I meant to."

"Tell me what happened, Benjamin."

"It was Jethro I was after first and foremost, and I had decided if I found Singer to be as dangerous as Boatwright was beginning to think he was, then so be it. I would deliver him to his fate too."

Violette flinched. So had Boatwright told him about the thinly veiled threats from Singer last week?

"Davey had mentioned he thought his father was back in the town of Natchez proper. Said it was likely he had something to do with the hanging of Davey's half-brother. Jethro's own son. Can you imagine anything more vile than hanging one's own son? Davey speculated his father was sleeping at night in one of the old slave quarters at Riverwood and more or less hanging around the docks during the day trying to blend in."

"So you went out to Riverwood to search him out."

"I went part of the way. But the moment I heard Jethro's voice snickering and boasting in the woods about a third of the way there, I knew my search was over. I hadn't planned on what happened next. Turns out, there were three of them seemingly at their leisure in some kind of crude camp they had constructed with saplings as a roof. And while I didn't really know the new banker well, I knew the history of the other two. Knew there was nothing they wouldn't do for liquor, women, and a white man's pat on the back."

Violette wanted to scream. She had chosen to keep Chester Singer's threat to herself—a threat not only to Emerald but to every slave struggling to benefit from freedom—when if only she had told Benjamin, then maybe none of this would have happened.

"I ought to be the one in here."

"What?"

"Oh. Nothing. I was just . . . just thinking of how filthy this place is. I ought to be the one in here so I could give it a good cleaning is what I meant to say."

Violette jumped at what she deemed a stray roll of thunder. Of all the deceit she had infused into God's world—spreading the news about Jonathan's missing papers, leaking information to the goons that pushed him into the river and within an inch of his life, spying on Dinah's and Jonathan's romance, pretending to be a sister to Emerald when she was her mother, and going to the river with Chester Singer all those years ago—nothing had come close to rattling her the way she was rattled now.

"Wh-who do you think the banker might have been? His real identity, I mean."

"I don't know. What I do know is I heard him brag to his 'boys' in those woods tonight that he was part of a new fast-growing sect, formed in Tennessee and called the Ku Klux Klan, that would 'restore the South to its former glory.' He said they would hang every ex-slave in the South before they would let the North ram that idea of being equal with a mess of subhuman creatures down their throats."

"And what did they say, the two ex-slaves? Surely they must have asked to be exempted from that life-sucking label."

"They laughed. Said how lucky they were to be out there in the 'little Riverwood' they had carved into the woods. Behaved just as you might have thought from two men who equate survival with sellout. Men who pattern their souls after what they see as success."

Sambo and Quimbo.

Violette pulled up straight as Benjamin halted his description. Something much bigger than the accusation hanging over his head seemed to weigh on him. But what could be larger for a black man than a charge of murdering a white man in Mississippi? A white woman, perhaps? Violette squelched a rueful smile. Remained silent as long as she could before trying to reengage Benjamin.

"They really do remind me of two characters I read, Sambo and Quimbo."

"In *Uncle Tom's Cabin*."

"So you really did read it."

"I read it. Years before I ever came to Mississippi."

"And what did you think?"

"The paternalism bothered me. It still does. The fact that the author, well-meaning though she might have been, could presume to know the proclivities of our entire race disgusted me. One state-ment she made, in particular, one of many I might add, etched itself across my brain and never left: 'The principle of reliance and unquestioning faith, which is the Gospel's foundation, is more a native element in this race—the African—than any other.' Faith in our Lord is always a good thing, but how would she know what elements are native to every man and woman of the race?"

"I myself have wondered the same thing. But Benjamin, you were going to tell me what happened on the Riverwood Road." As much as she loved him, murder was murder. Though he had said he didn't shoot him on purpose, she had to know if he had taken Chester Singer's life, even accidentally.

"It was quite straightforward, really. The weather was coming in, but they guffawed and caroused so gustily they paid no attention to it. Never even heard me walking up on them, their boisterous voices punctuating the wind with slurred speeches and tirades which I followed into the woods. I was to discover that they had been drinking overmuch. I cocked the pistol. Set myself to mow down all three if need be. That must have been when they sensed someone was near.

"But the strangest thing happened as I stood just out of their sight gun in hand. In the midst of the brewing thunderstorm, I started to hear the night sounds. Clear sounds of life seemingly magnified tenfold. It occurred to me that Jethro was still a man with a heartbeat. Still human, because just hours before, I had mingled my sweat with his in the arm wrestling contest, so I knew his body, the one God set him in, still functioned. And where there was a body that the Almighty had created, there had at one time been a whole soul, one that could still be repaired." Benjamin looked up at Violette.

"It simply was not my right to take his life. No matter the contemptible things he had tried to do to Dinah, had done to his own wife, to Davey."

The things he did to me, thought Violette.

"No matter how my flesh wanted him off the face of the earth, how my own justice screamed it was the right thing to do, I simply could not shoot him down. Perhaps my father could have, but I could not."

Relief flooded Violette. "So you walked away?"

Benjamin expelled a lengthy breath. Palmed his head from his hairline to his nape. "I wish it were that cleanly cut. But the truth is, that's where it really gets complicated." He paused. Shook. Seemed to step into a different place.

"One thing I learned tonight, Violette, which I'm not soon to forget. Years ago, I took shooting lessons, but I am not, nor will I ever be, a gunfighter. In the midst of the increasing wind, I must have done some more woolgathering, three, four, five seconds, maybe a minute. I don't know. Long enough, I expect, for the banker to send Sambo and Quimbo to see what was out there—to get in back of me, the side nearest Riverwood Road, to try to get the better of me. Still, I had a cocked gun in my hand, and I knew how to shoot. When I heard them trying to rush me from behind, I turned. Taller than both of them, I opted to fire over their heads, scattering them back toward the road. By now, the weather was fierce. Loud. And when—partly from instinct, I suppose—I trained my eyes back toward the woods, I heard a strange popping sound. I couldn't believe what I saw. The banker, his form revealed through a singe of lightning that tore the bark from a tree, was falling a few yards from me, obviously badly injured or dead, for he made no sound. From the popping I had heard, I assumed lightning had struck him. Then suddenly the jailer was there. Gun. Manacles. Everything. Shouting through the rain. Said I didn't have permission to leave town. How he knew where to find me I will never know."

"But don't you see? If you had your back turned to him, you couldn't have shot him. And if you didn't, who did?"

"I wish I knew—"

"Catlett! Catlett, I say!" Violette could only describe the jailer's voice as uncanny, as stringy as his body build, his words sounding as though they were spoken through a spread of taut threads. Obviously pumped with fresh anger, as though a river had swelled and changed courses within the hour, he approached the cell.

"More company. This time of night." He stuck the key into the slot. "You sure do have the colored side jumping tonight. The girl's go'n have to leave, though. Mr. Yankee Boatwright's here. Says he has news."

Violette was ready to kneel, beg. "Please, sir. Can't I stay? Just long enough to hear what Mr. Boatwright has to say?"

"You cannot. Don't be greedy. I just let you stay five minutes over as it is."

"Then I'll just have to have my say right here. Right now, before she leaves," interrupted Paul Boatwright.

"Now, listen here. You can't just come in here and—"

"Benjamin, I have posted bail. By this time tomorrow, you will be free, if not before."

"Out, maybe. But he won't be free." The jailer half-grimaced, half smiled. "Trust me. This one ain't never go'n be free again, Mr. Yankee."

CHESTER SINGER'S was not the first person's life Benjamin had taken, albeit not meaning to. Jail was what he deserved. Hadn't he said so just the other day to Paul Boatwright? He shifted on the cot to his side, his back facing the cell door. Listening to the residual dripping of the storm, wondering how many truly innocent men, unlike himself, had lain here before him.

"How will I ever tell Jonathan? I won't. I just won't tell him until I have figured out a way to rebuild." Again, the recent words of the jailer intruded upon Benjamin.

"This one ain't never go'n be free."

He bolted upright, the idea of being hanged tightening around his neck like rough, new twine. He willed his chest to slow. Made himself several promises.

I will find a way to reconstruct Jonathan's dream. I will find a way to help Emerald get an education. And I will tell Emerald's mother that I love her more with my every breathing moment the very next time I see her.

That is, if you aren't swinging in the breeze this time tomorrow.

CHAPTER 23

Monday, November fifteenth
Eight o'clock in the morning

*V*iolette stared at the backs of Jonathan and Dinah Mayfield, her heart breaking as she watched them struggle to take in the smoldering loss. Mama Tavie and Mr. James stood off a ways, obviously trying to give the couple a moment to make real what must seem like a nightmare. But Violette hovered, unable to keep herself from lightly rubbing Dinah's back, touching Jonathan's shoulder. Knowing the building that housed Mayfield's Cabinetry could have been the testament to some twisted man's thwarted plan had she been woman enough to go to Benjamin with her suspicions.

"Well, looks like we're the ones who are getting the surprise." Jonathan forced a smile at his wife. They were as beautiful as ever, those two. And just as much in love. Mr. James moved a little closer, everything about his distinguished bearing shouting, "You deserve better."

"I am so sorry, sir. You worked so hard and long to build this business. I pray and believe it will be erected again."

Violette could only imagine what this bittersweet reunion between this unlikely father-in-law and son-in-law must feel like. Two strong men united around a woman they would both die for. And to think. *This is all my fault. I could have prevented this destruction, this unnecessary pain.*

"It's all right, Mr. James. Papa. The Lord sees the reason behind the reason." Dinah smiled at her father. Looked around at her husband. "We experience the wonderful occurrence of waking up to each other every blessed morning. That's the only surprise we truly treasure."

Jonathan fairly beamed at this wife's encouragement. Violette's heart lurched with longing to have what they had as Jonathan looked toward the front of the house.

"Where's Benjamin?"

"Why don't we all go inside?" Mama Tavie said. "I'm go'n fix breakfast. It'll be like old times."

"Not sure I want old times." Mr. James had a rare hard look on his face as he moved closer to Dinah, the daughter he had not known he had until several years ago. He reached for her hand.

"For hundreds of years, we managed to keep going as slaves. A people of endurance endowed by God with a strong enough love for each other that no whip, no indignity, could sever it. Still I can think of few reasons to ever want to go back."

"Oh, James, I didn't mean to say it like that."

"I know you didn't, my dear. But a bit of clarification is in order, I think. Dinah, you and Jonathan, I am so sorry. Why don't we all go inside and have that breakfast?" He draped an arm around his wife. "I'm still married to the best cook in the state of the Mississippi. Perhaps the whole country."

They all took a seat around the table. Gradually the smells of Mama Tavie's kitchen soothed the troubled gathering. Violette asked the obvious.

"Tell us, you two, what are you doing here? We couldn't be

happier to see you, though never would we have imagined your arrival, on a boat at dawn, to usher you up the hill to this."

"We meant to be here for yesterday's dinner on the ground, but the boat hit a snag in the river. But for the grace of God we would have all perished." Jonathan paused. "And truthfully, I've been a bit concerned about the business."

Mama Tavie placed cups of steaming coffee on the table before everyone. "Sure would have been nice if you all had made it yesterday. Best dinner-on-the-ground time I ever witnessed."

"Yeah," said Emerald, who had been unusually quiet. "Mr. Benjamin whipped the socks off that lowdown Jethro 'fore . . ."

Dinah appeared stricken as her husband looked on helplessly. Violette spoke through clenched teeth. "Emerald, the impropriety of bringing up subjects best left to adults . . . Have you not heard anything I've tried to tell you at all?"

She struggled to salve over the moment with a few high-flown words from her reading.

"Don't you remember how we discussed *decorum*?"

Her efforts fell dead, Jethro's name silently reverberating around the yellow kitchen. How can you place a scab back over a wound, the type of which Jethro had dug into Dinah's soul? Gagging her at dawn. Kidnapping her from Riverwood and dragging her to the cotton fields. Forcing her to work alongside his beaten, swollen wife and their son Davey, all the while promising to use that beautiful, innocent girl in unspeakable ways come nightfall of the very first day? It was Jonathan who had saved her then. Jonathan who saved the moment now.

"Where is Benjamin, anyway? I would have thought him first to come bounding out of the house. Is he out of town buying supplies or something?"

Violette froze. But she was the one who had made this awful mess. The least she could do was answer the man's question.

"He's in jail, Jonathan." The screech of Jonathan's chair pushing back from the table assaulted Violette's hearing.

"He what? What for?"

"For the murder of a man named Chester Singer."

Jonathan tore from the table like an injured bear. "Why didn't somebody tell me?" he roared as he picked up his coat and sprinted through the door, Dinah at his heels.

～

BENJAMIN SAT on the edge of the cot, where he had been for the duration. His eye, jaw, and shoulder throbbing from the random clubbing he had received last night from the jailer. His breakfast of one cold potato, untouched.

For the first time in his life, he was beginning to feel like a slave, not to feel sympathy *for* slaves, as he had done all his life, but to feel *like* one. He was starting to play the game of survival, which was what Africans in America had done for centuries.

Trying to help a slave is a far cry from being one, Benjamin.

He resumed the meticulous study of the dirt floor in which he had been engaged for hours. Even in the predawn, long after Violette had departed, he had watched random roaches and countless unnamed bugs, different ones, he supposed, from the vermin now running free course over his lone potato. Never in his twenty-nine years had he looked toward the ground as much as he had during the last twenty-four hours.

He allowed his head to drop further between his knees. Tried to concentrate on the first part of his three-pronged promise, rebuilding Mayfield Cabinetry. Couldn't.

Thank God the Mayfields are hundreds of miles south of here in New Orleans.

No way under the heavens could he look Jonathan Mayfield in the eye right now—

"Thank you, but my wife and I will talk to him together."

Benjamin froze. *It cannot be. Lord, please don't let it be.*

The jailer who had beat him grunted as the familiar voice

continued, the voice Benjamin truly realized for the first time he had long since claimed as a brother's.

"If that meets with your approval."

He could almost see the one eyebrow lifted in sarcasm. Jonathan. Unmistakably. Undeniably. The brother he had always loved and admired. The last person on earth he wanted to see right now. With the exception of a risen Rogers Catlett in order that Benjamin could take that swing he had always wanted before he was hanged.

He determined to keep his head down. He had always prided himself on a firm jaw. A chin held high. But in the short while since Sunday's sapsucking event, he no longer felt worthy to look into the eyes of a man like Jonathan. It had taken him less than a day to learn not to lift his face to his betters. As Father's slaves seemed to know instinctively, but, in truth, as Master Rogers Catlett's slaves were cruelly taught.

The door creaked. Took a thousand years to open. Jonathan walked through, the swish of a woman's skirt following.

Not Dinah, too. Jonathan could not have really meant to bring his elegant wife in here. This was no place for a woman. Especially one like Dinah Devereaux Mayfield.

Just keep your head down. Stare at the floor until they leave.

"Benjamin, my man." Jonathan Mayfield laid down a letter at the edge of the cot next to Benjamin.

"I don't want to see you, sir."

The sir had come from a different place than when he once used it to get under his friend's skin. Understanding dawned. Jonathan was indeed a superior man. Always had been. Deserved to be called sir, just as Mr. James had once said.

"Looks like you have no choice in the matter. I'm here, and I intend to get you out." Despite his lowered head, Benjamin could see the strong, extended hand. "And stop calling me sir. I thought we had gotten past that."

"So did I. But I was wrong. My father said . . . that is . . . I was taught that 'sir' was warranted when a man is addressing a better man."

He felt Jonathan's curiosity rise at the mention of his father. Watched him slowly withdraw his hand. "Benjamin, everything will—"

"Don't say it. Do not say everything is all right. It is not. We both know it. I don't know if I'll be hanged for this or not. Either way, I have the resources"—Was he really about to offer dirty money, money made on the backs of people whose blood he might have running in his veins, to rebuild the shop?—"to build a bigger better shop. I will see to it that you know how to access it."

"Will you shut up and just listen? I don't care about the shop. I already have what I need to make life worth living. So do you, if you'll just—"

"I appreciate it, but I don't need your help, Jonathan."

"From the looks of you, I think you do. There are a lot of decent people in this town, and I still know a few of them. I'm sure everybody hasn't lost their minds. I'll have you out of here in no time. All right, so what happened?"

"Why are you so stubborn?"

Jonathan chuckled. "We've had that conversation before. Decided it was a tie between us, remember? So talk. I know you didn't just walk up and shoot a man, so the more I know about what did happen, the easier it will be to find out who really killed this Singer man. Who is he anyway?"

"I don't know, but I have a feeling I know who does."

"Well, speak up, man."

Benjamin felt his head snap up. "Would you stop with the bossing for a minute?"

Benjamin's face must have horrified Jonathan. "We have to get you out of here fast. But first tell me who it is you think might know something."

"A friend of mine. A white fellow named Paul Boatwright from Ohio who came South speculating after the war. Wrong motives, good heart. He's the one who introduced me to Singer as a banker who wanted office furniture built. Boatwright gave me an offhand, albeit intense, warning the other day about Singer. I should have listened."

"Yeah, you should have."

"Now, wait a minute, Jonathan. I don't need you telling me—"

"No. you wait. Obviously, you need somebody with a clear head to—"

"A clear head? More like a swollen one if you ask me."

"I didn't. And speaking of swelling, where did you acquire those lovely—"

"Jonathan, dear."

The sound of Dinah's voice fell like a flutter of rose petals. Soft and fraught with the scent of a woman's temperance and wisdom. Benjamin felt ashamed.

"What about Henry?" Dinah continued. "We have yet to see him this morning. Why don't you go see what he might know while I stay a while longer with Benjamin? And what about Mr. Boatwright? Perhaps you could be of service to him in securing bail. I understand Eli and Jethro are out there somewhere. They know something. I'm sure of it."

"Dinah. I, uh, almost forgot—that is . . . we shouldn't be discussing anything around you that might conjure up memories of those two."

Jonathan sputtered the way Benjamin would have, had he dared to say anything else on the subject. He lowered his head back between his knees where it should have remained in the first place and would have had Jonathan not riled him.

"I apologize, Dinah. You don't have to stay."

"But I want to stay, and I demand that the two of you start treating me less like a piece of porcelain and more like a thinking human being. We have a few minutes before that jailer returns. I admit something about him scares me, so when he comes, I'll leave immediately. He commented under his breath about something brewing in Tennessee for several years, designed to kill the 'uppity-ness' of men like you two. Did you hear him, Jonathan?"

"No. But that sounds like a good enough reason why I can't leave you here alone."

"You shouldn't have brought her in the first place."

"Shhh, you two. There you go again. That's enough. I can tell you are as worried about each other as you've ever been because you're both striking out in that way you do when you care." She gave Jonathan a look that transformed him. Said he was a goner willing to jump out of the window if she insisted. "I'll see you in a half hour, honey."

CHAPTER 24

"What's going on between you and Violette?"

Benjamin heard Dinah pull up the splintered wooden box. She took a seat and reached for his hands much as Violette had done. She pointed toward his feet.

"And if you don't lift your head, I'm going to move myself from this box and sit on that floor because I mean to see your face when I talk to you."

There was nothing for it but to look at her. It occurred to Benjamin that she and Violette were not so different after all. Different backgrounds, perhaps. But the same eyes probing clear to the soul. Same fierce heart always fighting for the ones they love.

"Now tell me about you and Violette."

"What do you want to know?"

"Everything. Don't leave anything out."

A breath of resignation whistled through Benjamin's nostrils. "It's just as you and Jonathan said it would be. She is wonderful with numbers." He couldn't help but chortle at the next thought that popped into his head. "Terrible in the kitchen, though. Cooked the nastiest food I ever tasted. Makes you look like a born chef."

"That bad, huh?"

"Worse. Which makes her all the more endearing because she wants so badly to be like you. But her gift is numbers, not designing and not food preparation."

"You're in love with her."

Benjamin was long in answering. Desperately wanted to deny it for every reason imaginable. Knew it was useless. Dinah would see right through it.

"Yes. Plain and simple. But it's no good. There are so many reasons why we could never be together, not the least of which is what she did to you and Jonathan. As much as I want to believe otherwise, I'm not sure a person can totally change from that kind of behavior." Dinah shot to her feet. Definitely the old Dinah now.

"Benjamin Catlett. I don't believe I heard what I just heard. Don't tell me you're still holding the fact that she told a few people about my accidentally burning those manumission papers of Jonathan's against her."

"It's not that simple."

"It is that simple. You, a Christian gentleman, are harboring something that happened nearly ten years ago against a woman who has fought every obstacle to get where she is. A woman, I might add, who did what she did because she was more desperate than you could imagine."

Indeed. Benjamin could not imagine a good enough reason to nearly destroy a man's freedom and his business right along with it, solely out of spite, especially a man who had never done anything to deserve that kind of malice.

"Right you are. I can't imagine, and I'll never understand."

"Oh, yes you will, and I'm about to enlighten you right now."

Benjamin drew his hand from hers. Raised it to a halting stance. "I know you mean well, Dinah, and I love you for it. But you should know that Violette is, as we speak, living an unresolvable lie. One that, admittedly, might be considered streaked with bits of off-color admiration. But a lie nonetheless."

"Benjamin, you need to listen to what I have to say."

"What would you say if I told you that Emerald is not her sister but her daughter?"

"It wouldn't surprise me at all because I already—"

"And what if I told you the father was someone you know only too well?"

Dinah paused. Stretched her eyes in unbelief. Benjamin thought perhaps he had finally struck a chord dissonant enough to make her move on.

"How . . . when did you learn about this? And since you have, I should think there would be a softening in the Benjamin I thought I knew."

A softening? Had Dinah gone daft?

"A softening? After learning that the baby's father is none other than our own quiet, capable Henry Livingston?"

"What?"

Benjamin was almost sorry. He hadn't wanted to destroy Henry's image. He expected any minute his friend's wife would dissolve into a feminine collapse. Instead Dinah pressed her fingertips to her lips and giggled. Giggling. About one of the most painful utterances ever to leave Benjamin's mouth.

"Henry? Where in the world did you get that from?"

"I'm afraid I don't see the humor, but I actually got it from Henry himself."

"Oh, I rather doubt that, since Henry is at least two years younger than Violette, and at the time of Emerald's conception was perhaps ten or eleven years old and most likely unable to sire a child yet, let alone with a girl he had always viewed as a sister."

Benjamin went hot to his toes, suddenly mortified to be talking to his friend's wife about such things. His mother would have to be resuscitated if she got wind of this discussion. Dinah, however, seemed more and more amused.

"You . . . you can't really mean little Henry."

Benjamin snapped back to the crux of the conversation. Wondered at how much his parents teaching had tilted his views.

Heated up again after processing what Dinah had just said about the impossibility of Henry's siring Emerald.

"In case you've missed it, he's not so little anymore. Besides, if not Henry, then who?"

Dinah's countenance turned quickly serious. She looked as though she wanted to weep. "Benjamin, have you ever known what it feels like to want to fit in?"

He had. Lord, how he had known what it felt like to want to play with the slave children, to want to be a child. Period. But Benjamin Catlett could not possibly admit to all that. Not even on his way to the hangman's noose. So he simply stared at her. Waited.

"Slave or free. Black or white. Rich or poor. We all have that need to be accepted into the group in which we find ourselves. Violette McMillan was no less. Only instead of finding her place among her peers, she found herself the subject of ridicule because she had always been a child that struggled with her size. The sparse rations that barely seemed to sustain many slaves turned to excess weight in her, resulting in names like pig and cow digging into her soul like a leech.

"But then she lost weight in her adolescence, and along came Eli Duggan."

Shock, visceral and crippling, nearly flattened Benjamin. He gripped the edges of the cot. No. Not that gardener that was in cahoots against Jonathan.

"A self-styled ladies' man who tells her she's fetching. Gives her something to look forward to at a time when her whole family, except her mother, would be carted off to the auction block like so much cattle. She was about to turn fourteen. And very soon into the family way."

No wonder she could so easily pass for an older sister. Benjamin knew many slave girls became early mothers. Still, this was Violette they were discussing. Bright, eager, sometimes too sensitive. Violette, barely a child herself when Emerald was born.

"She just happened to be a girl whose pregnancy was easily overlooked. Nobody knew. Even her mother who had become addlepated at the sudden sale of her husband and children didn't notice."

Henry's mother knew, but bringing that up was pointless right now.

"Then came that watershed moment in life that we all face, Benjamin. That time when we make a decision and we live with it or we rue it until the regret turns to poison and eventually kills us."

Like Lucie. It was as though Dinah knew about the girl whose life was snuffed out because of Benjamin. But how could she? No one except his mother, and now Boatwright, knew about Lucie.

"Benjamin?"

Pull yourself together, man.

"You look ill. You're holding your midsection. It's going to be time for me to leave soon anyway. Shall I go back to the house? Try to see if I can find something to relieve your symptoms?"

He wanted to hear the rest, though he sensed he already knew. "Please, no. I'll be fine. Go on."

"Violette and her mother delivered on the same night, but Violette's mother and her baby brother did not live. Heart stricken, yet already in possession of maternal instincts, fourteen-year-old Violette decided to give her baby the best chance at life she could offer. When the old midwife told her she was likely to more quickly become one of Jethro's breeders—possibly used by both Jethro and Eli to replenish the stock of human property—if she admitted the child was hers, the young girl agreed to tell everyone her mama had died in childbirth and left Violette to care for her little sister, when in truth Violette's only hope for a replacement of the siblings she had lost was dead, and the baby waiting to be cared for was her own Emerald."

"So . . . the father is . . . Eli Duggan, then." He could barely utter the words.

"The father is Eli."

The father is Eli. It's Eli—

Boom!

Another shock of thunder—unlike that of the Riverwood Road experience, more spring-like than wintry—jarred Benjamin's hearing. Sheared the edges of his thoughts. But hope, swift and unaccounted for, infused Benjamin's soul. He felt lighter knowing his rival was not his friend, Henry. All those accusations he had made about Violette's character seemed hollow now, made-up excuses to release her from his heart. For the first time in hours, he stood to his feet.

"If I can just get out of here, maybe sit and talk with her."

Dinah smiled. "I know, Benjamin, I know."

"Do you really think there's a chance for bail?"

"I think if God says so, it's done."

CHAPTER 25

$\mathcal{T}$he drama of the pounding rain was comforting to her, invoking a warm memory as rare as Mississippi snow. Violette hugged herself. Snuggled into the window seat beneath one of the dormers she had so quickly claimed and looked out the pane of the attic room onto the slanted downpour. Snatches of isolated moments, when the McMillan's slave force was shut down because of inclement weather, rode in on the sounds of the violent storm. Her mother, father, and siblings all under one roof in the middle of the day, waiting to be re-summoned to the fields, but feeling, in that warm, unexpected cocoon, like a free people. A liberated family stopping for dinner at their own command.

Thinking back to those rare times, times that marked the nearest Violette had ever come to a chance to build a cache of golden moments, gave her a delicious shiver. Rain. Wonderful and demanding, it had the ability to send people to their shelters. Stop the world for a moment and allow dreamers to dream. Here with her child safely downstairs, Violette craved a moment to dream.

If only she could stop the race to nowhere sallying forth in her thoughts.

No question remained about the source of last night's fire.

Furthermore, she knew in her heart who was responsible for the hanging of Davey's brother. Had known since the day Chester Singer had accosted her. And she knew what wicked alliance had burned down Mayfield Cabinetry. But now that the ring leader was dead, why did she hesitate to expose those other two?

What is there to fear?

Violette raised a shrug of withdrawal. Did a brisk rub of her triceps. The rain picked up, matching its intensity to the breach of calm steadily assailing her. She felt a push to run down to her daughter's room. Look on her as she took an afternoon nap during the storm as she had always loved to do when Emerald was a tot. No. It would be foolish to check on Emerald. Foolish and faithless.

I have to conquer that, dear Jesus. Precious Emerald is no longer a little girl. Truly, Lord, she has reminded me of that often enough.

Violette startled at the gentle rap on the door to the small space. Benjamin? Released already? Her heartbeat quickened. How many times within the hour had she imagined just the two of them in the matching window seats, a book in hand.

"Yes, who is it?"

"It's me, Dinah. May I come in for a moment?"

"Dinah? Why, of course."

Pure foolishness. Daydreaming about Benjamin in the middle of the afternoon, in another woman's house, albeit there was no place else for her to go with the shop in shambles as it was, even if the woman was the only friend in the world she had that was remotely close to her age. She leapt from the window seat. Ran to the door and stood at attention.

"Dinah? Is something wrong? Do you and Jonathan need me for anything?"

"Slow down, will you? I just made another trip to the jail." Dinah looked down at her soggy apparel. Laughed. "I suppose you don't need a statement from me to decipher the truth of that. I have good news. Benjamin should be home within the hour.

A surge of hopeful anxiety nearly toppled Violette. "Really? And truly?"

""I was wondering if you'd like to help me with supper?"

Violette chuckled. "So he told you, huh?"

"Told me what?"

"Come on, girl. Don't try to jest the court jester. I know he told you about that disastrous soup and all its accompanying horrors."

Dinah pressed her hand to her chest? "My, what high flown language. Jest? Methinks my friend has read a bit past her quota."

This time Violette giggled outright. "All right. Maybe I can learn a thing or two in the kitchen if I simply watch and not try to help. And Dinah?"

"Yes?"

"I know you've become the consummate cook, but just be sure while you're cooking nobody's coat is next to the fire this time."

They both laughed at the remembrance of Dinah's accidentally punching Jonathan's coat into the fire on the first day they met all those years ago. In the midst of a turn toward the door, Violette halted. Knew her eyes swam with tears.

"May I make a confession?"

"Of course. Whatever is on your mind."

"I was once so envious of you. If you said go left, I was compelled to go right. But I can finally truly say I'm so glad you're here, my friend. I don't know that I could get through this without you." And I must tell someone about Singer, or I shall lose my senses.

Dinah wrapped her in a hug. Violette tensed at the thought of another shameful admission to this woman.

"Could we sit for a few minutes? I need to tell you something."

It seemed only a short while ago Violette had bared her soul to Dinah about Emerald's birth. She allowed herself to be led back to the window seat where Dinah lifted Violette's chin with a gentle finger. Infused courage into her with a smile.

"Take all the time you need."

"I think you know Emerald means everything to me. Sometimes I think she is the jewel of my life and the source of my very dread and sorrow all at the same time." Violette accepted Dinah's handkerchief. Exhaled a lengthy breath. Dabbed at her eyes.

"I look at her and I see myself when you met me, a shell of a girl with 'bully' stamped on the outside and fear raging on the inside. Yet, though I see it in my own daughter, I don't know what to do about it."

Violette was deeply grateful that Dinah had the wisdom to remain quiet, for comment—any interruption—might make Violette flee these things she dreaded saying and never gain the nerve to say them again.

"I don't know if I ever really thanked you for teaching me to read and for teaching me my numbers, and Jonathan for a chance to work with the shop's books even before the war ended. Numbers are second nature to me, and that early chance to set down on paper what I had always somehow known I could do was the beginning of a realization of what it meant to respect oneself. Who but your wonderful husband would make the trip to Riverwood to teach me how to balance accounts, then return again and again so that I could keep them balanced, and then pay me the first wages I had ever received? Only as I have aged have I realized that it was more for me than the two of you."

Dinah shook her head.

"Oh, yes. It's true and you know it."

A sweet silence set in as Violette gained strength to tell this woman what needed to be told so that, no matter the consequences, she could, as she had done so many years ago with Dinah when she admitted to her Emerald's true parentage, free her soul.

"You remember that day near the middle of May of '65, don't you? When Jonathan found out that Lieutenant General Richard Taylor had surrendered his Confederate forces from Alabama, Mississippi, and a portion of Louisiana?"

Dinah nodded. "Of course, I do. Everyone had heard the

IN PURSUIT OF AN EMERALD

rumors. We knew about Appomattox. But that feeling, at least for Jonathan and me, that Mississippi, our own state, had finally stopped warring against us, its own people, was one of disbelief and exhilaration the likes of which I have not felt since."

"How well do I recall." Violette's heart raced at the memory. "Your husband gushed the news when he came to Riverwood, and I couldn't stop myself. I begged him to take Emerald and me back to town with him on the wagon. On the spot. The push in me to experience how it would feel to get away from Riverwood, to walk as an entity that belonged to herself, was almost physical. I wanted to celebrate. Felt the need to skip and dance like a child. I squeezed Emerald so hard until I nearly bruised her. I had never really celebrated anything in my life. So I wanted, just this once, to lay down all my guilt and celebrate like King David did in the Bible after winning the wars."

Violette cocked her head to the side teasingly. "Trouble was when Jonathan got us to the town of Natchez, all you two wanted to do—you and Jonathan were so in love—was hold hands and stand by the river. But me? I was like a toddler in a yard full of toys. The excitement of it all might have slammed me to the ground, but I just couldn't stay down there. In my mind, I was all over the place with possibilities.

"Knowing that, given the angry mood of the Confederacy, walking alone at night was probably not the wisest thing for a young slave girl to do, I decided to sneak away from you lovebirds anyway. Despite the fact you two had told me not to wander too far, I grabbed my baby's hand and walked toward Silver Street for the first time as a free woman. That was when I ran into Chester Singer."

"Chester Singer? Who is this man anyway? Did you know him then?"

"I knew him, all right. Chester Singer—whom people around town only knew as the McMillan's "Chet" before the war and until a day or so ago knew as the new banker in town—was once the manager of the slaves at the McMillan plantation where I was born. He was the despot that commanded Jethro, shaped him into the evil he became, the reprobate he remains. The overseer the McMillans overlooked while he did as he pleased with their chattel. The one that marked my mother as the best cotton-picking pickaninny on the plantation, working her throughout her pregnancies without a thought for her condition.

"So yes, I knew him. But the person I didn't know was myself." Violette paused. Let the new sounds of the intensified storm soothe her.

"In my haste to go to town with Jonathan, I had not forgotten to bring my handkerchief of money he had paid me over time. I had put together for myself a pitiful-looking "reticule" like the ones I imagined in the novels I read. Money was so very scarce back then, but your husband had somehow managed to share with me, making certain he always paid me in money he'd saved up before the war. As I sit here, Dinah, I swear to you that I didn't fully understand the draw of money, the evil it can unleash in those susceptible, until I started to collect it."

"Don't forget, Violette. I, too, was a slave. Perhaps not a field one, but when it came to money—and the rule of masters to keep it away from their human property causing it to be even more attractive—a slave was a slave was a slave."

"I suppose you are right."

She talked about the enticement of money. How the lure of it hurt her. How it hurt the slave holders. How it has the capacity to produce people like Simon Legree and even people like Harriet Beecher Stowe's Augustine St. Clare, a so-called benevolent master, who succeeded in numbing himself to his own humanity. How it causes people to set themselves up above other humans. And when their souls tell them to come down, their greed holds them fast.

"That night when I ran into Singer on his way under the hill, he told me he was headed toward a gambling den. Said he had seen the light about the evil of owning chattel and wanted to make enough money to turn his life around. I should have known that a man who had once set loose dogs on a six-year-old runaway would ever be a dog himself. But he said I could quickly and greatly enhance my savings if I gave the men down there 'a good time' while they gambled."

Dinah shifted her weight. Seemed uncommonly rattled. "He said this in front of Emerald?"

"In front of Emerald."

"And you let him?"

CHAPTER 26

$\mathcal{T}$he old familiar guilt washed over Violette anew. She stood. Paced. She must quickly resume the story before the unspoken alarm in Dinah's eyes silenced her.

"But I had been that route with Jethro. That route of selling for temporary gain what really was an endowment from the Lord. Had vowed afterwards, each time I immersed myself in water and came up still dirty, that I would never make that bargain with the devil again. I understood what gambling meant. Reckoned it a better way to look out for Emerald's future than selling myself to a man. Told myself that I just wanted to help my child go to a school up north with the money Jonathan had paid me by doubling it. Perhaps even tripling it. Who knew? On a night when it had become official that Mississippi had been forced to free its slaves, anything was possible.

"He asked me about the reticule. I told him I had money. The glint in his eye was barely contained as he set me up at a table in a back room up against the bluffs. He knew me, and I knew him from the old plantation. Hated him as fiercely as I always had. Called myself using him.

"But the gambling brought out something in me. Something

ugly and seductive that I didn't know was there. All too soon, with my baby sleeping on the floor of a stinking, smoky room full of men looking on, Singer had orchestrated the taking of every penny I had earned from you and Jonathan. He laughed at me. Informed me that I should always remember that no matter the war's outcome, darkies were stupid. Always had been. Always would be."

"Lord, forgive me." Dinah's voice was hoarse. "At this moment, I think I hate Chester Singer. I think I hate a dead man."

"Despite what he said, I will always believe that I had truly gained a little momentum at Riverwood in figuring out who I was after you and Mama Tavie married and moved away. But that night under the hill I lost whatever respect for myself I had gained, and I lost the chance to make a better life for my daughter, to get her to another place. One night of freedom, and I was forced to return to Riverwood more slave than ever."

"Darling girl. Don't you know we are all susceptible to the pull of money? To one degree of the other, we believe it makes not only life around us but life itself better. The more we get the more we want until money takes on a life of its own, making us watch over it, treat it as though it has a heartbeat. The key is to recognize and to forgive ourselves, as Jesus forgives those who sincerely ask Him, and to 'go and sin no more.'"

Dinah stood abruptly. "Come on. Let's get to that kitchen."

Panic swelled in Violette. She hadn't gotten to the part about Singer and the manner in which he forced her to pay her gambling debt that night. Nor about Jethro, Eli, and Singer and what she knew they had done to Davey's brother, to Jonathan's shop. It could very well be Jethro or Eli, or even that fourth man, who killed Singer.

It was now or never. She either acted this moment on the nerve she had mustered, nerve that she knew could forever sever ties with the people she loved, or she would never be able to rally it again.

"But . . . but I'm not finished I have more to say. Please Dinah. A few more minutes."

Dinah laughed. "What? That you're in love with Benjamin Catlett?"

"How . . . how did you know that?"

"Possibly because your every other word is 'Benjamin,' and you light or cloud up depending upon what is said about him. I declare. You two are really a pair. You must think the rest of us are blind."

"I don't deserve him. Even if he cared for me, which he doesn't, he like everyone else knows some of the mistakes I have made, and he just can't stomach them. But I think I can help clear up some things for him, and that's one of the things I need to talk to you about—"

Before she could finish her statement, Violette's shoulders were in the grip of Dinah's hands. She wondered if her friend were about to shake her.

"Violette, will you let that go? That stuff from ten years ago about the manumission papers is just that. Stuff. Stuff that God has forgiven but the enemy of your soul fluffs up with hollow meaning so that he can torture you. That's what he did to me all my life until the Lord let me meet Mr. James who told me he was my father and assured me of what a truly wonderful mother I had when all along I had thought her just a lowly prostitute. He let me see how much of my life had been wasted worrying over nothing. I don't want that for you."

"But Dinah, I still need to clear some things up for Benjamin. Ask for forgiveness."

"All right, all right. If you insist. And I know the perfect place where you can share the rest of your concerns about this man who is so right for you and obviously as much in love with you as you are with him. The kitchen." Dinah clasped her fingers around Violette's wrist. Tugged softly. "Hurry, Jonathan and Benjamin will be home soon. We only have a short while to get supper ready." Dinah hustled her down the steps to the second floor. Violette paused.

"You go ahead. I promise I'll be just a minute. I want to get Emerald up from her nap. She can help us get ready for when the men get here."

She knocked. Then remembering she had left an apron in her room, she abandoned her search for Emerald. Retrieved the apron and put it on. She didn't knock at Emerald's door this time. She simply pushed it open.

"Emerald? Honey?" Her eyes swept the darkened, disheveled room in a fraction of a second. Fear struck like a river flood, covering over every ounce of her reasoning with thick, debilitating fog.

Where could she have gone in all this weather? Davey. It had to be Davey. She flew toward the stairs. Heard Jonathan's voice mixing with another man's. Was it Henry? Why would he be out on a day like today when there was nothing he could do in the shop anyhow?

"Dinah? Jonathan? What is it? What's wrong?"

"It's me, Davey, Miss Vi'lette. Something bad done happened."

To ask "what" would be about as profitable as counting grains of sand. She already knew what the "bad" was. She just didn't know how bad. So she dug her fingernails into her palms. Waited wordlessly.

"My papa 'nem, they done took Emerald to some place or other they call the 'little rivertree or riverwood' or something like that. They say they better have some money to run with before daylight or they go'n take Emerald over the river to Louisiana, and Lord knows what else they planning to do."

My papa 'nem. Jethro. And Eli.

Violette heard herself asking the most normal, yet the most irrelevant, question she had ever asked. "In all this weather? My baby, she'll catch a chill in all this rain. She doesn't like cold."

She struggled to know even where she stood let alone why she had asked about the weather. Her mind was raw batter. Fluid and thick with all kinds of ideas that had become one unbearable thought.

My baby is ruined. Possibly by her own fa—

"No. NoNoNo."

"Shhh. It's going to be all right." Dinah's arms were about her leading her into the yellow kitchen. Odd. Tonight, yellow seemed odd in November.

"They want money from Mr. Benjamin."

The boy's voice shook. Violette wondered why. Did Davey care about her baby? About her being cold?

"Said you, Miss Vi'lette, would know where to get it even though Mr. Benjamin's go'n hang. One of them said tell you that Emerald is bound for the streets of New Orleans if they don't get what they want. Said she no longer precious to nobody but you and that when they was finished with her, she, like you, would no longer be that 'girl-like green.'"

The boy was crying now, the sounds of his sobs outstripping the slowed rain. He understood that nasty, crude attempt at symbolism as well as she did. There must be some way she could escape this pain that she feared would destroy her soul and body.

You have destroyed the two people you love the most.

Violette's last thoughts before the yellow swirled into a sun-like disc and the floor met her half way.

IT WAS SINGER.

That's who Benjamin had nearly bested in '63 when he and Henry had set out to join Grant's army.

"I knew something about him was familiar. I must have been the one to put that triangle on his head."

Feeling the suffocation of the cell, for a moment at least, Benjamin could rally around the sense of justice he felt at the realization that he had once tied up with Chester Singer and left his mark.

The storm lashed out with the strength of his father's whip, causing the small barred window touching the ceiling to look like the face of a laughing ogre. Though the clouds had already rendered the sun mostly useless, Benjamin sensed night was coming on. Clearly, he would not be released this day. Thinking he had never felt quite this cut-off, he wondered if the jailer had not simply gone home and left him there alone. The rain must have shut down everything, including the jail, and he had begun to feel hungry, his eyes searching the near-darkness for the potato. He found it pocked since last he had looked with the latest marks of rodents he didn't even remember.

Seeking mind leverage, Benjamin inhaled. His shackled hand brushed a piece of paper. No. Not just a piece. It was thick, a letter. He had forgotten Jonathan had left it. Oh well. No time like the present to read it. Perhaps it would be of interest, even entertaining. He craved entertainment especially since within minutes he would be plunged into total darkness where, while he had somehow suppressed their daytime presence, the rats had become so bold over in the night last night that it had been all he could do to keep from screaming.

It was awkward, but he was able to grasp the letter. He shuddered. And in the failing light, bent to the contents of the familiar hand.

My dearest and only son,

That you are faring well, escaping the trials of life, is always the joy of my existence, but I find the time has come that I can no longer manage the sizable inheritance that is yours without some semblance of assistance. Of late, I spend much of my time within my bedchamber under the doctor's care.

The doctor's care? When had Mother become so ill? She had always been so robust. So strong in her duties.

Always have I known your feelings toward the choice your father made in building up capital by what he told himself was the American prerogative. But it has become imperative that you know another choice he made which has and shall continue to affect you for the rest of your life. Unbeknownst to me, dear Benjamin, your father bought his first and last slave in the name of Benjamin Catlett, his will clearly stating his desire to force you to reckon with "what you have enjoyed all your life and will continue to enjoy after I am dead." It pains me beyond description to tell you that you have ever been a slave owner until the defeat of the Confederacy four years past.

Benjamin released the letter to his lap, an unnatural cold seeping into his bones. A slave owner? He had been a slave owner? Seemingly of their own volition, his fingers again took up the paper.

Of course, except for a handful of house servants who are now paid, your property has long since dispersed itself in the manner of free men and women everywhere, rendering your status as slaveholder moot. However, Rogers managed to hold on to the sizable assets throughout the war and, left in your name, they will have to be claimed and managed at my demise which without God's intervention, dear son, is imminent. My fondest hope is to see you before that time and to beg your forgiveness for a lifestyle imposed on you from birth.

On my deathbed, I would be derelict in not mentioning how proud I am of what you tried to do for our people. Every child you managed to smuggle to Virginia, I managed to find a home for in a northern state. Even our misguided attempt with Lucie has some merit, I believe. Please, if any regard for a devoted mother is in order, I implore you to respond quickly by post so that if I should be called to meet my Maker before you come, I will have the warmth of knowing you were on your way.

Your ever adoring mother,
    Anna Benjamin Catlett

The letter dropped to the dirt floor as an ominous calm settled over Benjamin, drowning him in the shame he had fought all his life. Now, between the clash of day and night, sitting in a dank, low-ceilinged jail, he sensed he had finally been removed from a struggle which so clearly had always been futile. He was and ever had been Rogers Catlett disguised as someone named Benjamin. Aspiring southern gentleman. Buyer and seller of human beings.

Humans with the same blood as his.

The thunder rolled eastward, the voice of the Almighty, as Benjamin had always been taught. But the winds of truth he thought he felt carried nothing of the Supreme, the strange calm he had felt moments ago now removed to despair. Benjamin Rogers Catlett sank back against a wall greasy with human oils and trembled like a colicky baby. The slaves he envied as a child—the ones he had stripped himself naked trying to imitate, the ones who had ultimately enabled him to have the wealth to free others all these years—all this time actually belonged to him according to the laws of this free country. And each dime of the wealth at his home in Virginia acquired via the slave labor was amassed in his name, rendering all he had tried to do to make up for it as meaningless as mown grass chased by the wind. In all his inbred polish, he was less of a person than Henry and Violette, who carried no such secrets. And every other slave he had tried to improve and subconsciously felt superior to.

"Jesus, I am in need of healing, forgiveness."

His hands shackled, he scooted forward. Fell clumsily to his knees.

Father. Lord Jesus. Only you can deliver me from the bias I was taught by my earthly father. I find that although I fault him, I realize that he, too, was moved to a place of evil by slavery. I have tried in my own strength to remove myself from my upbringing, only to finally see my attempts for what they are. Human pride and human failure.

He ignored what felt like moving fur around his ankle. Rats.

I know now, Lord, that only eternal deliverance can help me get past the lie of bought superiority that my father wanted me to see as truth. And he has succeeded, dear Jesus. For I now see clearly that not only had I wanted to change poor Lucie for Mother and Father, I had wanted to change her for myself. I thought myself better than she.

The deep, wrenching sobs that Benjamin would be loath to release anywhere else melded with the dampness of the cell. Could barely be heard for the storm. But Benjamin felt their power break open the hard places. Places that had been reserved and cultivated for that evil fleshly need to see oneself as better than his neighbor. Something deep down inside him had lorded it over Violette, Henry. Even his boss Jonathan. Simply because he had been taught to believe he was better.

And now, my Father, I have become the worst kind of slave. Chained to the wickedness of my heritage. So whether hanged or freed, I ask for Your forgiveness and that I am granted the blessing of asking the same of the woman I love. I pray this in Your Name and for the sake of the upbuilding of Your kingdom. Amen.

CHAPTER 27

Tuesday, November sixteenth
Riverwood Road, early morning

*V*iolette was disgusted with herself. Fainting twice. Having to sneak out to find her child. She really was turning into a novel character. She had lost count of the times she had checked for the small sack of coins she had earned during the last few weeks as she made her way toward Riverwood.

To think that Jethro and Eli are stupid enough to think I have access to Benjamin's money.

God bless Benjamin. He had paid her so much more than she was worth. She thought about the books, the ever-increasing sparseness of Mayfield Cabinetry's income, and halted her steps.

"I wonder if some of this is his own money. It has to be."

She ignored the involuntary chill that quickly possessed her. For sure, she was soaked to the bone, though from the looks of things, the storm was mostly spent. Its clouds sullen and exhausted from the energy expended throughout last afternoon and evening. Quickening her pace again, she struggled to hear through the residual rain.

Jethro and Eli, they have to be out here somewhere. Let Emerald be here, Lord. And let her be safe.

She had passed the spot when sounds of high-pitched moaning brought her to attention. People sounds. The kinds of sounds often made during nightmarish sleep or some other subconscious state. Human sounds. Ever conscious that she was a field hand turned washerwoman turned bookkeeper, Violette knew she was no expert on distinguishing animal cries. Still, the moaning sounded more human to her than she would have thought to find coming from deep in the woods of a soggy morning. And feminine, they sounded feminine.

Thanks to the weather, her footsteps were noiseless on the leaf-padded earth. She followed the sounds, more and more punctuated by sporadic snoring. Hitting her eardrums like the noises of war. Then she was upon them.

Jethro. Eli. And Precious Emerald.

What now? She had not thought through that she had no weapon when she'd sneaked from the house alone. Wouldn't know what to do with it if she had. Through the dim light, she stared half-sighted, yet knowing beyond doubt that it was the trio she sought.

Jethro McMillan. How had she been able to share the same name with this creature for so long? Because slaves had no such choices, that's how. And Eli Duggan. Two men she had thought— hoped, God forgive her—were eliminated from the surface of the earth. Two walking breathing nightmares, the incarnation of Quimbo and Sambo. Stretched out on either side of her baby. Their filthy limbs, as well as a sprinkling of twigs from the storm-battered tree limbs, sprawled all over Precious Emerald. Obviously, they were drunk, or had been. Bottles strewn like dark empty souls. Emerald seemed caught between sleep and a defensive wakefulness. Moaning. Her body taut with alertness. Jerking from whatever possibly unspeakable horrors filled her dreams. Violette fought the dizziness trying to claim her as she saw her little girl tied to a tree, her braids totally untwined, the collar of her dress slanted toward one shoulder.

"Vi'lette!" Emerald's scream split the air. She strained against the rope. "Vi'lette, that you? They trying to hurt me!"

In a fractured second, Violette was there, stepping on Jethro's trunk-like thighs. Heeling into his chest. Grabbing for Emerald. But Jethro prevented her, snatching her ankles from beneath her and flipping her onto her back as he pinned her to the ground with his elbow then got to his knees. Eli only grunted. Shifted his position and threw his leg over Emerald's knees. Jethro grinned.

"Well, well. If it ain't big sister come to save the little pretty one." He took a moment to bathe Violette in a leer. "You ain't looking so bad yourself these days."

"I don't know how you managed to crawl out of the grave. But I'm here to see to it that you let Emerald go. Do what you want with me, but let her go." She turned to reach into her bosom. "I couldn't get hold of Benjamin's money, but I've got coins of my own."

"It won't do." Insult formed a snarl. "Keep it, whatever you got. What chu think I am? A fool? You ain't got enough money to get me where I got to go. Now that the boss is dead and that other one is liable to take over . . ." He broke off his thought, a touch of fear in the pause. "Ne'er mind him. I need money to get over into Louisiana. Go west where I can get me a piece of that free land. Start my own kind of plan'ation out there somewhere."

Stupid man. He wouldn't know what's on the other side of Louisiana if someone wrote it across the heavens.

"Don't say nothing, Vi'lette." Emerald shivered like an hours-old puppy. "He mean. You just don't know how mean. He real, real mean. Just like that man under the hill."

She remembers. The screams, the beating. Violette's head pounded along with her heartbeat. Though it continued to drizzle, she felt dust in her eyes. Some crazy mechanism to stop her from having to look at her child. Still she saw her.

"Don't worry, honey. I know only too well how mean he is."

Jethro cackled like a storybook witch. "Aw, now. You done hurt my feelings. Is that what you called what happened 'tween us? Meanness? And there I thought I was being a real gentleman that night in the warm dirt of the fields."

Emerald whimpered. Tried to put her hands to her ears. Violette trained her eyes on her child.

"Shut up, Jethro!" Violette trained her eyes on her child. Her heart beat so loudly now, seemingly pressing against the insides of her ears, until she wondered if the others heard it. She smiled at Emerald. Surmised her own hearing ruined forever.

"Shhh. Hush now. It's going to be all right. We'll be home soon, back in Mr. Benjamin's warm, pretty house. I promise." She tried to infuse hope into her voice, hope that was running out of her like water. "Did you ever dream you and I would be so blessed, living in a house almost as tall as Riverwood? With our own attic? Everybody's waiting for you, honey. Davey, Aunt Dinah, everybody."

Help me, Jesus, to keep this promise to my child. I know I've been the worst mother in Your book, but I need that grace Brother Paul always talks about in the Bible. Help me make this one promise real.

Other Scripture surfaced from her past, Scripture she didn't know she remembered. "God resisteth the proud, and giveth grace to the humble."

Yes, Lord. I am desperate. I need Your grace Some of this my pride has gotten me into. I humble myself under your mighty hand.

In her heart, she prayed further that Jethro's love for power and his obviously desperate need for money would make her plan workable.

The lecher in Jethro took over again as he seemed to allow himself to take her in. Was he about to make her an offer? The same offer he made years ago in exchange for Emerald?

Oh, God, this couldn't be Your grace. Oh, Lord, I can't. I can't—

"You looking good, you know that?"

A voice followed Jethro's, tinged with deception yet soothing as the sounds of chirping birds at dawn.

You will. You know you will if you must. You'll do anything for her. Precious Emerald's life for yours.

No, dear one. My life for yours. You are Mine.

Thank you, Lord.

Jethro's voice tore through the fragile peace.

"How'd you sniff us out?"

She wanted to tell him it didn't take much since the odor from their little hideout was at skunk level. She decided against that rejoinder just as a series of grunts added to the threat.

Eli. Awake too.

He bolted to a perfect L, his person reeking of old sweat mixed with liquor. "Well, what do we got here?"

Her daughter's father. A greedy, shallow excuse of a man. Breath and britches, as Mama Tavie used to say She steeled herself. Subconsciously noted herself about to act as though Eli was the woodrat he really was.

"I'm not quite as dumb as the two of you always thought." Emerald gasped but didn't say anything. "I slipped out of the house and tracked you through your own loose words. Remember what you said unbeknownst in Benjamin's hearing about 'little River-wood?'" Violette looked around the shabby spot they had carved out for themselves. "Indeed. That you should be pitiful enough to be still dreaming of working on a plantation is both laughable and nauseating. But this is no more than a pieced-together children's playhouse. A mound of dirt is smarter than both your brains put together."

Emerald screamed as Jethro hit Violette so hard she saw stars. Shooting stars that should be hidden behind those sulking clouds. She struggled to remain clear. Prayed again. Thought to herself, how faithful is a Maker that listens to the prayer of someone whose worship is as inconsistent as mine. Her brain reeling, she spoke through bloody, smarting lips, further stunned by the slur of her own voice.

"Whas the matter? Don't you appreciate that I was s-smart enough to figure out where your 'little Riverwood' was even in a storm?" She fumbled to unpin the handkerchief from her bosom. Tried and failed to gain her feet, her thoughts fuzzier by the second.

"Here's the money. All I have. Enough to get you across the river. Now, give me my child, and I'll be gone."

My child. *Lord. Have. Mercy. On Me.*

Contrary to what Violette would have thought possible one second ago, her thoughts were suddenly as sharp as a knife point. She knew beyond question she had just said "my child." Crossed that dreaded thirteen-year-old bridge whose gate she had just opened and heard permanently shut behind her. There was no going back. Not with these two reprobates clearly having heard her. They stared speechless while Emerald took up the conversation.

"Vi-lette? Why you keep saying that?"

"Don't pay me no mind, honey. What I meant to say was—"

"Naw." Jethro grinned. Looked like a starving cat who had just run upon a bowl of stinking fish. "Uh umm. You meant to say just what you said. Took the mud out of something I been wondering about for a long time, why that old midwife was acting so off the night your mama died. Wouldn't even let the other womens, 'cept that Livingston woman, come near the cabin to help, and when I asked about that second pile of dirt 'longside the grave that one of them slave boys dug for your mama, that old granny shut up tighter than a old maid's bed chamber 'fore she finally blabbed some big whopper about your mama losing one of her twins."

Jethro stopped. Guffawed at his own twisted humor. "Hmph. Back then, I just let it go. Didn't make me no never mind. Wasn't nothing left that me and Mr. Singer could get out of your mama, no how, crazy and weak as she had got."

Like lightning, Violette was on him. Scratching, kicking. Thinking, Yes, I want him dead. I want the earth freed of him. Whompf! He flipped her onto her back again. Impaled her with knee and elbows again. Looked at Eli then back at Violette. "And I think I know who the papa is to this little pretty one, too. My old friend Eli, here." He winked at Emerald. "What else could have made your mama hate Miss Dinah so when she first met her? Thank goodness, 'cept for his color, you ain't got his looks, but Eli's your papa, all right. Yes, sir. Here you been sleeping next to him all night and didn't even know he was kin."

Eli's jaw dropped. Emerald fainted. And Violette, lying there beneath the weight of this monster, wondered if she and her child had begun their last day of relative peace on this earth. Or was it their last day, period?

CHAPTER 28

*B*enjamin screwed up his face and prepared to bite into the potato. He chuckled. "It can't be any worse than Violette's soup."

He felt better than he had since he'd been marched into the cell days ago. Better, in fact, than he had felt for a long time. He grasped the potato and bit into a chunk with no obvious marks. The less chewing the better. All he wanted now was sustenance.

And a chance to see Violette before I die.

He thought of that morning a couple of weeks back when he had gone out to Riverwood to see her. The change in her, her lady-like carriage, had rocked him. Yet, though he had been loath to admit it, it was more than that. Seeing her had anchored him to a firm reason to wake up mornings. The idea of never seeing her again, even in her anger, pierced him. Brought back sinister probabilities. After that talk with God last night, those worries had receded to a place so far in the distance that he had slept like a mildly scolded child at nap time. Now they had come barreling back.

You're going to hang, never be able to offer the affection to

Violette and Emerald that they so crave and that you desperately need to give.

He stood to his feet. Turned toward the tiny window. Even with the layers of dirt mixed with grime from the town, the sun slashed through with the authority of an ancient well-crafted sword. He thought of the river, not much farther than a stone's throw. Jonathan had always loved the Mississippi River. No matter the times and the way that massive maritime roadway was used, for unbridled classism and the transport of his race to painful and unknown places, the man had always taken the opportunity to stand by that God-given stream to clear his head.

"What I wouldn't give to be able to walk to the river. See the sunlight adorn the dark waves." He reached for his pocket watch. Remembered it had been taken from him. "It must be getting on to nine o'clock by now."

Where could Jonathan be?

Benjamin would never have been considered the embodiment of patience, but over the years, he had cultivated a sense of how to bring calm to clearly-ratcheting anxiety. A Bible verse repeated to him from one of the house servants when he was a child—sacred words from the lips of an old slave preacher who was reputed to have sneaked into the woods with the few of his father's slaves bold enough to follow him—bounded to the top of Benjamin's thoughts.

"The Lord is good unto them that wait for him, to the soul that seeketh him."

He would seek the Almighty again. So he turned. Sat down on the cot and waited. And waited. Unexpectedly remaining awake, given the amount of sleep he had lost. He had just caught himself nodding when he heard the voice of his friend.

"Benjamin, my man."

Jonathan. And . . .

"Paul?"

The jailer he hadn't seen since the night of the beating opened the door without a single word.

"You're free to go," said Paul. "This gentleman here says your things are up front." Benjamin rubbed his eyes like a child. Wondered if he had dozed back off.

"Do you mean . . . are you saying . . . for good?"

Paul clapped him on the shoulder. "Whoa, now. Not so fast. This is bail and not a cheap one, I might add. You have all those weeping women back at the house to thank for it. It took skill, but they convinced us you were worth it,"

Benjamin's laugh reverberated around the cell along with Jonathan's. He had done some weeping himself, but these two didn't need to know all that. He watched his friends while the scowling jailer unlocked the manacles. Banter notwithstanding, they seemed a bit shaken. As anxious to leave this place as Benjamin, if not more so. As though they sensed his sudden embarrassment, they stepped outside while the jailer did an officious, unnecessary frisk. They entered into some rushed whispers, as the jailer took the opportunity to level a whisper of his own into Benjamin's ear.

"This ain't near 'bout over, you know. A darkie can't just kill a white man and walk off without paying up."

"How do you know so much about my future?"

Instantly Paul was back at Benjamin's side. He raised a cautionary hand. Completely Paul the lawyer, now.

"No more questions, Benjamin. No comments either."

He glanced at Jonathan who stood just inside the door, his fingers interlaced as he took his thumbs through a series of cartwheels.

"Besides, we have far more important things to discuss."

Paul turned to face the flame-faced jailer. "May we have a moment?"

"No."

"Why not?"

"Because I said so, and I'm running this jail until the sheriff comes back. He won't be back for another week, so y'all git on out of here." He looked at Benjamin. "By that time, we ought to have a hanging scheduled. If it ain't already over."

"Mr. whatever-your-name-is—"

"Lawless. Deputy John Lawless."

Fitting name, thought Benjamin.

"Mr. Lawless, I hate to have to remind you that you along with this jail are still subject to the laws of the land, and the Union forces still in place might have something to say about your not-so-veiled suggestion of hanging procedures."

The atmosphere of the small square Benjamin had occupied for days crackled with tension. He expected, along with his friends, to be shot at any moment, so outraged was the jailer.

"Now," Paul continued, brows furrowed in authority, "if you'd be kind enough to have Mr. Catlett's effects ready, we will meet you shortly."

The jailer stomped off while the churning that had taken center stage in Benjamin Catlett's gut hardened into an iron fist.

It was as clear to Benjamin as the ray of sun slanted across the dirt floor. Something was very wrong.

"What's the trouble, gentlemen? What's so urgent it can't wait until we clear this place?" Paul nodded to Jonathan.

"There are a couple of things we need to discuss. But once we clear the door, we can't stop to talk."

"Why?"

"Because there seems to be an undercurrent brewing," said Paul. "We can't be sure, but we think there's some kind of offshoot from a hate group from Tennessee called the Ku Klux Klan trying to assert itself in Natchez."

Benjamin recalled what he had heard out at "little Riverwood" about the group formed in Tennessee.

So that's the name of the main group.

"Within the last few days there have been more men than usual hanging around the jail as though waiting for something, and that jailer has made no attempt to scatter them."

"And it's me they're after."

"Afraid so. You're the only prisoner right now, my friend." Jonathan looked pained. "The only other jail mates here came in from the docks last night to dry out from a brawl."

Benjamin tried to keep it light. "All right then, shall we make a run for it? See who the old man is in the bunch?"

The two men looked at each other. Again Paul gave the nod.

"There's more," said Jonathan. "Emerald has been kidnapped. They're threatening to take her down river to become a . . . woman of the evening." Jonathan's voice croaked. He jammed his fingers into his vest. Turned toward the cell door. "Sometime during the night, Violette slipped out of the house, obviously to look for her."

"'They.' Who is this 'they?'"

Benjamin flinched at the hard edge of his own voice. But he had no control over it right now. He felt murderous. And as guilty as ever a man who stood on two feet.

"Jonathan? Who are they?"

"Please, Benjamin. We all know who they are."

"I need to hear the words! WHO. ARE. THEY?" He had yelled so loud that the rats behind the several holes seemed disturbed.

"Jethro McMillan and Eli Duggan."

"Let's go." Benjamin made for the door. Sensed his two friends still standing near the cot. Spoke with his back turned. "What's the matter with you two? I said let's go!"

"Benjamin, we don't know where they are. We have to make some plans, put some thought into this." It was Paul's voice, but it shook something loose in Benjamin.

"For I know the thoughts that I think toward you . . . thoughts of peace, and not of evil, to give you an expected end."

Benjamin stopped and turned back toward his friends. Men who themselves were risking their lives for him. He felt the wetness on his cheeks just as he had when he'd laid bare his past to Paul a few days ago. Again, he didn't care.

Would he run out ahead of God again? Would he again try to fix what only the Lord could?

He stumbled to the cot. Fell to his knees. Heedless of his two friends who knelt beside him, Benjamin poured out his heart to the Lord, seeking and straining for guidance until his very soul felt raw. Past doubts, he prayed. Past fear and agonies that he could very well still end up trying to decide in his own strength and intellect, he prayed. Past his driving will that fought to do something— anything except kneel in a filthy, rat-infested jail with the door flung open while the two people he loved most in the world might be dying—he prayed.

Then the words he'd lived an eternity for, not knowing if they would ever come, came. Stiff and humbled, refreshed and rejoicing, he rose from the cot.

"I have my answer from the Lord."

Neither man spoke. They simply rose along with him. Listened.

"I know where they are. I am going to get them. And I am going alone."

CHAPTER 29

"*T*hat's a lie!"

Eli looked like a child accused of stealing, his mouth twitching somewhere between fear and contempt.

"I ain't never married no woman. Ain't got no children."

"That's right, you ain't got no children. All them little pipsqueaks of yours pretty much grown now." Jethro eased his massive hands from Violette's shoulders. Slapped his knee. Seemed about to die of his own humor. Repeated it through gleeful choking.

"'Pretty much grown.' That's good. That's real good."

Now would be a good time to lam him across his head. If only she could get her hands on a weapon. She had seen no shovel. No gun. Nothing. Still wouldn't know how to use it if she did.

But anybody could use a knife. Surely there must be a knife around here somewhere.

"Vi'lette?"

The sun, fast taking control of the sky now, cut through a space between the limbs used as shelter, right across Emerald's face. Her eyes, usually the color of honey, had deepened to rich cane syrup.

"Vi'lette, is you my mama? I thought you said my mama died?"

"She did. She did die," said Eli. "I remember. She did die."

"Hush yo' mouf." The language of Violette's youth rushed forth more forcefully than she'd heard it in a long time. "You don't git to talk to her. Not now. Not ever."

She stood on wobbly knees, not knowing what the few steps toward her daughter would cost her with Jethro. Afraid to get too close, she knelt before her. Twisted her hurting body around to face the two of them.

"Can't ch'all take these chains off her? Just for a minute? I promise I won't do nothing. If you would just—while I talk to her —if you would just . . . please."

"Yeah, I reckon."

"Naw." Jethro growled. "You better be glad I'm letting you talk a'tall. And if Benjamin ain't here by the time that there sun reach the top of the sky, it ain't go'n matter, 'cause all four of us go'n be headed toward New Orleans if we have to walk."

"I thought you had changed your mind. Were going west."

Jethro looked befuddled. Obviously thought New Orleans was west too."

Eli grinned. "You don't know where west is, do you, Mr. slave driver. Think 'cause Vidalia, Louisiana is west New Orleans, Louisiana is west too."

"Shut up, you mangy lowlife! I changed my mind again, is all. More money in New Orleans." Violette reached out to touch Emerald, but her child turned away.

"Honey, listen. I was fourteen and ugly. Sure enough I was a slave, but, doncha see? I was a young girl just like those girls I now read about all the time in England and other places, with the same mixed-up feelings. Slaves had feelings like everybody else. Always have had. I know white folks wanted to think there was nothing between a slave's ears but colored air. Some of 'em still do, but that just wasn't true. Still ain't. I wanted to be pretty like all girls that age, not just a replica of my father and all my brothers. It's hard enough in a country where your color and hair are thrown aside like some aberration. But add to that an ungainly form and a black girl's life can get to be a mighty cruel one."

Eli lowered his chin. Coughed loudly as though to drown her out. But Violette was patient. He couldn't cough all day.

"Just at fourteen, honey. That's how old I was when that man over there coughing said I was 'right cute.' Practically the same age as you are now. I had lost the childhood fat at the time, so I guess I grabbed at the rare compliment. Emerald, d-do you know what it means to want to be pretty? To have boys look at you in that way that says you count?"

Emerald nodded while Violette surprised herself with a chuckle.

"Probably not. You are already and always have been so-o-o pretty." Violette found herself rewarded her with a stingy, lopsided grin.

"Aw, Vi'lette."

"But you are. You and Dinah, you are what I imagine queens of our ancestry looked like. Anyway, I let feelings get the better of me, and that's how I ended up in a situation with Eli over there that resulted in you."

Nobody, not even Jethro, said a word, though his constant shifting said he was getting antsy. Finally, Emerald spoke, her voice smaller than the four-year-old that had once fallen in love with Benjamin Catlett.

"Y-you sorry about me, Vi'lette?"

Violette's heart swelled with something inexpressible. "Sorry? Oh, no, honey. Would I name someone I was sorry about 'Precious Emerald?'" Violette was crying now. "I am sorry about so many things. Sorry that at my birth I opened my eyes to a world of slavery. Sorry my mama was used like a breeding mare and worked even harder. Sorry my papa and siblings were hauled from our lives like so many cows." She turned toward Eli. Stabbed him with the point of a poisonous stare. "Sorry I turned for comfort to a man who never knew, and, sadly, still doesn't, that he *was* a man."

"Now, just a minute. I ain't got to sit here and listen to this."

"Sorry that I took you under the hill that night and likely damaged you for life. Sorry, so sorry, for letting jealousy and fear drive me to nearly destroy Jonathan and Dinah Mayfield. Sorry that, four years after a war was won which was supposed to make things better, I still feel like the most pitiful of slaves. Sorriest of all that I've been the worst kind of mother."

And sorry beyond description that I will most likely never see Benjamin Catlett again.

"But there's one thing in my life I am not sorry for and that's the bundle of hope that old midwife put in my arms thirteen years ago. You are my world, precious gem. You always have been and always will be."

Emerald tried to reach for her. "My mama. I got my own mama?"

All in the world Violette needed before she collapsed onto her daughter still chained to a tree.

"That's enough," said Jethro. "I just wanted to hear you admit it." He scratched himself. Retrieved the knife Violette so desperately wanted and clambered to his feet. "Sun's high enough. Let's go."

"But don't you think it would be safer to wait until night?"

"Yeah. I agree with that," said Eli.

"What do I care 'bout what you agree to?"

Jethro eased down to the covered box on which he had rested his head the night before. He opened it. Pulled out a gun to the gasps of everyone, including Eli who leapt to his feet.

"Where'd you get hold of that thing? Put that down."

His eyes taking on a half-crazed, milky stare as though he fought to keep just enough light in his soul to see his way, Jethro shook the gun in Eli's face.

"You forgetting who I am? You must be done lost your mind.

You go'n push me one time too many after while. I should 'a done put you in your place long time ago. Should 'a kil't you out there at Riverwood 'neath Vi'lette's window few weeks back."

Violette's body did a shiver. Remembered the foul smells the night the kerosene ran out too quickly. "So it was you."

"Yeah. 'Twas me, all right. Me and this here fool scrapping like two young bucks over which one of us was go'n have you and that gal of yours first. Now we gotcha, we too wound up to care. Just you wait though. Your time coming in New Orleans."

So they had planned to pierce her world way before now. The Lord had been her protection all along. Not Riverwood.

"So what kept you from breaking in that night?"

"That there new owner. He come up just as I was about to get the best of Eli—"

"Ain't so. Just ain't so. I'd ' licked you sho's honey's sweet if that man hadn't showed up."

"Hush up! Last time I'm go'n say that to you. Yeah. That new fellow come off the back veranda just about the time I was winning, and he seen me too. Had a lantern in his hand like he was looking at the place a bit. That's why I got to keep out of his sight 'til I can get away from here.

"But iffen he push too hard, I'll kill him. You don't mess with Jethro. Don't care who you is. I was a driver one time, remember? Folks did what I said when he wasn't around."

Violette knew he had switched pronouns. Wanted to ask. Thought better of it.

"He forgot that, old Singer did. 'Twas old Singer hisself who taught me how to shoot, just in case, doncha know, some of them slaves boys got a mite too out of hand. Thought he had old Jethro so far in his pocket until it didn't matter. And it didn't. For a long time."

"I reckon it didn't."

Eli glanced at Violette and Emerald, a flicker of what might have been lit his face. He started to back away and then stopped.

"Since you stood there and watched Singer hang your own boy, I figured nothing must not have mattered to you." Eli broke and ran. Without so much as another glance.

"No-o-o!" Emerald screamed as the father she had known for a quarter of an hour fell to the still-soggy ground with a shot dead center of his back. Jethro moved toward Eli. Poked him with the toe of his boot. Spat on his face.

"Like old Singer, that'll be the last time I'll have to tell you not to mess with Jethro." Holding his gun in one hand, he fished for something. Rocking Emerald as best she could, Violette could only guess at what he searched for.

"Since you two seem to like to hug up on one 'nother, I'm fixing to put y'all together, at least whilst we walking through these woods."

Jethro held up a key. Violette said nothing. It was no use. But she prayed. Harder than she had ever prayed about anything in her life.

CHAPTER 30

"*I*t smells like old times in here."

Benjamin's head jerked up as Jonathan clapped him on the shoulder and patted his midsection in anticipation.

"Time was, I would do just about anything for one of Mama Tavie's teacakes."

"I still would," said young Davey.

Benjamin heard the hum of voices in various corners of the room. Dinah and her father holding forth about goodness-knew-what. Others keeping the chat just out of range of fellow hearers. All of it irritated him beyond expression.

"Now tell me again why I'm sitting here waiting for breakfast when Violette and Emerald could be out there anywhere, suffering the most heinous kind of degradation at the hands of two of the worst degenerates this side of the Mississippi. Or perhaps even—"

"Don't say it." Jonathan stayed Benjamin's nightmare death word with an upraised palm. "We've been over this at least a dozen times since leaving the jail. With the undertow of the Klan-related group, to go out there during the daylight hours would be next to suicide. Have you forgotten what happened to Davey's brother in broad daylight? Just for expressing an opinion?"

Davey's face had taken on an alarming puffiness. There was no beard yet, leaving him to look like an enraged child in a man's body. A scary enraged child.

"First my half-brother. Now po' Emerald."

Benjamin had not known that the victim of the brutal hanging had not been Davey's whole brother.

"All he did when he wasn't cracking that whip was drop babies in places he had no business. And now . . . po' Emerald." He turned his back. Muttered just loudly enough. "I'm go'n kill him one day."

Not if I kill him first.

"Besides," continued Jonathan, "as Paul and I explained, Jethro and Eli smack of the type who are much more bluff than stuff. They are broke and will likely not go anywhere until they receive some kind of word from you, Benjamin, because Violette won't have the kind of monetary means they seek."

"Jonathan, have you forgotten just how mean and vicious Jethro is?"

Benjamin wanted to bite his tongue, remembering what Jethro had done to Dinah, how he had kidnapped her, put her in the fields then attempted to ruin her almost under the noses of Davey and his mother. But it was too late. He watched as his friend paused. Slowly turned to drink in his wife. Benjamin had to admit she was still something to behold, the most beautiful thing about her being that inner light that seemed to diffuse her surroundings wherever she went.

"That's where you're wrong, my friend. I cannot tell you how many times I look at Dinah and rage courses through me at the thought of how close she came to being ravished by that animal." He lowered his voice. Stepped away from Davey, who at the same moment moved toward a window.

"I have even wondered if that ordeal with Jethro out at the plantation has somehow affected her ability to conceive." A painful memory showed up on Jonathan's countenance. "Or perhaps it is I who am unable to sire a child."

Benjamin tallied another failing mark against himself for unearthing Jonathan's past, recalling the so-called "circumcision" his friend had to endure on a ship so many years ago, simply because he decided to walk openly on the deck as a black man. How had he become that insensitive?

"Oh, now Jonathan. We've settled this one a long time ago. Let's not—"

"And that's what Jethro has become. An animal. And animals don't reason. They react to fear, to anger, to basic needs. Trust me, he won't go anywhere today. He's not that desperate yet. Furthermore, until the sheriff returns, I think you should make yourself as scarce as possible in the eyesight of that new jailer."

Benjamin couldn't argue with that. Something was definitely amiss where that jail keeper was concerned. Furthermore, he got the feeling that whatever he did, he needed to leave no room for Davey to try to help him. He didn't want the boy hurt. He exhaled resignedly as Mama Tavie blew into the room like a five-foot whirlwind.

"Breakfast is ready. Hmmm. Don't know if I can call this breakfast or not, high as the sun in now. Anyhow, I want only hungry people. If you ain't hungry, this ain't the place for you." She chuckled and looked toward Benjamin. "That don't mean you, though. You got to eat."

"Yes, ma'am, I thank you, but I don't have much of an appetite."

"You must didn't hear me, son. You coming whether you hungry or not. One more day and it won't be nothing left of you to decide whether you got an appetite or not. What they gave you up in that jail anyway? You so skinny you look like you could be placed in the fields and not a crow within a day's ride would come nigh it."

"Well, thank you, Mama Tavie," said Benjamin to the hearty laughs of everyone.

Mr. James's eyes twinkled. He gave Benjamin's back a gentle slap. "I promise you, although you don't look nearly that frail, you cannot win this one, sir. Best to just go along."

Benjamin allowed himself a turn. Tried to smile at each of the waiting company collected around him. Jonathan and Dinah, Mr. James and Mama Tavie, Henry, Paul, and even Davey. He knew he had been covered with the kind of love and caring he had wanted all his life. Instead of being in a home where people enjoyed life's humor and rallied when one of its members was in trouble, he had grown up in a home where imitating one of the most dehumanizing means of wealth possible had been the primary and only focus.

Remembering the silent dinners at the table of Rogers Catlett, Benjamin blinked. His throat at the edge of closing. What must it be like to live in a family like this?

"I thank you all. Truly."

He let himself be guided toward the savory smells of what had temporarily become Octavia McMillan's bright yellow kitchen. Ham and potatoes, biscuits, gravy, and jam. The little dictator had announced there was "no sense in messing up a dining room when there was this much room in the kitchen."

Benjamin stifled a chuckle, an obstinate tear slipping from the corner of his eye. Maybe he would be able to work up an appetite after all. Then when evening came, he would go fetch his own family, or at least the one he hoped would agree to becoming such.

And he would do it alone. Barring the problem of a very angry, young gentleman named Davey.

CHAPTER 31

Tuesday night

$\mathcal{V}$iolette listened to the buzz of an out-of-season mosquito and wondered what time it was. No telling, with the darkness so thick and liquid she could hardly see Emerald's face. The sun had long since hidden behind the Mississippi River, though the woods in which Violette and Emerald had been shrouded for hours had given no quarter to the sun's usual evening show put on across from the bluffs of the river in Natchez.

Pain shot up Violette's neck. Emerald had been asleep for hours, her head against her mother's shoulder, their backs sharing a tree trunk. Violette eased her exhausted daughter's head an inch or two as best she could without waking her.

As best I can with these chains on.

Never in her life would she have imagined finally becoming a free woman of color. A woman with a paying job, only to end up chained to a tree by another ex-slave while waiting to start a walking tour to the city of New Orleans to become a lady of the night. New Orleans. As foreign to Violette as the English shires she had read about from the McMillan library all these years. Like

218

Jackson, the notorious city was a place she had merely dreamed of one day visiting. Ha! What a turn of events this was.

Emerald startled. Rubbed her eyes as though she thought it would erase the darkness.

"Vi—I mean, Mama."

Violette smiled. "Honey, you don't have to try to call me that this soon. Truthfully, I would understand if you never did."

"But I want to. I want to call that word. I like how it feels on my tongue."

"Well, go 'head and call it, then." Contorting as best she could in chains, Violette tried to goose her child the way she did sometimes when they were still living at Riverwood and Emerald was little. Contorting as best she could in chains. Emerald set loose a string of giggles.

"Stop! Stop! Stop! You go'n make me lose my manners."

"Well, that would be a miracle since old slewfoot's grandson seems bent on starving us to death."

Quiet tried to get a foothold while crickets did their best to disturb it, and a steam whistle blew, letting Violette know they couldn't be too killing far from the river. Emerald repositioned her head on Violette's shoulder.

"Vi'lette?"

"Yes, honey."

"Can I ask you something? I know you say I ask too many questions, but this one is something I really want to know."

She's honoring my request about asking too many questions? Violette swelled with love and thanksgiving. Just to know that something she had pounded over the years was starting to stick. No matter the future, maybe she had done something right. Anything that would qualify her as having mothered.

"Don't look like we'll be going anywhere anytime soon, so ask away, honey."

"Do you like Mr. Benjamin?"

Like him? Oh, if her daughter only knew. If Violette allowed herself to think of him in that jail cell longer than a fraction of a second, it would be her total undoing. Her melting, like butter on a July-hot day. She couldn't do that, dwell on the love that had slipped sideways into her heart and consumed it but for Precious Emerald. She had had to make a choice. Stay and fight for the man whose very presence stole her good sense or save the child of her loins. She had chosen. Would never look back.

"I . . . well, I do, yes. Why do you ask?"

"I was just thinking. I just lost one papa that I only got a chance to know for a few minutes. He wasn't worth much, I reckon, but it kinda felt good to learn a little about who I am. Who knows? Maybe since we free I might one day find out he had some good kin, and maybe I could meet 'em."

"That would be nice, honey. Sometimes I think about the same thing concerning my family they sold away. Wouldn't it be something if one of our kin turned up wherever we end up?"

"Sho' would. Anyway, I'm glad you like Mr. Benjamin, and I just wanted you to know that if y'all had gotten a chance to love each other, I would have loved the whole thing."

Violette kissed the top of Precious Emerald's head. Turned the tears over to a state of freefall. "I thank you." My baby.

"Vi'lette?"

"Yes, Emerald."

"Wonder what's keeping old slewfoot's grandson so long? I thought we was leaving for New Orleans sometimes this afternoon."

Sniffing and trying to wipe her eyes, Violette laughed out loud at the moniker they had assigned to Jethro.

"Good question."

Maybe he got caught in a river current.

For shame. In truth, she had scrabbled her brain all day trying to figure out why Jethro had not got them going yet. In preparation for the journey, minutes after he had shot Eli and stepped around his body as though the man was a rotted log, something had spooked the fearless slave driver in the section of the woods he had chosen for his necessary. Sent him sprinting back to little River-wood like a frightened deer, his pants practically around his knees.

"Just going to take a little pee 'fore we go," he had announced beforehand grinning, "unless-en y'all want to watch. That being the case I can stay here and do my business."

She and Emerald had said nothing. Still too stunned by the dead body that drew their gazes like the center of a gross magnetic field. Couldn't figure out why a lecher like Jethro was being that sensitive to their sensibilities in the first place. But true enough, he had finally left without putting on that show. And, in no time, had come tearing back into the woods dismantling the recent statement of his plans to vacate little Riverwood right away.

"We ain't going nowhere just yet. I got scouting I got to do."

As though it were one of Mama Tavie's soup ladles, he picked up the gun that had just taken the life of a man. "You ladies mind keeping house for me while I'm gone? You'll get paid good for it once we get to New Orleans." Again, he reveled in his own twisted humor as he alluded to their future lives as harlots. Took up his weapon and headed toward the road.

That had been hours ago. In vain, Violette tried to probe the darkness beneath the thick canopy of leaves for some sense of time.

"I wonder what time it is, Emerald."

"Time for you ladies to get up from doing nothing and let's go."

Help us, Lord. Slew J. Foot is back.

Inwardly, she laughed at her creative name for Jethro. Then nearly fell apart, her unacknowledged hope that someone had detained him for some crime he must have committed somewhere in his past disintegrating into crumbs. But her outward reaction was meticulously schooled.

"May I ask where we are going? I thought you didn't approve of night travel."

"I don't. But how was I supposed to know the new owner of Riverwood would show up again today and spend the whole night drinking and carrying on in his newly-bought house he's fixing up? I tried to wait him out but looks like he's there for the duration."

Violette's breath caught. What if she could find a way to get loose from him and get to Riverwood? It couldn't be more than a mile from here. Perhaps when—if—he removed the chains so they could make better time.

"And don't get no ideas. I ain't got no intentions of loosing you two. You just go'n have to learn how to walk with them chains like any other slave woulda done."

"We ain't your slaves, you old long-tooth slew footed—"

"Shhh! Hush now, Emerald." Violette thought she might prefer a supper of worms served over rat tails than to have to offer this next statement. "If you will help us up, we'll be ready to go. As you know, we didn't bring any clothes trunks."

Jethro unchained them from the tree. Violette reached out her hand as best she could. "Do as I'm doing Emerald." Slew J. Foot tried pulling them up with their wrists shackled together and toppled to the ground beside them, eliciting a poorly-restrained set of giggles from Emerald. Obviously shamed, Jethro sprang to his feet. Started to pace like a revival preacher.

"You know who you laughing at, li'l girl? Huh?"

He grabbed his knees. Bent to Emerald's face. Violette wondered if she herself would survive without spitting in Jethro's eye.

"Lots of folks done made the mistake of thinking old Jethro something to be poking fun at. Think he ain't nothing but a old flunky. Yeah. That's what Singer thought all these years too, huh? And I let him think it 'til he started talking about killing up every darkie in the South. He should 'a said every one 'cept old Jethro 'cause Jethro was the reason he'd come up in the world as far as he had."

Jethro paused. Seemed to think he had said something profound.

"Tell you what. Why don't chu go ask him now? Go out to that graveyard and ask him how I managed to think quicker than a schoolteacher when I found a chance to make him pay. Circled back round behind him through all that thunder and knocked that gun outten his hand. Yanked it up just before that strange bolt of night lightning made just the right popping sound to match them bullets I put in Singer's gut with his own gun what he taught me how to shoot. Lightning that blinded Mr. Big Man Benjamin. Never had such a feeling in my life, not even with women, to see old Benjamin rubbing them high and mighty eyes of his, trying to figure out what just happened, while I thought on whether to run and catch up with old chicken-liver Eli who was hotfooting it toward Riverwood Road. Just to be on the safe side, I would have shot Catlett too if Mr. Lawless hadn't showed up when he did, reckoning that Benjamin had just killed Singer."

Violette thought to ask who Mr. Lawless was. Decided against it. Jethro

backed away from Emerald. Fumbled for something in his pocket. "Just had me another thought. I'm go'n loose y'all after all 'til we can get a head start toward New Orleans."

Gun in hand, he struggled to lift them to their feet. Then, clearly as dumbfounded as he had just been boisterous, he hit the ground with a thud, Davey on top of him.

"Ain't nobody going nowhere 'til after I finish killing my papa."

"What?" Jethro seemed mystified as he easily shook off the boy. Davey latched onto his back. "I'm go'n kill you! I am!

A litany of grunts and sobs infused the scuffle until Jethro managed to plow his son into the ground. "You little good for nothing stinking hunk of dirt. I should've got rid of you years ago along with that mama of yours."

Davey kicked him in the groin. "Don't you call her names. I'm gonna kill you just like you did her. Just like you did your own son!"

Emerald's mouth was opened in a silent scream, while Violette watched in horror. As pitiful a fighter as Jethro was turning out to be, Davey was far worse. Instead of using his advantage, he floundered and kicked, alternately sobbing and screaming. His voice seeming to go in and out of adolescence.

"You killed my mama. I saw you choke her to death with them big awful hands of yours."

Jethro recovered more quickly than Violette would have guessed. Threw the boy back to the ground like a sack of rotten potatoes. "Same way I'm go'n do you if you don't shut your mouf'. Right now."

Like a bloodied rooster, the boy sprang into action again, the sound of gunfire jerking his youthful body back to the sodden earth.

"Davey! Please, Lord, no-o-o-o-o." The only sounds to come from Precious Emerald's mouth before she, too, went slack. And the father of the still form at Violette's feet disappeared into the woods, murderous weapon in hand.

CHAPTER 32

*T*wo. Dead. Bodies.

Not quite, Violette spoke to her own spiraling thoughts. After spotting the set of keys Jethro had dropped and unshackling herself from Emerald, she searched methodically. Looking for an empty liquor bottle. Separating her rampant emotions from the boy on the ground whose lifeblood ran with abandon, so that she could try to think. Anything that might give Davey a chance.

Her mind raced against the flow of blood, dredging up everything she had ever heard about emergencies. She would have to ignore her heart. If it got in the way, if she started to think about what Dinah had told her of Davey's past—how concerned he had been over the bruises his mother tried to hide from the other field hands that day—she would simply lie down next to this poor child, gather both him and Emerald to her breast, and die.

How could she ever have resented him? Blamed him for the scum that was his progenitor?

Oh, God, please forgive me.

"There!"

She snapped back to attention at the sight of the shiny bottle beneath Jethro's sleeping bundle. She uncorked the half-empty bottle and poured its contents onto the wound. The boy never flinched. Neither did Precious Emerald, who was still out cold.

"Come on, honey. Don't give up on me. Don't give up on God."

Relieved to hear Emerald's moans, she barked out orders as she stuffed the wound with as much of her damp torn hem as she could.

"Quick! Get up, girl. Over there. Get some of that Spanish moss. Good. Now find the cleanest oak leaves you can." She had no idea whether she was helping or finishing his life. Only that to do nothing was certain death for this child that, like herself, never gained a foothold on happiness. Emerald obeyed like the dear little girl Violette once knew, her tears dropping onto the small bundle of moss and leaves.

"W-what I'm supposed to do with these?"

"I don't really know. I just thought they might help stem the bleeding."

Violette took the small bundle from Emerald. Laid it atop the stuffed wound and bound it with the apron ties she still wore from Dinah's kitchen. A scripture floated in from the Book of Isaiah. Fragrant and hope-infusing.

"The Spirit of the Lord God is upon me; because the Lord hath anointed me to preach good tidings unto the meek; he hath sent me to bind up the brokenhearted."

"It's go'n be all right, honey." That "honey" was for Davey."

She sat back against the tree. Wrapped her arms around her daughter. Whether God chose to heal this precious boy in this life was totally out of her hands. But she had done what she could to bind up the brokenhearted. Now she would wait. And pray.

~

JETHRO RETURNED and forced Violette at gunpoint to leave Davey for dead. His own son.

"He's a goner. Ain't a thing you can do for him no how. I ought to just go 'head and put him out of his misery.

Why hadn't she left when she had a chance? Because the one thing in her that remained whole was her knowledge of motherhood. Because she could never willingly leave a mother's child in that condition. And because, fool that she was, with all she had seen from this evil man, she still somehow imagined he would try to save the life of his son upon his return.

Shackled together again, she and Emerald had been walking for hours, and Violette had no idea where they were.

And neither does the Mr. Slew Jethro Foot, the all-knowing bigwig slave driver.

Dawn was imminent, its quiet buildup as dramatic and beautiful as the birth of a child. The waning moon was to their left causing her to conclude that so was the river, but in all this time they had never come anywhere near Riverwood. At least not that Violette could tell. And having lived on that plantation for the last nine years, she sensed she would have been able to tell.

Even though she knew nothing of the city of New Orleans except what she had read, she knew it was south of Natchez.

"We are headed north."

"What'd you say?"

She wanted to shout in his grimy, hairy ears. "I said we are headed north," you old addle-headed, murderous sycophant.

Although it was November, the weather was in a teaser. Summer in the throes of death, fighting with all her remaining strength. Hot and stormy one day. Sunshiny and miserable the next. And with it came a resurgence of Mississippi's friendly mosquitoes serenading Violette and Emerald with bloodthirsty songs as they stumbled along, tripping over night things. Each patiently helping the other to her feet.

Violette swatted. Hers and Emerald's hands, now re-shackled, often clumsily striking each other. Finally, Emerald became so sleepy that she practically sleepwalked. Violette knew when she had had enough.

"I don't believe you know where you're going, Jethro."

"And I don't need no woman like you telling me what I need to do."

"You need somebody, or if the sun doesn't rise soon, you just might take another turn and march the three of us into the river."

Jethro halted. Made a spiteful abrupt turn to the left. Lost his balance and screamed like a child in pain.

"See. That's what I mean. We are now headed west toward the river. Just keep walking. Maybe you can walk us through the river. Get us to Vidalia after all."

She was beginning to enjoy this. Could almost feel the clammy nervous sweat radiating from the ill-formed body in front of her, squirming in pain. All Jethro had ever really done was follow the leader and bully the followers. Maybe she could ease into that leadership position without his knowing it.

"One more turn and you'll be headed in the right direction."

"Sit down, both of you. Move and I swear I'll split your pretty li'l heads in two."

Silence, as mother and daughter eased to the ground.

"Uh, Jethro. You ever heard of a former slave woman called Harriet Tubman?"

"Naw. And iffen you know what's best for you, you won't tell me about her. Can't you see I done did something to my ankle?"

Violette smacked her lips. "Now, let's see. Where shall we start tonight's lesson. Harriet Tubman was born in Maryland. Ever heard of it Jethro? I know you must have learned to read by now, lover of freedom that you are. Anyway, back to the lesson. Harriet was abused. Know anything about that, Jethro? But she didn't let that stop her. She found a way to escape her slave master, and not only escape but return into slave states numerous times to set free hundreds of oppressed people from animals just like you. No one knew *directions* better than Harriet Tub—"

Crack! Emerald whimpered. Screamed as Violette's shoulder imploded into what felt like a misshapen lump of quivering dough. She fell to a bed of damp leaves.

"Shet cho mouf! If I didn't need you in New Orleans to get me started, I'd kill you right now and keep on going with this gal of yours."

Emerald recoiled to a moan. "Mama, Mama, let me help you."

Violette shook off Emerald's help. Struggled to a sitting position, the chain binding their wrists causing Emerald to remain close.

"The one th-thing I m-most admire about Harriet Tubman is how v-very smart she was. K-knowing how to strategize how to . . . how to run at night to avoid de-detection. Imagine that. A woman who was s-s-smart enough to figure out how to elude p-patrollers and slave drivers at night."

She heard when the gun clicked. Reached to kiss her child goodbye. Then, along with Jethro himself, recognized the back side of Riverwood. The house was quiet. The entrance familiar to all three of them. Most easy to access from this side. Knowing Jethro craved rest, she could see the yellow of his grin as the sun bounced up from the east.

"Well, I'll be. Done run right into what I thought at first I needed to run from."

BENJAMIN HAD DETERMINED to keep just inside the woods. He had traveled the road to Riverwood enough times not to get lost, and he could not chance the noise of a horse. Now, with this poor boy on a skid, Benjamin had no choice except the middle of the bumpy road. A self-inflicted image of Violette and Emerald brutally victimized was his companion. For the hundredth time, he railed against Jonathan and Paul.

"How could they, men who are supposed to be my friends, allow me to sleep until near midnight when they knew the stakes?"

He pulled the skid onto his street and patted himself down for the key.

Not there.

He tried to ignore the boy's gurgled breathing. Noticed for the first time a low light next to the settee beneath the stairs. Beat on the door with all his might.

"Open up in there!"

The door was open before he could finish the yell, Jonathan and Dinah looking more haggard than he'd ever seen. Dinah inhaled sharply, likely remembering what she and Davey had suffered from Jethro all those years ago.

"Davey! What happened to this child? Where are Violette and Emerald?"

"I don't know and I don't know. We need a doctor. Now."

"I'll get him." Mr. James appeared from somewhere. Grabbed his coat from the coat tree, Mama Tavie at his heels. "I fetched him many times before in the past when I . . . belonged to the McMillans."

Even now it is painful to admit he was once owned, thought Benjamin, as well it should be. He looked at Davey. Doubted if the boy would make it to dawn. Vaguely recognized Mr. James's disappearance.

"I have to go. I found Eli dead at the camp along with what you see of this poor child. There were signs Violette and Emerald were there." He nodded toward the skid from which Dinah and Mama Tavie had already begun working to extricate Davey. "If you look closely there, you'll recognize that the boy's wound is bound with an apron string," though it was so bloody as to have nearly given up its original color. Still Dinah must have recognized it.

She looked up at him, fear, begging, and stubborn faith in her eyes. "Go. And God go with you."

CHAPTER 33

Wednesday, November seventeenth

$\mathcal{T}$he woods back of Riverwood were heavily blanketed with fallen soggy leaves. Violette and Emerald walked past the crumbling cabins once used for a portion of the town estate slaves. Violette's thoughts bloomed with memory, prompting the cabin doorways to come alive with women of a Sunday morning. Tired yet determined to attend the church meeting allowed by the McMillans. The spaces between their knees filled with the backs of little girls waiting and complaining through the sometimes painful process of having their hair braided, while little half-naked boys chased one another with stick guns.

"You trying to ignore me, Miss Vi'lette?" Gun cocked at the ready, Jethro's attempted whisper fell hoarse and gravelly on Violette's ears. "I asked, ain't you been working out here in the old wash house for a while?"

Dry, swollen lips encouraged Violette to say nothing.

"Answer me or I'll make that hurt shoulder howl without lips."

Silence.

"Or maybe I just show the li'l miss how to have a good time."

IN PURSUIT OF AN EMERALD

"Yes."

"'Yes,' what?"

"Yes, I worked in the wash house as you well know."

"Good. That be good." He looked smug. "I thought I remembered hearing that. We can stay in there 'til sundown. Make it nicer knowing you stayed in there, and you can find some rags to see about my leg."

"What if the new owners hear us? You thought of that?"

Jethro hesitated. Tried to redistribute his weight to favor what seemed an ever-increasing pain in his leg. Pierced her with a nervous, indecisive glare. "Ain't no new owners out here. They gone by now. I heard the new master say he had to catch a boat to Vicksburg at dawn. Wasn't no women with them on the road last night what could hold 'em back with a lot of frills and stuff to haul. Just the owner wanting to show off his new property and maybe drink with his friends, so they bound to be gone by now."

Violette considered the truth of it. Though much improved, there was nothing about the place that looked inhabited yet. No sound of horses. No flickering lights. No busy servants.

"But Vi'lette." Emerald managed to tug at the sleeve of Violette's good arm. "I thought I seen a shadow just now moving across the back verandah. Maybe Mr. Benjamin done found us."

"Hush! Hush, Precious Emerald." Violette's heart tried to take a leap of faith. Failed. In any case, Jethro didn't need to be alerted. "Probably just an early bird, honey. You know Mr. Benjamin is still in jail. He couldn't possibly come out here."

"Yeah. And unless-en he coming with the money I need . . ." Jethro ratcheted up his volume to meet what Violette suspected was another threat. He had obviously heard all they had said. "Y'all better hope Mr. Big Man Benjamin don't show up out here. Do and I'll put a bullet in him just like I done Singer and Eli."

And your son.

Arm clasped next to her to support her injured shoulder, Violette moved toward the wash house, Emerald in tow. Jethro limped alongside her, every now and then poking the gun barrel into the small of her back. He had proved he would use it if pushed too far, so she moved slowly. Stealthily.

Except for the new curtains of spider webs draped and swooped haphazardly across the tiny space, the wash house was just as she had left it weeks ago. Jethro fell onto the dusty clothes-folding bench Violette had used for nearly ten years. Closed his eyes and displayed an astounding round of weak writhing, the gun dangling carelessly from his hand. Violette withheld a gasp. Issued a quick, silent prayer. Thrilled to the best possibility for escape she had seen in days.

Should she? She knew better than to try to grab it by the barrel. The gun could go off or Jethro could simply shoot it, killing her or Emerald.

Words that Singer had whispered in her ears that night under the hill so long ago when she lost every penny Jonathan had paid her, every cent toward Emerald's future, came back to confront her.

"Your only chance to improve your pitiful situation. You win or you lose."

Hesitation born of that flawed advice and ultimate decision to be made swayed her exhausted body. Emerald bunched a section of Violette's shift in her hand. Kept Violette on her feet and furiously mouthed her own suggestion.

Now! Now! Now!

A streak of early morning light landed on the gun. Now was indeed the time. Wasn't it? Emerald on her heels, Violette lurched toward the gun, knocking it from the ham-like hands of Jethro. It skittered a ways across the floor.

Oh, praise the Almighty. Teeth gritted, heart pounding. If. She. Could. Only. . . put her hands on it. She groaned under the impossibility. Struggled against the sudden shifting of Emerald's obviously tense body. Kicked the gun from Jethro's near-grasp.

Hallelujah! Her daughter finally righted and pressed in to her back, Violette reached for the gun. Felt the slick warmth remaining from Jethro's hands.

"You can just drop that right now, li'l lady."

Violette froze. Where had she heard that angry, fibrous voice? In recent days too.

"Turn around now. Nice and easy. You wouldn't want to throw away the few minutes you and your young'un got left, now would you?"

Nice and easy. Foreign words since not a thing in Violette's life had ever been either nice or easy. Still, she managed to somehow turn toward the voice without falling to the floor and bringing Emerald along with her.

The jailer. Heavenly Father, it's the jailer! It had taken only that one visit to Benjamin's cell to see that he was a mean one. But why was he out here at dawn? Wouldn't it be Benjamin he wanted? And wasn't Benjamin still in jail?

"My, my, Jethro. Y'all have been a mite hard to find."

Jethro? How does this man know Jethro's name?

Jethro sprang to life. Pain seemingly eradicated as though this foul-smelling skinny jailer was some kind of warlock. He lowered his head. Hobbled to the door, every whit the spineless leech he had always been. Quimbo and Sambo leaping off the pages of Harriet Beecher Stowe's book with the alacrity of a hyena. His every instinct trained to slavery, clicking in place like the chambers of a firearm.

"Yes suh. So glad you could make it. Been waiting for some help with these ones." He pointed toward Violette. "Wrastled this here gun offen her just after she shot and killed po' Eli."

"Liar!" Emerald made a dash for Jethro. "He's the one. He's the one what killed everybody!"

"Everybody?"

The jailer let out a heartless, raspy chuckle. "Well, that don't seem quite right, does it, li'l lady." He looked at Jethro. "Good job, boy. We'll get to the bottom of all this. But right now, I've got more important things to take care of than these two darkies. I'm trying to find the killer of a white man, Benjamin Catlett."

"Find him, suh?"

'Cept for a few minutes the other day when I went home to see what the missus had cooked, I'd been guarding him ever since I caught him in that storm Sunday night with the warm gun in his hand out here near Riverwood. But yesterday some of the men of the town caved in to a few pleas, and Catlett was let out on some kind of bond arrangement with that carpetbagger Boatwright. And now he's missing.

"I tried to tell them he would run. Tried to make them see that a honest darkie is as rare as hens' teeth, but no one wanted to listen to me. Felt like I was just some babbling dirt farmer who'd been given a chance to baby-sit for the sheriff. Wouldn't they be surprised if they knowed what an important organization I done got to be a part of?" The jailer paused. Made a turn to let that sink in.

"Truth is, they was so caught up in gazing at that money Boatwright put down that they wouldn't've been able to notice their dying mama take her last breath. And now that cabinetmaking killer's done took off."

The words seemed to slip from Violette's mouth, her need to make sense of something, anything, outstripping what little good sense she had ever possessed.

"And why would he stop out here, mere miles from the jail, when there's so much more distance to be gained on this planet?"

The jailer stretched his neck like an overfed rooster. Laid down his gun. Took his time approaching her. Spat in her eyes before slamming his fist into her jaw. Before Violette felt her legs fold and the weight of her child come crashing down on her. Before her brain could get hold of the fact that the keeper of the law had literally just tried to snuff her lights out.

∾

IT COULD NOT BE. That fool jailer had just laid his gun down at the door. Two feet from where Benjamin crouched beneath the window, careful to avoid the advancing light.

Lord, I knew he was evil. But I didn't know he was evil and stupid. And a part of the hate group.

Benjamin inhaled to set himself. Thought of Lucie. Determined he could not mess this one up. God had given him another chance at love. At rescue and protection of a woman that deserved so much more. He had never considered what fatherhood might mean to him until the last few weeks. Suspended between childhood and woman, Emerald's laughter had charmed him. Warmed him so completely that he could almost swear her capers were slipping into his own behavior, surrounding him with a cloak of pleasant expectation like he had never felt before. Even the comfort of the not-so-dapper clothes he had worn lately had amazed him. At night, when he turned over, a smile claimed him as he thought of watching her grow into a capable woman in the age of freedom. A teacher? A lawyer? Maybe even a doctor like Elizabeth Blackwell, the first woman to graduate from a medical college some twenty years ago.

Ah, and Emerald's mother. He had loved her for a decade. He couldn't wait to show her the love and care she didn't even know she deserved.

Careful, man. Don't get ahead of yourself. There could very well still be a noose waiting for you.

He peered into the window once more at the lovely back of Violette McMillan, drawn once again to the fight he had glimpsed in this woman he had stupidly thrown to the wind all those years ago, simply because, unbeknownst to him, he thought she needed fixing. Then he had decided she was not fixable, when the one who had so desperately needed to be repositioned on the Great Potter's wheel was Benjamin himself.

He watched in anticipation as she turned slightly. The sun, like Benjamin, seemingly drawn to her fierce beauty and determination.

Lord, help me.

Her face was beyond battered. Her usually perfect lips gravely misshapen twice their normalcy. One of her eyes was shut. The other barely a slit. And the arm opposite the closed eye was plastered to her side like that of a tin soldier. Still, to Benjamin, she was beautiful. Words from days ago resurfaced with hatred that Benjamin knew to be ungodly yet could not contain.

I will kill Jethro. I will kill him. The both of us cannot inhabit this earth at once any longer.

In one fluid move, Benjamin crowded the door to the wash room and scooped up the jailer's gun.

"Move, Mr. Lawman, and it will be your last one."

CHAPTER 34

"*M*r. Benjamin!"
Violette could hardly see a foot ahead of her,
let alone make out who filled the door with such taut determination. But that voice . . . that voice . . . . she would know it
anywhere.

Emerald dragged her along. A set of oxen could not have
matched the child's strength at that moment, while Violette, both
eyelids forsaking her, struggled to see if it was really true, if the
shadowed, handsome, arrogant stance she had so come to love and
admire, consuming the doorway of the wash room, was really the
one she knew in her heart it had to be.

"I told you, Violette. I told you I saw him. Mr. Benjamin. You
came to get us. You came. You did it. He came, Mama." Emerald
pulled herself and Violette between the jailer and Benjamin.

"No!" Benjamin's voice rang through the cobwebs as the jailer
snagged Emerald to his chest and laid a knife to her throat.

"Jethro!" he yelled. "Get over here and loose the mama. Then
—I don't know where you got it—but pick up that gun of yours."
He stared at Benjamin, a near incredulous look on his face.

Affected a humorless grin. "Boy, don't you know you've just confiscated a white man's gun and a deputy's at that?"

Through the diffused light, Violette strained to keep up as Jethro sprang into action, unlocking her from Emerald while Benjamin, now within a foot or two, still held onto the jailer's gun.

"Let the child go, or I will empty your own white bullets into that sunken belly of yours."

"Ha! Real clever talk for a darkie. Same kind of uppity talk you put to my boy a week or so ago when he came into your shop to see Mr. Singer."

The blond-haired youth who spoke of the organization that had gotten started in Tennessee and spread so quickly.

"Hear tell you really insulted my son, and now you threaten his pa. But you won't do it. Ain't got it in you to put li'l miss darkie in that much of harm's way. Too much the black goody-goody who likes to play the white man. Everybody in Natchez says so. That's why a few of us have come up with our own secret organization that's go'n show darkies like you that imitating the white man will never drain you of the blood that makes you black, don't care how near white some of you happen to be."

He shot a look at Violette. Was he thinking of her light skin?

"Imitating might would have been all right 'til you started thinking about trying to be the best furniture makers and senators and every other god-given right the white man is due. Now drop that gun or I'm gonna write my name up and down this girl's windpipe."

"For an ignorant hellion like you who probably can't get further than the letter C, that would be a real feat, I'm sure."

"Benjamin, don't! Please don't say anything else. He will kill her."

Violette caught sight of Jethro, who had managed to pick up the gun he had obviously taken from Singer and point it at her head.

"Then Jethro will likely kill us all."

Morning sunlight had finally completely claimed the room helping Violette to see Benjamin's face. The struggle that reflected his soul. Eyes snapping, jaw clinched, Benjamin dropped the gun to the floor. Jethro scrambled to retrieve it. Passed it to his latest master. Glowered at Benjamin.

"Since you here, Mr. Big Man. You mayst well come on in. Join us for the breakfast we wish we had."

"Shut up, Jethro." The lawman was suddenly insulted. "Just because Singer's dead, don't forget yourself here. Easy enough to swing you from that same tree as that boy of yours if need be."

A streak of barely discernable anger sat over Jethro's brow, causing Violette with her impaired sight to wonder if she had seen it at all, then passed just as quickly. She had to do something, but what could she do when she could barely stand?

You can pray. You can always pray.

Torn for a moment between the rough handling of Benjamin and the uncontrollable shaking of Emerald, Violette forced shut the remaining eyelid, only partly opened anyway. Something much bigger than her and anyone in this room was urging her to go within herself. Search diligently for that "true Light which lighteth every man that cometh into the world."

Strange that in the midst of such turmoil she would remember a scripture from John that had always puzzled her.

"What does that mean, Lord? How can I who have mostly walked in darkness, only turning to you at such a desperate time as this, still have that Light within, if I ever even had it?" Words, seemingly springing from her very soul, claimed her thinking.

I Myself put that Light in you. I have been waiting for you to fan the flame. My patience, like My love, is longsuffering.

Violette felt a smile blossoming in the depths of her. A visceral, tangible smile that defied anything she had ever experienced. She wanted to sing aloud. Pray aloud. This instant.

No. Not yet. Be patient. The enemy of your soul surrounds you right now in the persons of his disciples. Hearing about our conversation would only infuriate him more.

Then what am I to do?

Wait. And loose Precious Emerald.

Loose her? Didn't Jethro just do that? Ooohh! Loose her, like that. But I am chained to her. She is my life, and even if I wanted to, how can I unshackle myself when I don't have the key?

But, dear one, you do have the key.

Violette felt laughter infusing her, filling her with good will and unfathomable understanding. It echoed through this wash house where she had spent so many years trying to figure things out. It echoed through her being. Through the dependency across the square where she had struggled to understand a society like the one described by Miss Stowe. And finally, across the acres of Riverwood and beyond.

I feel free, like a single person. One that matters by herself.

My point exactly, dear one. You have been chained to Precious Emerald—and bitterness and guilt and self-loathing—for so long until you have forgotten what it is to be the magnificent, single creation I formed you to be.

Violette knew it was time to pray aloud. Though it had only been moments since that Voice had whispered to her soul that she must be patient, a lifetime of wonders had been set forth in the laughter and the conversation about Emerald that ensued with her Creator. She whispered in her child's ear.

"Emerald, precious girl that you are, kneel with me."

"What?"

"Do as I say. Kneel here with me." Leaning on her daughter for support, Violette dropped awkwardly to the floor, Emerald right along with her.

"And just what do you two think you're doing? Get up from there or I'll shoot those black knees right out from under you."

"Lord Jesus, I thank you for your servant David and his legacy of a psalm that I now have the blessed privilege of speaking as my own."

Violette heard Benjamin's intake of air. Prayed silently for his strength. She touched her fingertips to Emerald's lips and repeated portions of the Holy Psalm number thirty-four.

"O magnify the LORD with me, and let us exalt his name together.

I sought the LORD, and he heard me, and delivered me from all my fears.

They looked unto him, and were lightened: and their faces were not ashamed.

This poor man cried, and the LORD heard him, and saved him out of all his troubles.

The angel of the LORD encampeth round about them that fear him, and delivereth them.

O taste and see that the Lord is good: blessed is the man that trusteth in him."

"Get up from there! Do you hear me? Stop that right now!" The jailer's rasping voice hit against Violette's ears. She heard him shuffling toward her.

"Mama? Mama, don't let him shoot us."

"The eyes of the LORD are upon the righteous, and his ears are open unto their cry.

"The face of the LORD is against them that do evil, to cut off the remembrance of them from the earth. The righteous cry, and the LORD heareth, and delivereth them out of all their troubles."

Grunts, it seemed to Violette dozens of them, drowned out the sound of her scriptural prayer. But she kept going.

"The Lord is nigh unto them that are of a broken heart; and saveth such as be of a contrite spirit." "Many are the afflictions of the righteous: but the Lord delivereth him out of them all."

BENJAMIN FOUGHT like an heir of the biblical King David. Most likely he was going to die, either now or by a rope, and he knew it. Felt strangely good about it.

If only he didn't have to leave Violette.

While Violette was praying, he had managed to grab Jethro and slam him against the wash tub, stunning him into a sprawl on the floor. And now he was engaged with the jailer. Had knocked the gun from his hand just as he had turned to threaten Violette and Emerald. Then Benjamin had gone at his midsection with a punch he didn't even know he possessed. The jailer let fly a series of staccato grunts that sounded like a litter of hungry pigs, as he heeled backwards, stumbling toward the window.

God, you are truly a wonder.

Benjamin smiled. Felt that last communication with the Lord buzz through his brain as the butt of a pistol slammed against his ear. Jethro.

Knowing he was outnumbered, he fell to the floor. Waited to be assailed. Still there was no fear of death. Either now or at the hanging, should it come to that. His only regret was that he wouldn't live to see the Righteous One deliver Violette and Emerald, for he sensed strongly they would be delivered. Had embraced it the moment the love of his life sank to her knees. For some reason, he felt rather than heard laughter in the room. Good cleansing laughter. He decided to join in.

"All right fellows, it seems you've won. So what's next?"

BENJAMIN LOOKED at the length of chain between his ankles. A first for him. Somehow, they had ended up together, he and Violette and Emerald. All three of them sitting on the floor, their backs against the folding bench. Bathed in a swath of sunlight coming through the door. Linked by a lone chain to the wash tub stand.

Benjamin managed to reach far enough to cover both Violette's and Emerald's hand with his own, massage their bruised fingers with what little strength his thumb could offer. Odd. For the first time in his life, he felt he was a part of a family. Truly caring for others. Looking out for someone as best he could. Not to fix them but to love them. Simply love them.

And now he was about to die. Why wasn't he dead yet?

"Powerful prayer you prayed, my sweet."

"Powerful fight you fought, my love."

"I knowed you two was sweet on one another. Knowed it all along."

Violette tried to smile. Grimaced instead, her distorted mouth protesting, sending Benjamin's gut into a clench at the sight of it.

Please, Jesus. Deliver her quickly.

He looked at the backs of the two men standing across the room. Jethro nodding vigorously at every whisper coming from the jailer's mouth. What were they discussing and how long would they keep his family in this place? Violette and Emerald looked so starved. So torn. Placing a finger as close to his mouth as he could, he signaled them to remain quiet while he caught snatches of the jailer's words.

"Trying to figure out what to do with the women. Don't want no jawing from none of them goody-goody officials back in town."

"Yes suh. You sho' right."

"But Catlett hangs. No two ways about that."

Emerald's eyes went wild, but she managed to restrain her mouth as though an invisible hand had rested there. Thank God.

Lord, I thank you for a foretaste of the graceful and self-contained young woman that is to come. I know in your own timing you will continue to teach her to listen to her mother after I am gone.

"Best get rid of the woman and girl."

Benjamin lurched, the chains tinkling in the still air. The comfort of his prayer about Emerald's self-containment suddenly flying out the door with the early-morning chill. A word of desperation escaped Violette's blood-crusted lip.

"Please."

"Quiet over there! You'll get your reward for that prayer soon enough." The jailer set forth his best snarl. Resumed his scheming. "We'll make it look like they came upon some kind of danger wandering around out here. Not much risk in that story."

The sound of the slightest depression of soggy leaves came from just outside the door. Benjamin's body went taut. He wondered if the jailer had heard it. Wondered if it was friend or foe.

"And making no difference whether they're jawing or not, pretty soon all the big men who run Natchez are go'n know who I am and the worth of the organization I'm a part of."

Benjamin's anticipation of the visitor outside was getting the better of him. His mind skipped like a twister across a field, knocking down every pleasant possibility in its path.

Mr. James? No. Boatwright? Possibly but not likely. Jonathan. It had to be Jonathan.

"Morning, all. And welcome to Riverwood Plantation."

Lord? A white man he had never seen in his life poked his head through the door, gun in hand. Smiling. His southern accent was as thick as Chester Singer's had been though it was far more polished and didn't quite ring Mississippi. He cocked his head to the side. Seemed to survey the wash house. Locked onto Jethro's face.

"Can y'all imagine? In all my visits, I have yet to look in this wash house."

Benjamin's heart sank. The man was toying with the whole group. Was most likely a closet Klansman come to help his lackey jailer.

I felt so confident you would help us, Lord.

The man acted as though Benjamin and Violette and Emerald had melded with the clothes-folding bench. Given the manner in which he scanned the room, he didn't even know they were there. Finally, he set sights on the jailer.

"'Fraid I didn't get your name, sir."

"Lawless. Frank Lawless. Temporary deputy for the county of Adams."

"Jesse Compton. A pleasure, sir. Then as the new owner out here, I can help you with the arrest."

Benjamin glanced at Violette. Saw his growing confusion mirrored in her face. Why did Mr. Compton continue to hold the weapon? How would he have known there would be an arrest? For the first time, the stranger looked at Benjamin and company. Then back at Jethro whose eye had assumed the slightest tic.

"I suppose y'all are wondering about me, too, huh?"

He ran his free hand through a thatch of hair that obviously hadn't seen a comb this morning.

"I had a little too much to drink last night. Overslept and missed my boat." He lifted the same hand in quasi-warning. "But that doesn't mean I don't have a conscience, though I admit to doing a good bit of spying and eavesdropping within the last half hour or so since I couldn't seem to go back to sleep after I missed my excursion to Vicksburg."

He chortled. Walked the room's circuit, gun in hand. Eyes never leaving Jethro.

"Must have been the Almighty who woke me because after the kind of . . . ahem! . . . celebrating I and my friends did last night, it usually takes a while for me to reenter society. Been in town several weeks overseeing the purchase and decided to see how it would feel to finally sleep all night in the house I bought. Lost my wife two years ago. Moving here from Savannah, you see. Lovely place, Savannah." His words were languid and wistful. "Something about Natchez kind of reminds me of home."

The jailer said nothing. But Jethro inched further toward the door.

"Halt, there. It's really you I'm about to arrest. I should have taken you in that night a few weeks back when I was out here doing some final business with the McMillans. I saw you and another fellow wrestling near the kitchen dependency. But I'm thinking I'll make an even better witness against the kind of fellow you are, now that I heard you bragging earlier about killing two men. One named Eli and the other Chester Singer." The new owner paused. "Do I have those names right?" Emerald nodded, then yelled.

"Yes, sir. You got 'em right!"

Not quite self-contained yet, thought Benjamin, a smile about to break loose.

Violette released a sob she had obviously been holding while Benjamin gave in to laughing outright.

"You do indeed, have it right, sir. You ambassador of right-eousness!"

In a flash, Jethro had gained the back of the jailer, locked his forearm beneath his neck.

"Ain't nobody go'n take old Jethro, not even you, Mr. Jailer. And I ain't forgetting myself when I say I ain't go'n let no underfed gravy-sopping white trash like you swing old Jethro from no tree."

CHAPTER 35

Friday, November nineteenth

"Old Jethro" had been taken. Shot in the leg by Jesse Compton and now waiting in jail to be sentenced. Most likely to be hanged.

Violette shook loose her thoughts from Jethro and all the Jethros in the world. November had finally and completely dismissed summer as every bowed head lifted to the fragrance of delightful dishes and Mr. James's blessing. The men had built a fire in the fireplace, and thoughts of Christ's birthday next month had begun to color everyone's anticipation. All of Violette's family —well, she couldn't call it family exactly, but it was the closest thing to it she'd had in a very long time—were gathered around the table, Mama Tavie having decided Violette's and Benjamin's and Emerald's safe return was worth eating in the dining room. Not to mention Davey, who was upstairs healing quite nicely, Emerald by his side struggling to read to him.

All praise be to God.

Violette dug into the collard greens Dinah had labored over all day. She added a piece of cornbread and looked at her friend. Dinah lifted an eyebrow.

"Leather?"

Violette's laughter nearly spewed the greens. "Hardly. These are right up there with Mama Tavie's." She closed her eyes. "Umm um. Make you want to hurt somebody, they're so good."

"So what's this about leather?"

Poor Benjamin. There was still a lot he didn't know.

"A joke for another time," Jonathan said.

Quietness took over except for the clinking of tableware. Mama Tavie beamed. Urged everyone to eat more. Choked on her emotions.

"I can't believe we once-upon-a-time slaves and others of God's people black and white is—"

"Octavia?"

"Oh, all right, James. We *are* sitting here together in heavenly places like this."

Paul Boatwright laughed. "I think you are communicating just fine, Miss Octavia. As much with this potato pie as with your improving grammar. In my mind, they are of equal importance. Well, no. I think this chicken outstrips verbs all day long."

So this was what it felt like to be at home, if only for a little while. Violette understood that the Simon Legrees were still out there, lurking in the alleys and on country roads. Waiting to serve evil. But for this moment, she would savor what her people would have to continue to fight for. Life, liberty, and the pursuit of happiness.

She thought further. A shadow passed over her happy thoughts. Violette could call this group neither family nor home. Not yet. She probably would never be able to once she told Benjamin about her history with Chester Singer. And it was Benjamin, not Mama Tavie, not even Dinah, that she would tell first. And Benjamin, gentleman that he was, would let her down easy. But he would want no more to do with her, and she and Emerald would be on their way to Jackson.

~

BENJAMIN GLANCED up from Mama Tavie's smothered chicken to find Violette's gaze intent on him. Her eyes whispered a need to be alone with him. At least that's what he hoped. Prayed. She stole from the table. Entered the vestibule. Held out a hand to him, one which trembled so in the effort that Benjamin wondered if she would be able to sustain her upright position as he moved quickly across the space. A hand which, he thought, had become much less water-wrinkled in recent weeks. Not that he cared, but Violette was forever trying to hide them.

She slid the quivering hand into his. Held on seemingly for dear life. "Walk with me?"

The walk to the river was quiet, the crisp November air rapidly heralding the season.

"Cold?"

"A bit." She attempted a smile, but her lips trembled, rendering it a failure. "I guess I should have stolen another one of Dinah's shawls."

"Had Mama Tavie seen you out here uncovered, the only thing you'd need to steal would be some ointment to soothe the tongue lashing you would get."

She laughed. For real this time. Benjamin wrapped her in his coat. Gently squeezed her shoulders. Slipped his fingers back between hers. Determined he would not let go her hand until she forced him."

"Better?"

"Perfect."

She tugged him toward a tree. Sat down on the chilled brown grass. Benjamin sensed a reckoning.

Is this it then, Lord? Have I been found out for the arrogant, tainted rogue I and my father have always been?

Without warning, she started to talk, still holding his hand as though to let go would be to silence herself forever.

"Please understand that when I begged Jonathan to follow him back to Natchez that day, I knew nothing of its nightlife."

Benjamin no longer wondered. He knew a watershed moment was upon him. A parting of the ways. His life would either end or begin from this moment forward.

"I didn't know the pull of money. Had never had any other than the small amount I had collected from Jonathan for the book-keeping work. All I knew was Jonathan had come to Riverwood and told me Emerald and I were free. Appomattox had happened. Slavery was no more. At first, I wanted to celebrate. That was all. I tried to get Jonathan and Dinah in on it, but as I've been told married people often do, all they wanted was to be together. Alone."

Benjamin felt her trying to remove her fingers, as though about to bolt, but he wasn't ready. He sensed she wasn't either. "Please," he said. "Please, let me hold on."

She batted away the threatening tears. Relaxed her fingers which had indeed become more soft and delicate.

"Holding fast to Emerald's hands, I walked toward Silver Street, savoring the free air. Somehow, I knew I shouldn't, not alone. Knew that feelings in town were far from warm. The very walking surface itself felt like not an innocent hill but a dangerous precipice.

"But the elixir of freedom to a lifetime slave is intoxicating. So with Emerald, my one priceless gem, clasped by one hand and the money Jonathan had told me to hold onto held by a makeshift purse string thrown over my shoulder, I lowered myself, step by step, toward the docks. I had almost reached the bottom of the hill when I saw him."

Benjamin felt his shoulders tense, but he held on to Violette's hand as she continued.

"'Ain't you a McMillan?'

Emerald and I stopped abruptly. 'Yes, sir. Who you be?'"

~

THE STRAIN of remembering this pointedly was more than Violette had bargained for. She had thought to just tell the story and be done with it. But with the speaking came the attendant emotions.

"Give me a moment. I am sorry. It's just that—"

"Shhh! You have a story. I have an ear for hearing it. End of story. Well, no. Not truly. That would ruin things, wouldn't it?"

They both smiled. And oh, what a smile that Benjamin Catlett owned, straight gleaming teeth that had obviously been cared for since he was a child. She would love to have seen him as a little boy. Violette savored the smile, secreting it away for the times later in life when she would need it. When Benjamin would have the wife he deserved and the children he would adore. So much for empty wishes. Time to move on. Violette picked up the story.

"'Come on now, gal. It ain't been that long since we was together out at the McMillan Plantation,' he said.

"It had begun to get dark and the setting sun put him in shadow. But the closer Emerald and I got, the more I recognized Chester Singer, the man who had been the heartless overseer of me, my mama, my whole family. The man who had arranged the sale of my papa and my siblings, leaving Mama and me alone to fare for ourselves. You would think I would have run, wouldn't you? And I would have but for the questions that flew from his mouth like the devil's own arrows.

"'What's that you got on your shoulder? A coin sack? Want to make some more tonight? Double, maybe?'"

~

BENJAMIN FELT A SHUDDER. Couldn't tell if it was hers or his or both. Only that her need to tell this was as great as his to tell his story when the time came. He needed strength from the Source that was larger than the both of them. Else he would beg her to plug up her story right now. And he would plug his. And they would live . . . miserably ever after?

"Double?" Violette's telling heightened. "Was it possible to double one's money in one night? The sheer power of it lit my consciousness like a bonfire. In that moment, it meant everything to me. Everything to Emerald. We were free, but what was freedom without money? With money, I could do so much. I could walk away from the McMillans and not have to worry about how Emerald and I would eat. I could pay Dinah back what I owed her for so many things.

"I could send Emerald to school."

Thus far, Benjamin had not put in a single word of questioning, but the words came before he knew it. "So you've known for this long that you wanted her education?"

"I knew the first time I laid eyes on her." She shifted. Burrowed into his coat. "Singer led us into what I now know was a brothel as well as a gambling house, all the while promising to stay over my shoulder telling me how to play the game. On a night like this, I could well make enough money to take care of Emerald and me for years, he said. He would take no more than a fourth of what I made, he said.

"'And what if I lose?'

"He grinned. 'Would I let that happen? You won't lose. But if you do, I have an easy way for you to pay. Won't hurt a bit.'

"I gambled all night. Winning just enough to stay in the game. Every penny Jonathan had paid me for keeping the ledgers went into the pocket of a cigar-chewing, liquor-drinking, constantly-leering man across the felt table from me until I began to owe him. Finally, Emerald asleep in a corner, I was forced to ask the fatal question. 'What do I do to pay?' Singer whispered the answer into my ear. 'What? No,' I said. 'I thought I would wash dishes or clean or something.'

"I will never forget the look on nine-year-old Emerald's face when she awakened to my vocal resistance. It was as though she turned into a woman at that moment. Understood at the same time as I what the payment would likely be. Singer laughed. Called to the gambling attendant.

"'The pickaninny's awake now. Get rid of her, will you? Don't kill her, though.' His eyes licked Precious Emerald as though she were a stick of candy. 'Who knows? In a few years, she might be as useful as her mama.'

"And I saw as clearly as I saw the dingy, green felt tabletop where my hands rested that the innocence had been taken from my daughter. Nothing's been the same between us since."

Biting off the edge of a curse word, Benjamin searched her face. Smoothed her temples. Kissed her forehead. "I know there's more, but it can wait." He decided to try for a little levity. "It's time for me to take you home before Mr. James and Jonathan come looking for me with a shotgun."

"No. I want to finish then never discuss it again." She slid a little closer to him as though to shore him up for the last of it.

"Biting, kicking, screaming—using all I had in my unsophisticated arsenal while the other gamblers looked on in their salacious snickering—I fought Singer with all the strength left to me. But in the end, he won. At the close of my first day of freedom, I was chained to the bed and turned over to the evil cravings of a man whose name I didn't even know and who, outstripping even Jethro's demands, had taken all my money, and now would take the part of me I had worked so hard to try to regain."

Benjamin swore. Repented. Swore again. "Lord help me. I want to dig Singer out of his fresh grave, along with my father, and kill him again."

"There's more, Benjamin—"

He gentled a finger to her lips. "Shh. That's enough, sweet-heart. Enough."

CHAPTER 36

*V*iolette sniffed. Wiped her eyes. Felt the marrow flowing back into her bones. Had Benjamin Catlett just mentioned his father? "Benjamin?"

"That's right, I said my father. I know that all of you know I didn't drop down out of the blue. Like everyone, I have a past. But unlike a lot of people, it's not one you want to share if you hope to keep any friends. Yes, even Jonathan."

A strange new fear gripped Violette. What was Benjamin holding back that could cost him Jonathan's friendship?"

"I am a murderer and a slaveholder."

Violette shot to her feet. Sat back down. "I didn't hear you. The wind is picking up. Say it again, please?"

She stiffened as Benjamin did something shocking, at least in that moment. He pulled her to him. Cheek to cheek. Held her so fiercely it hurt. She relaxed against him. Listened. As he told her of the evils of slave owning, how the practice mixed with greed changes a man. Had changed Rogers Catlett. Had changed even him.

"Though I put up my best fight against being like my father, I have learned that the arrogance, the feel of superiority, somehow slipped in when I wasn't looking and made me try to play God to slaves just as smart and important to the Lord as I was. More so in many cases."

And then he told her of Lucie. What a lovely name. And the way he described her. Was he still in love with her?

"Beautiful Lucie who did not need fixing but whose lot in life it was to have my mother and her servants prod and poke and grease and straighten and dab until we killed her. We didn't mean to. In our attempt to atone for Father's sins, we meant only to dress her up as a lady. Put her in silks and stays so that I could marry her into a life of privilege, not knowing that last day, when Mother's maid corseted her into pain, that her appendix had already burst, spreading infection throughout her emaciated body. A body my father had used in his fields, then whipped at his whim. Hours later after she had complained to us in the drawing room, sweet Lucie died.

"Thing was, we never asked her if she wanted to be what we thought she must. That has ever been my problem with those I care about which, thankfully, the Lord has recently shown me."

Violette shifted as though she would leave his arms. Hoped to give him space if he needed it, though she had never been more comfortable.

"No, no, please. Let me hold you until I am done. I may never get this chance again." With all her heart, Violette hoped that would not be so. Wanted to blurt out her feelings right then and there. But as he had let her finish her narrative—almost—she would do the same.

"The one thing in my whole life I despised more than any other was the enslavement of human beings. After Lucie's death, to have a father who relished being a master, and over his own people at that, some of them his blood kin, was more than I could take. So I simply took off from my father's Virginia plantation. With Mother's help, I ended up in Natchez. All the while working for Jonathan, I started stealing slave children from the area and smuggling them to Mother, who found homes for them in freedom. I don't know why my mother never confronted Father about slave-holding, but at least she did some restitution after he died."

Violette thought her heart would disintegrate with pride. How she had misjudged this man.

"But the other day when I was in jail, all my efforts done in my own strength came crashing down. Jonathan brought me a letter from my mother." Violette watched his eyes mist over.

He loves her. He still loves her.

"She's dying. I need to go home."

"Not to stay, I hope. Oh! How callous of me. I mean . . . I am sorry about your mother. Truly I am. Benjamin? Did you hear me?" But Benjamin had cut her off, as though the telling had taken him to a sightless, soundless isolation.

"Mother's letter says every slave Father ever bought was purchased in the name of Benjamin Rogers Catlett. My name. I have been a slave owner all my life. He did it first to ensure my wealth. Later on, out of pure spite."

They sat there. Holding each other. Rocking each other. Letting the hurt seep into the winter grass beneath their feet. Finally, Violette pulled back. Explored every nuance of his handsome face with the tips of her washerwoman fingers.

"I love you, Benjamin Catlett. Nothing can alter that. Now. Will you let me finish my story?"

She felt his body tense against hers. Smiled. "I lost the fight with Singer who imprisoned me in that room with my creditor, but the man proved too drunk to harm me. He simply fell asleep, snoring and shuddering louder than the surrounding boats until Singer, thinking the debt was paid, freed me and sent me and Emerald on our way."

Though he said nothing, Violette could feel the tension receding from Benjamin's body.

"I know you deserve a lady, and I am no lady. But soiled though I am, I bring you all the affection of which my God has made me capable. I will understand if you leave and never return. But if you leave, my love will follow you—whispering to you each morning of the fierce pride I take in having known a man like you. Reminding you that I only want the best for you whether you're in Virginia, Mississippi, or China. I am forever spoken for, Benjamin Catlett, though the words may never have formed in your mind."

Ever so gently, Benjamin pressed her head to his shoulder. Remained silent for a bittersweet eternity while Violette, every moment, waited to be let down. Let go.

"Sweet, sweet Violette." She half-felt, half-heard, his chuckle above her ear. "I have loved you for so long. Since you turned and looked my way in that kitchen nearly ten years ago, I've met you countless times in my dreams. No matter the Catlett mandate, your charm and beauty would not let me go. And that morning in the wash room a few weeks back, you took my breath away, did you know that? I told myself it was improper to have you under my roof when the truth was I hardly trusted myself to share the same four walls with you."

Curving a finger beneath her chin, he tilted her head upwards. He looked at her as Violette had often envisioned in her own dreams. "I've decided to use some of the money my father left to rebuild Mayfield Cabinetry. The rest I will donate to that school in Jackson—Tougaloo, I believe it's called?" He grinned. "Contributing to a school for ex-slaves, that should please my father a lot."

The sarcasm vanished, replaced with an intensity of gaze that vanquished Violette's doubts, just before he lowered his head and kissed her into oblivion.

ABOUT THE AUTHOR

Jacqueline is a multi-published author whose works range from short stories to a memoir of growing up during and after integration. Wheelock has been a member of several writers and critique groups and is currently a member of the American Christian Fiction Writers, an organization which has afforded her valuable instruction and opportunity toward publication.

An avid reader and former high school and college English teacher, her first novel, *A Most Precious Gift*, debuted in 2014 via Mantle Rock Publishers. The sequel, *In Pursuit of an Emerald*, was published in August of 2017. Jacqueline and her husband Donald reside in Madison, Mississippi and have two adult children and one beloved granddaughter.

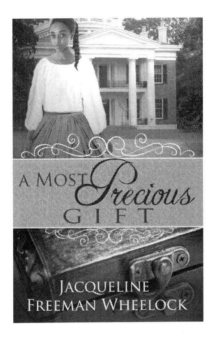

A Most Precious Gift

Dinah Devereaux, New Orleans-born slave and seamstress, suddenly finds herself relegated to a sweltering kitchen on the Natchez town estate of Riverwood. Having never cooked a day in her life, she is terrified of being found out and banished to the cotton fields as was her mother before her.

But when she accidentally burns the freedom papers of Jonathan Mayfield, a handsome free man of color to whom she's attracted, her fear of the fields becomes secondary. A gifted cabinetmaker, Jonathan Mayfield's heart is set on finally becoming a respected businessman by outfitting a bedroom at the palatial Riverwood—until a beautiful new slave destroys his proof of freedom and his fragile confidence along with it.

When the mistress of Riverwood orders Dinah to work alongside the sullen Mr. Mayfield, sparks fly setting the two on a collision course. Is their mutual love for God strong enough to overcome deep-seated insecurities and set the couple on a path toward self-acceptance and love for each other?

MORE HISTORICAL ROMANCE FROM SCRIVENINGS PRESS

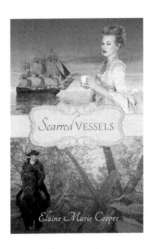

Scarred Vessels
by Elaine Marie Cooper

In a time when America battles for freedom, a man and woman seek to fight the injustice of slavery while discovering love in the midst of tragedy.

In 1778 Rhode Island, the American Revolution rallies the Patriots to fight for freedom. But the slavery of black men and women from Africa, bartered for rum, is a travesty that many in America cannot ignore. The seeds of abolition are planted even as the laws allowing slavery in the north still exist.

Lydia Saunders, the daughter of a slave ship owner, grew up with the horror of slavery. It became more of a nightmare when, at a young age, she is confronted with the truth about her father's occupation. Burdened with the guilt of her family's sin, she struggles to make a difference in whatever way she can. When she loses her husband in the battle for freedom from England, she makes a difficult decision that will change her life forever.

Sergeant Micah Hughes is too dedicated to serving the fledgling country of America to consider falling in love. When he carries the tragic news to Lydia Saunders about her husband's death, he is appalled by his attraction to the young widow. Micah wrestles with his feelings for Lydia while he tries to focus on helping the cause of freedom. He trains a group of former slaves to become capable soldiers on the battlefield.

Tensions both on the battlefield and on the home front bring hardship and turmoil that threaten to endanger them all. When Lydia and Micah are faced with saving the life of a black infant in danger, can they survive this turning point in their lives?

A groundbreaking book, honest and inspiring, showcasing black soldiers in the American Revolution. *Scarred Vessels* is peopled with flesh and blood characters and true events that not only inspire and entertain but educate. Well done!

~ Laura Frantz, Christy Award-winning author
of *An Uncommon Woman*

~

Under This Same Sky
by Cynthia Roemer

She thought she'd lost everything ~
Instead she found what she needed most.
Illinois prairie - 1854

When a deadly tornado destroys Becky Hollister's farm, she must leave the only home she's ever known, and the man she's begun to love to accompany her injured father to St. Louis. Catapulted into a world of unknowns, Becky finds solace in corresponding with the handsome pastor back home. But when word comes that he is all but engaged to someone else, she must call upon her faith to decipher her future.

Matthew Brody didn't intend on falling for Becky, but the unexpected relationship, along with the Lord's gentle nudging, incite him to give up his circuit riding and seek full-time ministry in the town of Miller Creek, with the hope of one day making Becky his bride. But when his old sweetheart comes to town, intent on winning him back—with the entire town pulling for her—Matthew must choose between doing what's expected and what his heart tells him is right.

Stay up-to-date on your favorite books and authors with our free e-newsletters.
ScriveningsPress.com

Made in the USA
Las Vegas, NV
11 May 2023

71850240R10151